SEA CHILD

Renny deGroot

RENNY DEGROOT

Toadhollow Publishing 7509 Cavan Rd Bewdley, Ontario K0L 1E0

Contact Renny at: http://www.rennydegroot.com

ALSO BY RENNY DEGROOT

FICTION:
Cape Breton Mystery Series
Garden Girl (Book One)

Historical Fiction:
Family Business
After Paris
Torn Asunder

NON-FICTION:
32 Signal Regiment: Royal Canadian Signal Corps – A History

*Dedicated to my team in Nova Scotia
who worked so hard to transform the raw land of my dreams
into the reality of my writer's retreat.*

*Thanks to: Barb and Bill, Mary and Sandy, and Stephen,
and all those service providers who
cleared, constructed and drilled on my behalf.*

CHAPTER 1

DETECTIVE GORDIE MACLEAN OF the Cape Breton Police Service sipped his second cup of coffee on the morning on May 18, 2021. When his cell phone rang, he jumped, almost causing him to spill hot liquid down his shirt. He set the cup down, pushed his thick mop of white hair back from his eyes, frowned, and dug the phone out of his top pocket. His heart beat a little faster because his first thought was that something had happened to his elderly mother. His brow relaxed and a slight smile creased his weather-tanned face when he saw it was his 'lady friend', as his mother liked to call Vanessa Hunt.

He swiped to answer the call and had just taken a breath to give a cheery 'good morning' when Vanessa started speaking, her voice fast and high.

"Gordie? I'm so sorry to bother you at work and so early. Are you in a meeting or anything?"

He pictured her pacing in her cozy living room, soft ash-blond hair pulled back in a loose tie at the nape of her long neck, escaped wisps framing her strong features. "No, it's fine. What's wrong? You sound frazzled."

"Oh Gordie, I've just heard that Adam MacDonald is missing. You know; Sharon's husband."

Gordie hesitated, trying to place the name. "Is that your quilting friend?"

"Yes, that's her. From Port Hood."

His mind cleared, and the names fell into place. "Right. I remember her now. I met her at one of your handicraft things."

It was a testament to how upset she was that Vanessa didn't correct his name of the artisan shows she sometimes went to. "That's her."

"What do you mean, he's missing?" Gordie held the phone to his ear with his left hand and with his right he one-finger typed into his system to see if there were any missing persons reports.

"He hasn't come home from fishing yet."

Gordie glanced at the time displayed in the bottom corner of his computer. "It's only eleven o'clock." He relaxed back in his chair and picked up his cooling coffee. "That's not late. Why are people are already alarmed? You say that MacDonald's missing, but aren't there usually three in a crew? Are they all missing?"

"No, no. They didn't go out together. I heard the boat was already gone this morning when the crew showed up at five o'clock."

Gordie frowned. "Maybe he took someone different this time?"

"Apparently not."

"How are you hearing all this, anyway?"

"I called Lynn to see if she wanted to come for a cup of tea and she told me she couldn't. She and her husband are going down to the Port Hood wharf to see if they can help."

"Let me look into it and I'll call you back, but this is something the Mounties would probably get the call for."

"I just feel so helpless. I wonder if I should go up there."

Gordie tried not to let the chuckle slip into his voice. "I know you mean well, but what can you do? I'm sure if the Mounties feel it's necessary, they'll get volunteers with boats out on the water to help look. Extra bodies standing around might be more of a hindrance than a help."

He heard the sigh. "I know. I thought the same thing, but I want to show I care."

"My advice is to wait for a while until you know more information. It may all resolve itself, and then you'd be making the trip for nothing."

"All right. You bring the voice of reason, as usual. But will you look into it and let me know if you hear anything?"

"Of course, Vanessa. Now, get yourself that cup of tea and relax for now."

Gordie hung up and sat for a moment. He had a stack of reports he should be working on, but if he was honest with himself, he'd been looking for a reason to put them on the back burner. Detective Roxanne Albright looked up from her computer screen when he stood up. Slim with short, glossy chestnut hair and high cheekbones, she had a petite exotic appearance, although, Gordie realized, she had been growing her hair and adding muscle to her frame lately.

She leaned back in her chair. "What's up?"

"Vanessa called me to say there's a missing fisherman in Port Hood."

She did what he had done and checked if there were any reports in about it. "Maybe the Mounties have it?"

"Probably. I might give my pal there a call."

"You thinking of going out there?"

He shrugged. "Maybe. I'll let you know if I do."

Gordie stood and stretched to his full five feet and eight inches and rolled his shoulders. He walked out the back door of the red brick building and stood safely out of view of the public and lit a cigarette. In the quiet of the early spring morning, he called his friend Constable John Stevens, at the Inverness Detachment of the

Royal Canadian Mounted Police. Gordie explained what he had heard. "Have you guys heard anything about it, John?"

He heard Stevens tapping on the keyboard. "Nope, nothing here. It's not likely we'd get the first call. It would probably be the Coast Guard if it was on the water. We might take a look at it for a hand-off, but otherwise we'd probably kick it over to you fellas. We're strictly non-emergency and backup support these days."

Gordie nodded unconsciously. "OK, just thought I'd check. I'll take a run out."

He finished his smoke and made his way back inside and down the hall to the office of his boss, Sergeant Arsenault. He tapped on the doorframe of the open door and waited, even though he knew Arsenault had noticed him there the second he approached.

Arsenault took his time to finish reading the page he'd been reviewing and then made a show of closing the file, sighing as he did so. His dark blue uniform shirt was crisp, hugging the contours of his muscular chest and arms. "Yes? What is it then, MacLean?"

Gordie felt his jaw clench at the sound of impatience in Arsenault's voice. "I heard about a missing fisherman out in Port Hood. I thought I'd take a run over there. Maybe take Albright with me."

"I haven't seen anything about a missing fisherman. How did you hear about it?"

"One of the locals called it in. It isn't official yet."

Sergeant Arsenault grunted. "Hmph. All right, go ahead, but don't make a picnic out of it. I expect to hear back from you once you're on the ground. If it ends up being nothing, I want you back to finish the reports."

Gordie knew Arsenault was just saying that to be annoying. His boss knew full well that both he and Albright lived north, and to go all the way to Port Hood and back to Sydney for the sake of some reports was madness.

"I'll take the computer with m Sarge and if it turns out to be nothing, I'll write up the report and carry on with the monthly stats from home."

If it were up to Gordie, he'd only come into the office once a month for the department meeting, but Arsenault went through these phases when he felt like he needed everyone right there, bums in seats, to be sure they were working. They had been in one of those phases for the past couple of weeks and Gordie was glad for a reason to get out from under the eye of his cranky sergeant.

Arsenault frowned when he heard the title 'Sarge', grunted again, and waved his hand, which Gordie took to mean the meeting was over.

MacLean walked back along the corridor to the open plan area where the detectives shared space in a series of workstations. He grinned at Roxanne. "Pack up your troubles. Road trip."

They unplugged their laptops and packed them into the issued black carrying bags. Gordie made sure he shoved the file of statistics he'd been working on into the bag as well, just in case he ended up working on it from home.

They walked out together to the parking lot. Gordie nodded to his partner. "Do you want me to meet you at your place and we'll go together from there?" Roxanne Albright lived with her grandmother in Big Pond, which was only half an hour from the office.

"No, go on ahead. I'll meet you at the Tim Hortons in St. Peter's and leave my car there."

"OK, thanks." They both knew that the more direct route to Port Hood was via the Trans-Canada highway 105, but taking that route meant that they would both have to take their cars all the way to the small coastal community north of Port Mulroy. Going to Saint Peter's added twenty minutes to the drive, but it was worth it to drive at least part of the way together. This way, they arrived as a team.

Gordie MacLean lived with his Great Pyrenees dog named Taz on Isle Madame, which was a short half-hour beyond St. Peter's.

By Roxanne taking her car all the way there, it would mean Gordie wouldn't have to drive so far to return her home.

They each headed out of the parking lot, but Gordie drove faster and lost sight of Roxanne in his rear-view mirror before long. Once he was past the outskirts of Sydney, he pushed the green button on the steering wheel of his Santa Fe and when prompted, said Vanessa's name to dial the phone.

Vanessa answered after the first ring. "Gordie?"

"Hi. I spoke with the Mounties and they haven't heard anything, but I'm heading up there now. Albright and I will check out the situation and I'll let you know what I find. Sound good?"

"You'll call me no matter what?"

"I will. Don't worry."

"Well, maybe I'll go out and do a bit of raking now that the sun's out. Being outdoors may help distract me a bit."

Gordie laughed. "Don't dig up any more bones."

"God, I hope not. Once was enough."

Gordie disengaged the phone and remembered last spring when Vanessa Hunt had an old tree removed, only to discover a human skeleton in the shallow ground beneath the dead tree. It was how he had first met her. After it was clear that she had nothing to do with the remains, the two of them had become good friends. Now Gordie didn't like to think about his life without her friendship, and sometimes thought maybe it was time they consider moving in together. The problem was, they each loved their own homes. He shrugged and put the thought aside. *If it's not broken, don't fix it.*

Gordie drove along Route 4, on autopilot; his mind wandering from thoughts of Vanessa to his dog Taz, to his mother and sister living in Halifax. He made up his mind. *I really must get down to visit them soon.* The 120 kilometers passed without notice and his car turned into the Tim Horton's coffee shop lot almost of its own accord. He parked and stretched before going in to use the facilities and pick up a medium double-double coffee for himself and a green tea for Roxanne. He stood outside by a picnic table with his coffee and enjoyed a quick cigarette, glad to be standing for a few minutes, when she pulled in and parked. She nodded to him as lifted her tea from the table and held it up. She nodded but she walked inside to make a pit stop herself before joining him.

He handed her the cup. "Do you want to drink it here?"

"No, I'm good to go. Looking forward to blowing out the cob-webs with the sea air."

He nodded. "Right, then. Let's see what's going on in Port Hood today."

CHAPTER 2

SHARON MACDONALD LAY IN the early dawn light of their room, the argument spinning around in her mind. She had awoken when he rose, much earlier than his usual four a.m. fishing season start; in fact it seemed they had just gone to bed. She had remained still with her eyes closed, though, not wanting to spark a conversation. She tracked his progress, listening to the familiar sounds of opening drawers for clean socks, underwear, and long-sleeved thermal undershirt. He took all his clothes with him down the hall to the bathroom to dress and after Sharon heard him go down the steps to the kitchen, she heard nothing further. Usually, she heard the faint sounds of the whistling kettle, drawers and kitchen cabinets opening and closing, but today, nothing. He left without making a thermos for himself or sandwiches for his lunch. There was a time she would have gotten up to get his breakfast and lunch organized, but somehow this season, that tradition hadn't been resurrected.

Sharon sighed and turned over, for about the twentieth time since waking in the faint light of dawn. She couldn't fall asleep again, her body jumpy, in tune with her mind. Her words haunted her, and she knew she'd been in the wrong with her accusations and complaints. Her words seemed to hang in a bubble over her head, like an image in a graphic novel. In her mind's eye, she saw the bold print and exclamation mark. "'I'm always the adult in this family. You need to grow up and take some responsibility!'"

Adam's face had collapsed. "I do my best."

"Well, maybe that just isn't enough. Maybe it's time to let Kyle take over the boat. Yesterday you were gone all day, tinkering with the boat or whatever you were doing. You can do better working at the pulp mill. They make great money, and it's all year round." Even as Sharon was speaking, she knew she was being unreasonable. The boat and the sea were his life, after her and their daughter Izzie, that is. The boat and license were still in his father's name, but Danny-mac, as everyone called Adam's father, had made it abundantly clear over the years that the business would be going to his eldest son one day. Sharon knew he couldn't give it up. As soon as she said it, she knew she was being mean, but she was at her wit's end.

Adam had slowly shaken his head. "I'll get the money. You don't need to worry. Izzie doesn't need to worry."

Sharon almost apologized then, but two glasses of wine and the letter from the Conservatory telling them that Izzie was accepted into the music program had stopped her. Their daughter's acceptance was wonderful, and the child was wildly excited, but the accompanying schedule of fees floored her.

Instead of saying 'we'll figure it out' like she might have, she poured herself another glass of wine, shook her head, and took her glass outside to sit on the veranda in the spring evening. Adam didn't follow her, and she knew he'd go to bed soon. The life of a fisherman didn't allow for leisurely evenings drinking wine.

Now, Sharon lay in bed with a sore head. She gave up tossing and sat up. She blinked as the hangover made her head pound even more. *OK. Just get up. Take a couple aspirins and have a hot shower.*

After that, breakfast. By that time, she'd figure out how to apologize and tell Adam the truth. She loved him and if he was less than great at making decisions and planning things out, well, that was OK. *He's so good with Izzie.* Being the adult was her job, and truth be told, she knew she was a bit of a control freak, anyway. If he actually started making decisions, she'd probably just argue with him. *Maybe I can sell that quilt.* She had spent two years making a beautiful seascape quilt that hung on their wall, but she could make another one. *I bet that would bring in a thousand dollars. A tourist would pay that.*

She stood in the hot shower and thought it through. She didn't know why she had resisted before this, but in fact was glad she had, because if she had sold the quilt before now, the money would have been spent. After her shower, she stood in front of the mirror and wiped the steam away with the corner of the hand towel. She pulled her damp, shoulder-length auburn hair back into a ponytail and secured it with a black scrunchie. Her face looked paler than usual despite the flush from her shower, and the small scar on her chin that she had gotten as a kid when she fell out of a tree, stood out as a thin red line almost like a cleft. She smiled at her image and her pale blue eyes crinkled, as she banished the anger of last night. She had a plan now. It was a new day, and everything would be fine.

The headache was almost gone and the old-fashioned kettle was just on the verge of whistling when the phone rang. It was five o'clock, and the sun lit the kitchen with a warm buttery glow. Sharon smiled as she reached for her cell phone that lay face down on the kitchen counter. *He's calling to make up. He can't talk because Kyle and Dab are right there, but I'll understand. I'll ask him what he wants for supper, so he knows I'm sorry too.* All these thoughts flashed through her mind even as she lifted the phone and went to swipe the icon to answer. She hesitated for a split second when she saw it wasn't Adam, but his brother Kyle, calling.

She shook off the unease that chilled the back of her neck, and the smile was in her voice as she answered. "Did you leave your phone in the truck again?"

She frowned when it was Kyle who responded. "Sharon?"

"Kyle. What's up? Did Adam lose his phone?"

"I don't know. We haven't seen him this morning, but Sharon," there was a hesitation before her brother-in-law continued, "the boat's not here and I wondered if you had gone out with him for some reason?"

"Well, no. Obviously not. Maybe he and Dab went out on their own? Or they picked up a casual to help crew for the day?" She knew her voice held an accusation when she continued. "Were you late this morning, Kyle?"

"No. I wasn't bloody well late. I've been here for fifteen minutes. And no, he didn't just go with Dab 'cause he's here with me."

Sharon felt her heart beat faster. Both her brother-in-law and their usual crewman, Dab Haan, were at the wharf, but Adam and the boat were gone. It made little sense.

"Did you ask around? Maybe someone saw him?"

"What do you think I've been doing this last fifteen minutes? I've asked anyone and everyone who hasn't gone out yet. One of the others tried to call him on the radio, but no answer, and before you ask, no. No one out there can see the *Sea Child* from where they are. He's not at his traps."

"Not at his traps. This doesn't make sense. Where would he be?"

"You tell me. Did you guys have a fight?"

Sharon felt ill. "Why would you ask that?"

Kyle sighed. "Forget it. I'm going to go. I'm going to catch a lift with one of the guys leaving now and see if I can spot him." Before she could respond, he had disconnected.

Sharon turned to see their ten-year-old daughter standing in the kitchen doorway, her pink pajamas with its ballerina images crumpled and askew. Izzie scowled. "What's going on, Mom?"

Sharon hesitated. This might all be resolved quickly, and then she would have frightened Izzie for nothing. She walked over and ran her fingers through her daughter's tousled shoulder-length blond hair, enjoying the silky feeling caressing her fingers. She leant over and kissed the forehead, still damp and sleep-smelling. "Nothing. You're up now. You might as well go and get dressed and I'll make pancakes for breakfast. Would you like that?"

Her daughter smiled. "On a school morning?"

"Only if you're quick."

Izzie beamed at her and turned to skip up the stairs.

Sharon picked up her phone again and tapped it to call Adam. It rang four times and then went to voicemail. She kept her voice low. "Adam, where are you? Kyle's worried and now I am, too. I'm sorry I was harsh yesterday. You know I didn't mean anything by it. Call me to let me know you're all right."

She pulled out the box of pancake mix and blended the ingredients for a few pancakes. Her stomach churned, but she knew she'd have to eat at least one with her daughter. Izzie was such a sensitive girl. She'd know right away that something was wrong if Sharon didn't make a big effort to act normal, so she went through the mechanics of making breakfast, even as her mind worked overtime to imagine where he could be. Put the kettle back on again to boil since she had been interrupted before she made the pot of tea. *He found a couple of people to crew for him. He wouldn't go out alone.* Pour a glass of orange juice. *He took the boat out on his own but anchored somewhere just to have some breathing space because I upset him.* Flip the pancake, take it out of the pan, put it on a plate and into the oven to keep warm. *Someone stole the boat, and he's with the Mounties to report it.* Pour a new ladle of batter onto the hot skillet. *He took the boat out on his own and has had an accident.* Flip. *He took the boat out and has done something to himself. Because I belittled him.* She scraped the last pancake; the burnt one into the garbage and fell into a chair, feeling the lump in her throat. She felt nauseous and knew she needed to get a grip on herself. In a few minutes, Izzie would be down. She rose and poured herself a cup of tea. *I'm letting my imagination run away. It's all fine. Focus on getting Izzie to school.*

She knew she was over-compensating with her cheerful behaviour with Izzie but it was that or break down, so when the canny ten-year-old asked her 'why are you acting so weird?' she grinned and declared that she was celebrating the acceptance letter to the Maritime Conservatory. That started Izzie talking about music and the possibility of a new viola and Sharon let her chatter away with only a minimum of uh-huhs and maybes required. Sharon stood at the front door and watched Izzie walk to the corner, and then when the schoolbus door closed, the red stop signs with the flashing lights folded back, and the bus rumbled off, she went back in the house and collapsed into a chair at the table, the pancake threatening to come back up. She sat for a moment and then jumped up, put her phone into the front, zipped pocket of her black leather purse and took her keys and jacket. *I'll go down to the wharf and then decide what to do.*

***

Sharon parked close to the berth that normally held their boat. She scanned the sea, and for a minute she felt the breath catch in her throat when she squinted against the sun and saw the red hull in the distance. She stared, her eyes watering in the wind and the glare of the sun on the water. The boat was churning through the water in her direction, and then a wave struck it and the boat rocked. It turned slightly, and she had a better view of the profile. This was the other red boat. It was brighter; wearing a fresher coat of paint than what adorned *Sea Child*. This one was bigger as well, the hull and pilot house stood taller than *Sea Child*. Sharon closed her eyes against the sight, the tears smearing in the creases at the corner of her eyes.

It wasn't him. She turned away from the disappointing view of what she now recognized as the boat *Cherry-Cherry*. She stood for a moment, undecided as to what she should do. A collection of onlookers stood near the hut that sold hot drinks and later in the day, would sell fresh fish and chips. When they saw Sharon look their way, two women detached themselves and surged forward, covering the distance in seconds. They weren't the hugging sort, but each of them touched Sharon; a slight tap on the arm or shoulder just to make a tangible connection.

Lynn Duggan spoke first. She was a small woman with the tight grey curls of a home permanent. Her tanned face showed the weathered look typical of a fisherman's wife. "Sharon. We came down to see if there is anything we can do." She nodded to the other woman, and they shifted together, forming a protective circle with Sharon.

Sharon shrugged; her voice clogged with unshed tears. "I don't know. Maybe there's a simple explanation."

Lynn nodded. "Of course there is. You've tried phoning, I'm sure?"

Sharon nodded.

The other woman spoke up. "The boat's broken down. That's all. Probably the phone's run out of juice and that just makes it all the more dramatic."

No one mentioned the fact that her husband had gone out without his usual crew. It was such a strange act, so filled with dark implications, that it was best not to remark on it.

They turned as one to watch as Cherry-Cherry pulled into her berth. Kyle leapt out to make her fast to the dock, but one of the regular crew took the rope from his hand and Kyle left them to stride towards Sharon. Not for the first time, she was a little surprised that he looked so different from his brother. Kyle's short cropped dark hair and glasses made him look younger than his 33 years. Adam was tall and lean; his salt and pepper hair hanging too long in the neck. Kyle was short and stocky. She took a few steps towards him, meeting him halfway, leaving the other women behind, their circle broken as they watched her.

Kyle waited until he reached Sharon before speaking. "We searched the dumps." Sharon knew that referred to the groups of traps marked out by buoys. "We even hauled up a few traps, but he hasn't been there today."

Sharon pictured the area that Kyle had visited and bit her bottom lip. "Where could he be, Kyle?"

"I wish I knew." He narrowed his eyes, the sun shining off his black-rimmed glasses. "Did something happen between the two of you?"

She took a deep breath, torn between denying it and telling her brother-in-law what happened. "Oh, Kyle. We had words last night. It was nothing. I know Adam called Dannymac last night, so you probably know Izzie's been accepted to the Maritime Conservatory?" She waited as he nodded. "I was just worried about the money. You know how it is." Her voice held an undercurrent of pleading. "I didn't mean anything by it. We'll figure it out. We always do."

He nodded. "I know. Adam is great at figuring things out. Did he say anything at all that might tell us what was on his mind?"

She shook her head. "Really, no. He left earlier than usual, but I didn't think much about it." Sharon put her hand to shield her eyes from the sun as she gazed out at the water.

Almost in a whisper she asked: "He wouldn't have gone after someone else's traps. would he?" Even to ask seemed shocking to her.

Kyle drew a breath before answering. "No. Never."

She nodded. "Maybe even just to scout out a new area?"

He shook his head. "No, he wouldn't, but all the guys are out there searching now. They're keeping their eyes open while they're working. Just about everyone's out there." He grasped her arm now. "Let's go get a coffee. As soon as someone spots him, we'll hear about it."

She turned to walk beside him up to the coffee hut, and her friends parted to let them pass. At the question in Lynn's eyes, Sharon simply shook her head.

Sharon sat at a picnic table as Kyle got them each a coffee. It wasn't until he set down the paper cup in front of her that she seemed to surface from the daze she was in. "Where's Dab?" It had occurred to her that the other crew member, Dab Haan, might know something.

"Dab went out fishing with one of the guys. He didn't know anything. It seemed better."

Sharon nodded. She understood. Dab, a man in his 60s, had crewed for Adam and Kyle's father for years and Adam kept him for that reason, but he drank far too much and keeping him out on the boat was the best way to keep him from his rum. "He didn't have any ideas?"

Kyle shook his head. "He almost went home when he didn't see the *Child*. If I hadn't shown up right then, he probably would have."

Sharon allowed herself a small smile. "As if you guys would have left without him."

He shrugged. "Any excuse, I guess."

She frowned. "Imagine if he had left. You might have been the one thinking they'd left without you, and we wouldn't even know he's missing."

Kyle sighed. "I wouldn't have thought that, and besides, we don't really know he's missing as such."

"I should call the police."

Her brother-in-law pursed his lips. "Let's just wait a bit. Once you get these officials involved, there's no end of paperwork for what might be nothing more than a broken- down engine."

"Oh Kyle, you don't believe that."

"I don't know what I believe."

Kyle stood as another boat chugged its way into the harbour. It was just after ten o'clock and the fishermen were starting to return. The snug, dark blue hull riding low to the water and the bright orange waterproof pants of the crew made a cheerful, postcard-like maritime scene as it came close.

Sharon turned to watch as the men in the buyer's truck jumped out to make their way to the pier. Sharon knew the process like the back of her hand and watched without really seeing. She knew they'd weigh the tubs of canners and market lobsters before providing the owner of the boat with a receipt. They'd load the catch into their truck and take it away for processing or shipping. It was a scene she'd watched so many times before. Often Adam handed the receipt to her to keep because she kept the books for their business. Unlike some owners, Adam paid both Dab and Kyle himself instead of having the buyer pay the crew at the end of the week. Adam liked to have control.

Now she wished with all her heart that it was *Sea Child* tying up at the wharf instead of *Lucky Girl*.

A grey Hyundai Santa Fe drove past her and down to the end of the paved wharf road, pulled in and parked in the lot for the RV campground. Sharon squinted to see who it was. By now, more cars had arrived and people milled around in anticipation of hearing some news. It didn't take long in a community like theirs for the word to go out that a fisherman was missing.

Kyle had already left her side to go down to meet the home-coming boats as each one pulled in. It was busy now as crews handed out their tubs and the two buyers weighed and issued receipts. Sharon's stomach churned as she watched Kyle greet each new crew and saw the same response each time. The head shake and shrug. No one had seen Adam.

She turned to join her friends when her phone rang. Sharon frowned when she saw the name. She turned her back to her friends and answered in a quiet voice. "Michael."

Sharon smiled a short, quick smile. "Yes, we got the letter yesterday. Izzie has been accepted." She felt her friends behind her, perhaps believing that Adam was on the phone. "Michael, I have to go. Adam's missing." She disengaged the phone.

She stepped close to the women and shook her head when Lynn raised her eyebrows. They turned to study the newcomers. A white-haired man, who looked vaguely familiar to Sharon, walked towards the wharf while his companion, a young woman she didn't know, looked at her and walked purposefully in their direction.

Lynn said it first. "Cops. I know him. That's Gordie MacLean."

Sharon nodded. "Vanessa's friend."

"That's him."

They fell into silence as the woman approached and pulled out her identification.

Sharon had a moment of vertigo and closed her eyes. *This is it. It's official now and whatever happens, things will never be the same again.*

CHAPTER 3

DETECTIVE ROXANNE ALBRIGHT WAS deceptively delicate-looking with her slim build and scraped back dark hair, but her hours of working out and running had built up her muscles. After coming close to losing her life on her previous murder case, Roxanne had created a regime for herself to ensure she would never be vulnerable again. At least, that was the plan.

She understood some people took her less seriously than her male colleagues, and not only because she was a woman. Her deep chocolate-brown eyes were slightly almond-shaped, suggesting a distant inclusion of Mi'kmaq heritage, although Roxanne had never traced it. She knew often, people, including some of her own workmates, carried biases that played against her. It was one of the reasons she was happy to work with Detective Gordie MacLean again. He was different. A quiet man and a bit of a loner, he accepted her and listened to her opinions with respect. It had taken some time for him to get used to working with a partner since he preferred to work alone, but they had gotten past that. Roxanne knew Gordie's real partner was his Great Pyrenees dog Taz, so, early on, she had made friends with the big white dog and now Roxanne felt Gordie accepted her as part of his select small group of trusted individuals.

On this sunny morning, Roxanne Albright knew she was being sized up by the group of women gathered by the dockside. She straightened her shoulders as she dug out her identification.

"Good morning. I'm Detective Roxanne Albright from the Major Crimes Unit of the Cape Breton Police Services."

She saw one of the women pale even more than she had already been. "Major Crimes Unit? Why are you here?"

Roxanne shook her head. "I apologize. We are just here making inquiries. We received a call about a possible missing person, and we came out simply to get a sense of the situation. May I ask your name?"

"Sharon MacDonald. It's my husband who may be missing."

Albright put away her identification and pointed to a picnic table. "Let's sit down, and you can tell me what's going on. You look very worried and maybe I can help get to the bottom of things."

She steered Sharon to a table and when the other two women looked like they would follow, Roxanne shook her head. "Give us a few minutes, please, and then I'd like to speak to both of you as well."

They backed off, although one frowned, and the other looked as though she would protest. Roxanne turned away from them to focus on the fisherman's wife.

Albright sat across from Sharon at the faded wooden table, the wind off the water at her back, pushing wisps of hair into eyes. "Your friends are concerned for you."

Sharon turned to glance at her friends and nodded, whether in answer to Roxanne's question or to send a silent message to her friends, Albright didn't know.

She waited, but Sharon seemed transfixed by the sight of the pier and the returning boats, so Roxanne pulled out her notebook, which made it less of a chat and more of an interview. "What happened this morning?"

Her eyes focussed, and Sharon sighed. "I don't really know. He went out, the same as every morning, but no one's seen him since."

"Did anyone go out with him?"

"No, that's the problem. Adam's brother Kyle crews for him along with another man, but Adam was already gone when they arrived this morning."

"How did you find that out? Do you usually come down here?"

"No. Not anymore."

Roxanne raised her eyebrows.

"I used to when our daughter Izzie was younger. I'd put her in the wagon and pull her down here, but now she's in school, so I get her ready and make sure she catches the bus on time."

"I see. So, did someone call you this morning to bring you here?"

"Kyle did. He couldn't understand where Adam was and thought I'd know."

"Is it unusual for him to go out alone?"

Sharon frowned. "Yes. Fishing is a three-person job. They could manage with two if they had to, but it's a lot of work. He'd never go fishing on his own."

"Did anyone see him?"

The wind pushed the wisps of Sharon's loose hair back from her face, for a moment giving the woman a skeletal appearance. "I don't think so. Kyle talked to those who were here, and then he radioed around to ask the ones who went out early."

Roxanne's phone rang, and she pulled it out of her top pocket to see who it was. When she saw it was Gordie, she climbed away from the table and turned to look at MacLean standing alone at the edge of the pier as she answered his call.

"I've had a call. The boat's been found. Sounds like they found a body, but don't say anything until we know more."

Roxanne nodded and hung up. She turned back to Sharon. "Is there anything else you can tell me? Any reason why Adam might take the boat out on his own?"

Sharon shook her head. "No, no reason. Maybe he just took it out for a run to test some mechanical thing and broke down."

"We'll leave it there for the moment, but we'll probably be in touch later."

Sharon stood, her bottom teeth chewing on her top lip. "Has something happened? Do you know something?"

"No, there's nothing to tell you. Maybe you should go home now. You look exhausted. Have a lie down before your daughter comes home."

By now, the other two women had crept closer again.

Before putting away her notebook, she turned to the newcomers. "Can I get both your names?"

The one who seemed most in charge reached for Sharon's hand. "I'm Lynn Duggan, and this" she turned to the other woman and introduced her "is Yvonne Farley." Lynn's short steel-grey hair and firm attitude spoke of a woman who was used to taking charge.

Roxanne appealed directly to her. "Maybe you can see that Sharon gets home. I don't think it's doing anyone any good to stand around here waiting for news. She'd be better off at home with a hot cup of tea or soup, don't you think?"

Sharon stood stiffly, resisting as if she might protest, but when Lynn put her arm around her friend's shoulders, she sagged and nodded as Lynn and Yvonne turned her towards the parking lot.

Roxanne hurried down the slope to where Gordie was waiting in the parked car. She climbed in and buckled up as he started the engine. She half turned to him. "Well? What did you hear?"

"Sarge called. He heard from the Coast Guard who had a call about a body on a boat. That's about all I know, other than it was out of Pleasant Bay."

"Is that significant?"

"The boat was in a different LFA than where MacDonald should have been."

"LFA." she repeated, and then nodded. "Right. Lobster fishing area. What area should he have been in?"

"He's supposed to be in 26B, but he was north, in area 27, off the northern tip of Cape Breton."

"Weird. What could have taken him there, I wonder."

"They towed the boat into Pleasant Bay. It's a couple hours' drive, but I think we should head right up. We can stop in Margaree Harbour for lunch."

She nodded. "Shall I let the boss know that we're on our way?"

He nodded as he pulled out on to Route 19.

MacLean waited until Albright finished speaking with Sergeant Arsenault before calling his friend Vanessa. She answered on the first ring and her voice sounded worried even through the speaker. "Gordie? Did you find anything?"

"Hi Vanessa. I'm in the car with Albright."

Vanessa's voice was warm. "Hi, Roxanne."

"Hi, Vanessa."

Gordie smiled at the sound of her voice. "Listen, we don't know much yet, and I can't have you sharing what I'm about to tell you, OK?"

"I understand."

"We're on our way north because it seems that they have found the boat. We know nothing more than that." Gordie crossed his fingers at the lie and Roxanne nodded.

"Maybe the boat just broke down?" her voice was hopeful.

"I'll know more when we get there, but again, please don't call Lynn and say anything. We need to be clearer on the situation, and then, of course, the family needs to be the first to hear anything, right?"

"Right. That makes sense. I'll just wait until you can tell me more." Her voice was subdued now. Gordie nodded. She got the message.

Gordie continued. "I don't know what the service is like along here, but I'll call you later when I can, OK?"

"OK, Gordie. Thank you. Bye for now. Bye, Roxanne."

They drove without talking for a while, listening to folk music on the satellite radio of MacLean's car.

"Did you always have satellite radio?"

"No, it's pretty recent. Vanessa signed me up for it."

Roxanne raised her eyebrows.

"For my birthday."

"Nice. When was that? You never said."

He shrugged. "Couple weeks ago. I'm not used to making a big deal of it."

She smiled. "Ah, but you're in a relationship now. I hope you know when her birthday is. You'll have to think of something nice to match this."

He nodded. "I wrote it on my kitchen calendar. It's not until October, so you have time to help me think of something." He looked at his partner and grinned.

***

They came into Pleasant Bay at two-thirty and followed the signs for whale watching tours to take them to the marina. Several fishing boats bobbed on the water; the work for the day done by now, but only one had yellow crime scene tape fastened to it. A wooden pier bordered the front of the small harbour, where picnic tables invited people to sit and wait for their turn on a whale and seal watching cruise. Despite it being very early in the season, a few tourists sat here with their cell phones held up, taking photos and videos of the police activity. There was also a large knot of onlookers who stood talking quietly in front of the building where they sold hot drinks, snacks and whale-watching tickets. Dressed in working clothes that marked them as part of the local fishing community, MacLean didn't see anyone amongst the sombre-looking group holding up their phones for photos.

Along the left side of the harbour was a long pier where the majority of boats were tied up, including *Sea Child*; her bright red hull and white cabin looking cheerful against the blue sky and aquamarine of the small harbour. Several officers gathered on the pier near the boat, their clothing a bright mix of colours representing the various units: blue-shirted Coast Guard, white-shirted colleagues from the marine unit of the Cape Breton Police Services and even the distinctive yellow stripe down the side of his pantleg identifying a Royal Canadian Mounted Police officer.

Albright leaned in to murmur in MacLean's ear. "Quite the crowd already."

MacLean grunted. "But room for two more."

"You sure?"

"If there's a body, it's a Major Case, not Marine or anyone else."

"You're the boss."

Gordie had his identification pulled out by the time they walked down the ramp and reached the edge of the pier. The RCMP officer strode towards them before they reached the knot. He was impossibly young-looking, the knife-edge crease in his trousers and gleaming boots a testament to the eagerness of his youth.

The young officer glanced at the identification cards for both MacLean and Albright and then introduced himself. "Constable Jeffreys. How can I help you, Detective?"

MacLean sensed the tension in the constable's voice. "Just here to take a look at the scene, Constable. Have you called the forensics team already?"

Jeffreys folded his arms across his chest. "Yes, they're on their way. Until then, no one goes on the boat."

MacLean kept his voice low and easy. "Absolutely right. I intend, however; to inspect the boat from the pier, so if you'll step aside so my partner and I can get closer, I'd appreciate it."

"With all due respect, Detective, this is my scene, and we have enough people tramping around already."

MacLean took a deep breath, exhaled, and then leaned closer, his voice a low rumble. "Son, you can be a professional and give up the scene now, and let us work together as colleagues, or you can give up the scene later and look like an ass. You choose."

The constable straightened his six-foot plus height and glared down at Gordie. "This is *my* scene, Pop, and when forensics has released it, you're free to take a look."

Albright touched MacLean on the arm. "Shall I call Sergeant Arsenault?"

MacLean scowled at her, and Albright left the phone in her pocket.

At that moment, one of the constables from the Cape Breton Police Services Marine Unit joined their trio, holding out his own phone. "Constable Jeffreys--call for you."

Jeffreys frowned as he took the phone, turning his back to MacLean and Albright to take the call.

MacLean nodded to the marine unit officer. "Hiya, Baker." He gestured to his partner to introduce them. "Detective Roxanne Albright, Constable Joe Baker. Who's on the phone?"

Baker smirked and answered in a low voice. "His boss in Inverness. I knew as soon as you drove up that it wouldn't be pretty. My buddy over in the Ingonish detachment told me they've had more civilian complaints in the six months Constable Mike has been in Cheticamp, than in the six years with the last guy."

MacLean nodded. "Out to make a name for himself?"

Baker nodded and then held out his hand for his phone as Jeffreys tapped the disconnect button and turned back to them.

Jeffreys stood aside. "Since you've driven all the way up here, you might as well look at the scene, but I'll say again, don't try to board."

MacLean tried not to sound sarcastic. "I appreciate your cooperation."

MacLean and Albright crossed the remaining fifteen feet to get to the rest of the group standing at the side of the boat. MacLean held up his identification again for the two Coast Guard and remaining marine unit officers. "I'm Detective Gordie MacLean and this is Detective Roxanne Albright." He turned to Albright. "Can you talk to these gentlemen and get the details of what happened, where the boat was found, all of that? I'll join you in a minute. I just want to take a look at the boat first."

Albright led the four men further along the pier to leave MacLean in peace as he examined the boat. Jeffreys stood watching, hands on hips, arms akimbo.

The sound of Albright's interviews and the presence of the glowering constable faded as MacLean focussed and began his examination.

CHAPTER 4

SEA CHILD'S BRIGHT AND cheerful exterior was not replicated within the boat itself. The decking was a gunmetal grey and while the exterior of the cabin had recently received a fresh coat of white paint, from Gordie's vantage point on the pier, he saw the interior was dirty white with chipped and peeling paint. Gordie pulled his notebook from his jacket pocket and focussed his attention on the deck which was empty aside from the large cold-tub which normally held the catch but now stood empty with its top open, a black plastic tote and the grey seaman's locker with two lidded buckets resting on top; one, a stained white, the other a yellow to match the constable's yellow pantstripe.

A bloody stain pooled on the deck, the blue and green blowflies busily feeding on the still sticky mess. Lying on the deck, tucked under the 'washboard' or boat's flat rim, lay a gaff hook, a wooden pole with a sharp hook at the end. Gordie took several photos and then stepped back a pace to walk along the length of the boat. He crouched down and took more photos of the hull, zooming his phone camera in to take detailed pictures. When he satisfied himself that he had seen all he could from the pier, he straightened and turned to Jeffreys.

"I assume the body is on its way to the morgue?"

"Yes, of course." The constable frowned. "I checked with my supervisor before letting the body go, and while it wasn't a full forensics team, they took a lot of photos, and bagged his hands before moving him. The rest of the team is on their way." He concluded with, "it seemed best to get the body out of here with the sun and all."

"I understand. Is he going to Sydney?"

"No, Port Mulroy."

"All right. I'll check if Dr. Allan wants it sent down to his lab or if he'll go up to Port Mulroy." MacLean made a note and then looked back at the constable, who was now standing with his arms crossed in front of his chest. "Have you made arrangements for the boat to be taken in after the forensics folks are done?"

Jeffreys nodded. "The RCMP has a trailer and a secure lock-up in Inverness where it'll go for now."

"That'll do."

The young man bristled; his jaw clenched, and eyes narrowed. "I know what I'm doing. I'm still not convinced that this won't remain under our jurisdiction."

MacLean straightened, tired of the younger man's aggressive attitude. "Constable Jeffreys, I won't wait here for the forensics team to do their work, but let me point one thing out to you because I want to ensure samples are scraped and proper photos taken." Gordie stepped closer to the boat again and pointed to a mark on the red paint of the hull. "See that?"

Jeffreys bent over and peered. "That bit of dirt?"

His voice hardened. "I know it's hard to see because you have draped the crime scene tape along the boat itself, thereby possibly destroying evidence, but I believe it is a fresh scrape made by something, possibly another boat, rubbing up against the hull." MacLean glared at Jeffreys. "If you are ever again first on the scene and need to mark it out, *never* contaminate the scene by touching it with tape."

Jeffreys visibly deflated, his crossed arms falling to his sides. "But I needed to surround the scene."

"No. You need to prevent contamination and you should have done that by posting the tape along the pier to prevent access to the boat. What you've done is possibly rub some of the trace evidence off the hull. Evidence that could make or break this case."

The young constable licked his lips. "Should I remove the tape?"

"For God's sakes, do nothing. You'll only make it worse. Just make sure the forensics address it first before any further movement, with people walking around on the boat."

Jeffreys nodded. "Right."

"And Constable?"

"Yes, Detective?"

"Get over yourself and let's just work together as a team."

He nodded, but Gordie saw by the flush and bulging vein in the younger man's neck that he had made an enemy.

MacLean turned to the group of other officers and saw them all watching. He left Jeffreys and stepped over to his partner's side. "How are you doing with the interviews?"

"We're done, I'd say. Did you want to go over anything?"

"Just one thing. When you first noticed *Sea Child* where you found her, did you see any other boats in the area? Maybe a small aluminum run-about?"

The two Coast Guard officers looked at each other and one answered for them both. "No, no one."

"That's it for me, then. Detective Albright can brief me on the drive back."

They walked as a group back to the ramp to leave the pier. "Good seeing you again, Baker. Thanks for your help today."

Joe Baker winked and nodded. "We CBPS have to stick together."

***

Roxanne briefed Gordie as they drove, and he only interrupted to ask specific questions. "Did they say if the *Child* was drifting or anchored when they found her?"

"Anchored."

He nodded. "So, he was in that spot, far from his assigned area, with no intention to fish since his traps are all in his usual place, waiting to be worked. What took him there?"

"Maybe he had done some repairs to the engine, and he was just out for a run to test it?"

"Maybe. Do we know if anyone fired up the engine?"

Roxanne shook her head. "I don't think so. They knew *Sea Child* was missing because of all the chatter on the radio, so when they saw her sitting there, the Coast Guard came alongside and hailed her. When no one answered, Officer Jordan boarded her. He was careful because by then they saw there was someone lying there, but they didn't know if he was alive or not. They saw the blood, so knew it was serious. Jordan didn't have any crime scene protective gear of course, but he said he stepped carefully to avoid the blood and only stayed long enough to check for a pulse and then he investigated the cabin below deck to make sure there was no one else there in need of assistance. He hauled up the anchor, they hooked the boat up to theirs and then he got out of there."

"Good. I noticed a scrape of paint. We know the Coast Guard boat is red and white, so no chance it came from them."

Her eyes widened. "Amazing it survived the tow to the pier."

"Right. We better call Sarge and see what he wants us to do from here."

Albright smiled. "Do you want me to call him?"

MacLean sighed. "No, it's all right. I better get it over with and tell him about the run-in with Mountie Mike. I'll just throw him on speaker."

He engaged the phone using his hands-free function on his

steering wheel.. Sergeant Arsenault picked up on the first ring. "MacLean."

"You're on the speaker, Sergeant. Albright and I just left Pleasant Bay and are on our way south again. The deceased had already been removed by the time we got here, but there was blood, so I'm guessing it wasn't natural causes like a heart attack or stroke."

"Where was the body taken?"

"Port Mulroy morgue. I should tell you that there was a young Mountie, Constable Jeffreys, in charge of the scene when we got there. He was reluctant to let us too near and seems to feel strongly that he has jurisdiction."

MacLean heard the sigh whisper through the speaker, followed by Arsenault's exasperated tone. "Did you wind him up somehow, MacLean?"

MacLean rolled his eyes. "Didn't do a thing, Sergeant."

Albright piped up. "I think it was just the guy's nature, Sergeant."

"Yeah, all right. So, what happened?"

MacLean continued. "Joe Baker from the marine unit was there, along with another constable. They were called in by the Coast Guard, who found the boat, and the marine unit contacted the local unit of the RCMP. When Joe saw that Jeffreys was going to be difficult, he called the county district for Inverness and someone there had a word with Jeffreys."

"Right. Get to the bottom line. Where do things stand now?"

"Forensics is on the way now and once they're done, the boat will be trailered to Inverness to a lock-up the Mounties have. I'm sure this will be our case, but for now, I've let Jeffreys carry on coordinating that."

"You did right. We'll get the autopsy done first and then we'll figure out jurisdiction."

"What do you want done about next of kin notification? Someone needs to go and tell her the news that we believe her husband is deceased and make arrangements for her to go in and do the formal identification."

"You've somehow inserted yourself into this case, MacLean, so you and Albright might as well carry on. It's up in your patch, anyway. Go see the wife, get some basic information, and then come into the office tomorrow and we'll figure out where we go from here."

"Right, Sergeant. Have a good night."

The phone disengaged without a response.

MacLean chewed his lip for a moment. "I better call Vanessa, just so she knows I haven't forgotten her."

"Once we get out of the National Park, there's a great bakery coffee shop in Petit Étang. Why don't we pull in there, and then you can make your call in private while I go in and check out what looks good?"

He nodded. "Sounds like a plan."

MacLean spent the half hour drive to the bakery reviewing the interviews again. "Did Joe Baker say anything about the crime scene tape actually draping the boat? He would have known better, and I wonder if he tried to intervene or just left buddy to it."

"He didn't say anything about it, and I didn't think to ask him." Albright's voice was low, as if embarrassed.

"Don't worry about it. I'm just curious if Jeffrey ignored advice or just didn't realize what he was doing. I suppose it doesn't matter either way."

When they pulled into the parking lot of the small bakery restaurant, MacLean had a hard time finding a spot with the half dozen cars already there. He let his partner out first and then squeezed in beside the dumpster. He watched her go in as he dialed Vanessa's number.

Her voice was breathless, as if she had run for the phone. "Hello?"

"Hi, it's me."

"Oh Gordie. It's bad news, isn't it?"

"I can't confirm anything until we meet with Mrs. MacDonald."

"No, I understand. Was there an accident? Can you say that at least?"

Keeping his voice neutral "It doesn't look like the boat had been in an accident, but we'll know more once forensics takes a look."

There was a second's silence. "Forensics. Oh, no. I won't press you for more information and don't worry, I won't call anyone. When I spoke with Lynn about an hour and a half ago, she had left Sharon dozing on the couch, but I imagine their daughter must just about be home from school now. I don't envy you your job, Gordie, but I better let you get on with it."

"I'll call you later Vanessa, if it isn't too late."

"Call me anytime. Do you want me to make up a plate of supper for you that you can swing by and take with you on your way home?"

Gordie was very tempted. He'd be driving right past her house on his way home. "No, thank you. It's very thoughtful but I better not. I'll have Roxanne with me, and I don't have any idea what time it'll be. We'll probably just pick something up on the fly."

He heard the smile in her voice. "Chili from Tim Hortons , maybe?"

"You know me too well."

She mentioned his dog then. "What about Taz? Do you want me to take her out for a bit?"

Gordie remembered how only six months ago he would call his neighbour to feed his dog, Taz, if he would be late, but just last month he had given a key to Vanessa for just such an occasion. "I don't want to put you out."

"Don't be silly. It will give me something to take my mind off what's happening in Port Hood. I'll go and take her out for a walk and give her supper."

"Taz'll be delighted to see you. If you're sure, thank you."

"Don't give it another thought. Go and do what you need to do, and I'll talk to you later."

Gordie disengaged his phone and moved the car now that a

couple of spaces had opened up. He walked in and saw that Roxanne was next in line to be served.

He joined her and peered at the menu board to quickly examine the baked goods on offer.

Roxanne ordered a tea and two cookies. "Oatmeal Raisin and a Jam-Jam please."

He raised his eyebrows "Jam-Jam?"

She shrugged. "It sounds good."

Gordie sniffed. "A double-double coffee, an oat cake and a molasses cookie, please."

His partner poked him with her elbow. "You're such a traditionalist."

"Tried and true. What's wrong with that?"

They took their snack outside and sat at one of the picnic tables at the edge of the parking lot. After he ate his cookies, he stood and made to walk away.

Roxanne waved him back. "I finished my cookies and there's a good breeze blowing. I don't mind if you sit and smoke your cigarette."

He sat again and enjoyed the last of his coffee with his smoke. He looked at his cigarette with a rueful smile. "One of these days, I'll give it up."

"I think that's the first time I've heard you say that."

He shrugged. "Maybe it's time."

"Vanessa giving you a hard time about it?"

"No. She's good that way. She doesn't bug me about it, but I know she doesn't like it."

"Well, good for you for thinking about it. It's a start."

He nicked the cigarette halfway through and put it back in his pack. "Let's get going. We need to get this over with."

CHAPTER 5

I T WAS EASY TO find the MacDonald house, just up from the harbour on a small lane off Main Street. The house was a typical two-story farm-style house, clad in white siding. There was a wrap-around covered veranda on two sides, and MacLean imagined peaceful evenings spent watching the sun sink into the water that glistened in the distance.

Sharon MacDonald pulled open the door as they climbed the steps. The auburn hair pulled back from her face into a pony-tail accentuated Sharon's ghost-like colour. In the few hours since MacLean had first seen the woman, dark circles had formed beneath her blue eyes.

Gordie spoke quietly. "Mrs. MacDonald, may we come in?"

She backed into the house and turned to the left, into the living room. MacLean and Albright followed, no one speaking.

Sharon MacDonald sat on the dark blue sofa and pulled a flo-ral-patterned duvet over her as if she were chilled. MacLean sat nearby on a recliner while Albright stood in the doorway.

She, Sharon, spoke first. "You found the boat."

MacLean knew she was ready to hear the news. "Yes, we did. It's been towed into Pleasant Bay."

"So far from here."

"Yes, it is."

Sharon shook her head, confused.

"Mrs. MacDonald." He stopped as she frowned.

"Sharon, please."

He nodded. "Sharon. I didn't see him myself, but the first responders who found the boat informed me that there was someone on it. The man was deceased. We will need you to go into Port Mulroy to make an official identification, but we believe it's Adam."

She clutched both hands in front of her mouth to stifle the keening sound.

"Sharon, did your husband have a history of heart problems? Anything to account for a sudden death?"

She shook her head and took a deep breath. "No. He's in excellent health. It must be a mistake."

"It's certainly possible, so the sooner you feel able to go to make the identification, the better."

Before she could respond, the door banged open and the daughter, Izzie came running through the door. The child threw herself on top of her mother. "Mummy! Michael MacInnes said that something happened to Daddy. He has his own cell phone, and he said his mom told him. It's a lie, isn't? He's a liar."

Sharon wrapped her arms around her daughter, pulling the little girl into her. "We don't know yet, sweetheart. Something happened to his boat, but we don't know for sure yet what happened to Daddy. These are police officers and they're trying to find out."

Izzie pulled away and stared at MacLean. "Where's my Daddy?"

"We're trying to find that out."

She stood suddenly and stepped away from her mother. Izzie pointed a trembling finger at Sharon. "It's your fault. You yelled at him last night and he doesn't like that. You made him go away. I hate you."

Sharon sobbed. "No. Izzie, that's not true. We had words, but all grown-ups do that sometimes." She stopped when her daughter ran up the stairs, leaving the three of them in stunned silence.

The distraught wife looked first at MacLean and then lifted a hand beseechingly towards Albright. "Everyone argues sometimes. It didn't mean anything."

MacLean stood. "I'll go make some tea for us." He glanced at Roxanne, who gave a slight nod before moving to perch on the edge of the sofa beside Sharon.

He walked down the hall to the kitchen and put the kettle on to boil, and then walked quietly back down the hall and up the steps. "Izzie?"

He heard sobbing from behind a door decorated with paper stars. He tapped softly. "Izzie? It's Detective MacLean. May I come in?"

He opened the door despite getting no response. "Izzie, I won't come in if you tell me not to. I'm just making some tea and I don't know if you drink tea, or if I can get you something else? Maybe a glass of milk?" By this time, he had edged inside the girl's room.

She sat up on the bed and rubbed her eyes. She nodded. "Milk and a cookie, please."

"Shall I bring it up here?"

She shook her head. "I'm not allowed to have snacks in my room."

"Let's go down then, and you can help me find everything I need in the kitchen."

She slid off the bed and trailed after him, still sniffling.

In the kitchen, she pointed out where to find the tea bags and cups while she herself got the milk from the fridge. She directed him to the package of chocolate chip cookies and then they sat at the table while the tea steeped. The girl drank her milk and nibbled on a cookie.

MacLean knew he shouldn't be interviewing the child without

an adult present, but he prodded gently. *We're just chatting.* "You sounded pretty angry with your mom. Do your folks argue a lot?"

She shrugged and then shook her head. "Not really."

"But last night they did."

"It didn't last long, I don't think. I had to get up to go to the bathroom, so I heard Mommy getting mad at Daddy for something, but then I ran back to my room and closed the door. I didn't want to hear."

"No. I can understand that." He stood. "I'm going to take in some tea to your mom now. I think she needs it."

The little girl's shoulders dropped, her anger spent. Her eyes filled with tears again and she leapt from the chair and ran down the hall to her mother. "I'm sorry, Mommy. I'm sorry. You know I don't hate you."

MacLean arrived with the tea tray and set it down on the coffee table. Mother and daughter were wrapped under the duvet together on the couch and Albright had moved to the recliner.

Gordie handed a cup to Sharon. "Izzie helped me, and she told me you take it with milk and two sugars."

"Yes. Thank you." She took a sip but put it down again almost immediately.

Maclean handed a cup to Albright and then took his own. "Sharon, do you have any idea why Adam might have been so far from his own fishing area?"

"No, I really don't."

"Do you know anyone up there? In Pleasant Bay, or Meat Cove?"

She shrugged and shook her head. "We know people everywhere, but I can't think of anyone that would warrant him going all the way up there on a morning when he should be getting ready to go fishing. Maybe his brother Kyle or his dad might know, but I don't."

MacLean took a couple more sips of tea. "Is there anyone we can call for you right now, Sharon? A family member or a friend?"

"No. My mother's in Halifax. I'll call her in a bit, but I can't face it yet. My friend Lynn is just down the street. I'll call her and she'll come." She closed her eyes for a few seconds as if to block out the world. "God, I'll have to call Adam's brother and father first." Sharon started weeping. "I'm not sure I can."

"We can do that notification. Adam's brother is Kyle, right?"

"Yes. His father's name is Danny. Danny MacDonald, of course, but everyone calls him Dannymac."

Gordie opened his notebook to a fresh page. "Please write their addresses."

Sharon took the book and wrote one address and handed it back. "They have the same address, basically. A couple of years ago Danny-mac severed two acres and signed it over to Kyle for a mini home, so their homes are side by side."

"That was generous. Was Adam upset that his father gave the land to Kyle?"

"No, not really. Adam and Kyle didn't always get along because things so often went wrong for Kyle and then someone had to bail him out. Not literally. I don't mean he was in jail or anything. Adam always worked hard, and he felt that if Kyle would stick with things, they wouldn't fall apart so often. As for the land, it wasn't being used. Dannymac still has several acres of his own. Besides, it was always understood that the boat was going to Adam, so he couldn't very well complain about the land, right?"

Gordie put his notebook away. "You rest. We'll go there right now, but we need to get the identification done as soon as you're able. Do you think you could find someone to babysit for you this evening?? It'll be late, but the Coroner's assistant has agreed to stay on this evening. I can have a community liaison person come to drive you if necessary."

The distraught woman bit her lip. "Lynn will look after Izzie for me and maybe Kyle will drive me."

"I'll ask him when we meet with him. I'm sure he'll want to talk to you, anyway." He pulled a business card from his wallet. "Call me later when you're ready, and I'll meet you there." He then tore a page from his notebook and wrote out the address for the morgue in Port Mulroy.

The two police officers left Sharon MacDonald hunched on the sofa with her daughter clinging to her.

It was a short drive to the address Sharon provided, for the Mac-Donald men. The main house was one and a half stories, with an attached garage in the back. They clad it in light grey siding with white trim. On the side near the garage, freshly painted dark brown steps led to an enclosed porch while on the long front side there was another set of painted steps leading to a covered over veranda. The driveway ran further into the property past the home before branching off into a Y, with the right branch leading to a tall, weathered boat garage while the left arm ended at what some people called a mobile home. From his vantage point where he parked the car near the open garage, Gordie saw that the second home looked quite new, meaning that they would consider it a mini home and not a mobile home.

Gordie led the way up the steps to the enclosed porch and knocked. When he opened the door, Gordie recognized Kyle from having seen him earlier in the day. "Kyle? We met earlier." Gordie held up his identification, as did Roxanne.

Kyle nodded and beckoned them to follow him into the kitchen. It was a clean and tidy room, although dated with white cabinets that had the somewhat quirky style of having the handles in the middle of each cabinet door rather than the more typical edge positioning.

An elderly man, thinning grey hair combed across his head and gaunt face, frowning, motioned them to chairs at the table from his seat in a large rocking chair.

Kyle spoke first. "Dad, these are police officers. They were at the harbour this morning."

Gordie nodded. "I'm Detective MacLean, and this is my partner, Detective Albright."

Mr. MacDonald made a sound that might have been a grunt of pain or a greeting. "Well, what news do you have?"

Gordie glanced at Kyle and then addressed himself to the father. "I'm afraid it doesn't look good, sir. As you may know, Adam's boat was found,"

"My boat." The old man interrupted.

Gordie nodded. "They found *Sea Child* quite a distance from Port Hood off the coast near Pleasant Bay."

"And Adam?"

"There was a deceased man on the boat when it was found."

His face paled. "And you believe it to be my son."

"I'm afraid we do. We do need to have a formal identification, though." Gordie turned to Kyle. "Mrs. MacDonald is prepared to go down this evening to the morgue in Port Mulroy. I believe she hopes you might take her. I think she could use the moral support. You can imagine that she's had quite a shock. You all have."

Kyle nodded but didn't say that he would. He looked at his father in shock. "Maybe it isn't him."

MacDonald Senior rested his head against the chair and closed his eyes. "Who else could it be?"

Gordie nodded towards Roxanne. "Kyle, would you mind showing Detective Albright around the property? I understand you have a separate residence here?"

Kyle frowned. "Why? Why do you want to look around?"

"It's always helpful to understand where a person spends time. The more we know about Adam's life, the more likely we are to discover what happened."

Kyle looked at his father, who had straightened up and now shrugged silently.

He stood, and with a jerk of his head, he invited Albright to follow him. "Fine."

After they left, Danny MacDonald narrowed his eyes and studied MacLean. "What is it you wanted to ask me without Kyle here?"

"Was there any jealousy between the brothers?"

"Show me brothers, or sisters for that matter, that don't have some jealousy between them."

"Fair enough. Was Kyle angry because he believed you planned to give the boat to Adam?"

He shook his head. "Nothing was written in stone. Kyle went through some difficult years, but he was coming out of it. He knew Adam was more responsible, and they work well together. For now, having Adam run the business was the right thing. Kyle understood that."

"You felt it necessary to give him some land, though."

"I did that for both our sakes because I have cancer. Although I'm not doing bad right now, over the last couple years I've had a lot of health issues and I liked having the boy nearby. He comes in a couple times a day to check on me or help with things."

MacLean nodded. "I didn't realize. That does sound like a good arrangement."

MacDonald sighed as if tired of the discussion. "I need to rest. This has all been too much for me today. Do you have any idea what happened to him? Maybe a heart attack?"

"I'm sorry, we don't know yet. We'll have to wait, first for the formal identification and secondly for the post-mortem." He paused and then asked one last question. "Mr. MacDonald, do you have any idea why Adam would have taken the boat way up to the Pleasant Bay area? It's out of your Lobster Fishing Area."

MacDonald shook his head. "No idea at all."

MacLean waited for more, but the silence grew, and it was clear that MacDonald was finished.

"All right. I'll leave you now and I'm very sorry for your trouble. Kyle and Detective Albright must be done with the walk-around so I'll join them outside. I hope he will take Mrs. MacDonald into Port Mulroy this evening for the identification."

MacDonald nodded. "He will."

MacLean met Kyle MacDonald and Albright as they came out of the boat garage.

The young man scowled. "D'ya really need to see my place? It's a mess and trust me, Adam hasn't been there in ages."

Albright spoke in a quiet, soothing tone. "We aren't here to judge your housekeeping ability, Kyle, so yes, please."

Kyle huffed in displeasure. "Huh. Come on, then."

They followed him to the home, which was done in white siding and dark brown shutters, and went up the steps, past a barbecue and into the home. Inside, it was surprisingly spacious, with the kitchen and living room as one large space with a peninsula and two chairs set up for eating, although one would be hard-pressed to eat a meal there now as it was covered with empty beer cans.

Kyle stood with his arms folded. "So here it is. If you want to poke around, you'll need a warrant."

MacLean held up his hand. "No, no. We don't need to look any further. As Detective Albright said, we just like to get a sense of things."

Kyle stepped to the door and held it open. "Then I guess you don't mind leaving. I need to go back to my dad."

MacLean turned and went back out, with Albright immediately behind him and followed by Kyle. They walked in silence back down the driveway to where MacLean had parked. He turned back to Kyle. "Will you call Mrs. MacDonald about driving her to do the formal notification later?"

Kyle nodded and went back up the steps into his father's home.

MacLean and Albright got in the car and as he drove out onto the road, Albright shook her head. "Was it just me, or did Kyle Mac-Donald seem more angry than bereaved?"

CHAPTER 6

MACLEAN TILTED HIS HEAD. "People react differently to bad news. I've even heard people laugh when given bad news before shocking themselves into shutting up. I wouldn't read too much into his reaction."

She nodded. "Fair enough."

"Tell me about your walk around with Kyle. Did you learn anything of interest?"

Albright pulled out her notebook and read through her notes. "He said it was just a normal morning for him. He had his breakfast, checked on his father, and then headed to the wharf and was surprised to see the boat gone."

"Was anyone else there? Someone who saw Adam leave?"

"Apparently not. He was one of the first there, but he did go around asking anyone who was already there if they'd seen his brother, with no luck. The other crew member was there before Kyle. That guy goes by the name of Dab Haan, and Kyle doesn't know what his full name is. He lives in an old cabin outside town."

"Did this Dab fella know anything?"

"No. According to Kyle, Dab's overly fond of rum and wasn't saying much of anything other than the boat was already gone when he got there a few minutes before Kyle himself. Seems like Dab worked for MacDonald Senior for years, so they keep him on as a favour to their dad."

"I wonder if Adam agreed with Kyle on that."

"I asked him about that." Roxanne smiled at the approving glance Gordie gave her. "Adam was even more keen about retiring Dab and had talked to his dad about it, but MacDonald Senior wouldn't hear of it, and although Adam's been running the day-to-day business, his dad still has the final say on major decisions."

"Well, that's interesting. Anything else worthwhile?"

"Not really. I tried to find out if Kyle resented Adam. What with their dad making it clear that Adam would be getting the business, even though it's Kyle who is essentially looking after his father."

"And?"

"He could be fooling me completely, but I don't think so. Kyle was reasonably forthright with his information. Until the past couple of years, he himself was a bit of a wild kid. He didn't even go fishing."

"Really? Did he elaborate? What did he do that was so wild? And if he wasn't making a living fishing, what was he doing?"

"He told me he lived in Halifax for a while, and after that he was in Toronto. He only said he did 'this and that'. "

"What brought him home?"

"His father got cancer. His mother died about five years ago, so when Kyle heard that Senior got cancer it shook him up and he came home. His dad went into remission, but Kyle was settled into his own place by then and he likes it. He took up fishing with his brother, and it sounds like they got along fairly well."

"Good work with all that. Senior told me about the cancer as well. Essentially, he said the same thing – that the brothers got along for the most part and Kyle understood Adam was the responsible one, but Senior mentioned nothing was written in stone about the boat and business."

Albright frowned. "You think something's changed recently?"

"I don't know. It's something to keep in mind. I didn't get a chance to ask the father if he knew of any enemies that Adam may have had, but I imagine if he knew something like that, he'd say. I asked if he knew why Adam might be way up there away from his own LFA and he said he didn't."

"I asked Kyle if Adam was well-liked. He was ambivalent. He said he wasn't liked or disliked more than anyone else, as far as he knew."

Gordie glanced over. "That's not much of a testimonial, is it?"

"That's what I thought. I'm not sure if he's just an understated kind of guy or if he knows something he doesn't want to share."

"It'll come to the surface sooner or later if there is."

"What now?"

MacLean glanced at the clock. "I'll take you back to your car and by then I'll call Sharon MacDonald again to see about meeting them at the morgue."

"I can come along."

"I know and if you want to, you're welcome, but I expect it to just take a few minutes and I'm a lot closer than you are. I suggest you head home, and we'll meet bright and early at the office tomorrow and see what the next steps are. Sarge may have even decided by now to give the case to someone else."

"True. I don't think he will, though. You've proven you're up to solving a murder."

"We'll see."

***

After dropping Albright at her car, MacLean sat in the parking lot of Tim Hortons and called Sharon MacDonald. He confirmed Kyle would pick her up and they would meet at the Port Mulroy morgue at seven p.m.

His next call was to Vanessa. "Hi there. I just thought I'd check in to make sure Taz didn't give you any problems."

He heard Vanessa murmuring to his dog. "A problem? What's he saying? How could you be a problem?"

He laughed. "I gather you two girls are still together, then?"

"I'm glad you called because I confess, I've stolen her away. She enjoyed her dinner and then I brought her back with me to the house. I was planning to call you later to check how late you thought you'd be, and I'll take her back close to when you think you'll be done. Is that all right?"

"That's fine and I'm quite sure Taz appreciates it. As it happens, I have about an hour to spare right now and I was debating running home for a few minutes, but..."

She answered quickly. "Oh, yes come here. Did you eat?"

"No. I'm in St. Peter's Tim Horton's, but I haven't gone in to get anything yet."

"Well, don't. Come here and I'll have something on the table for you when you get here in about 40 minutes."

Gordie started the car. "I'm on my way."

As he drove, he made a call to his boss, who picked up the phone on the first ring. "MacLean?"

"Just wanted to let you know where we are on this, Sergeant. Albright and I met with the deceased's wife and then went over to have an initial conversation with the brother, Kyle and father, Danny. We didn't discover anything significant yet. Kyle will be picking up the widow, Sharon, and I'm meeting them at the morgue at seven for the official identification."

"Did anyone know why this guy was so far from his normal area?"

"Apparently not. There are a whole lot of other folks to talk to still, but I told Albright we'll regroup tomorrow morning at the office and see where you want to take this."

"Good. Sounds like you've done what you can for today, MacLean. Come see me first thing when you get in tomorrow morning."

"Will…" The phone disengaged before Gordie could say 'do'.

He shook his head. "Typical."

Gordie drove through Port Mulroy, turned right into Parish Lane, and then right again into Vanessa Hunt's driveway. When he climbed out of the car, he stood for a moment to stretch. He lit a cigarette and walked a few steps to gaze through the trees lining the driveway at the view of St. George's Bay glittering in the early evening sun in the distance. Gordie swivelled at the sound of joyous barks that Taz let loose as she burst from the mudroom door Vanessa opened. The big white dog bounded to him and before she nudged him, he knelt down to wrap one arm around her, holding his cigarette safely away at arm's length with his other hand.

"Yes, yes. Here I am."

Gordie stood up again to watch Vanessa walk towards them. Her shoulder-length blond hair swept back from her face in the sea breeze, exposing her face with its dusting of freckles, laugh lines and blue eyes in a way that made Gordie's heart beat faster.

She smiled at him. "You made good time."

He dropped his cigarette to stamp it out and then reached down to pick up the butt and return it into his package. "I did. Not much traffic, even coming through Port Mulroy."

She held out her hand to reach for his, but instead he stepped closer and took her in his arms for a hug. She held him for a moment before pulling back to kiss him lightly on the lips. "Come in. Your supper is on a plate in the oven."

He released her. "I needed that, even more than supper."

"Come get settled and then tell me all about it."

He followed her into the house, stopping long enough to hang his jacket in the mudroom and take off his boots. He went to wash up and by the time he returned, Vanessa had placed a steaming plate of stew on the table.

She sat across from him with a cup of herbal tea while he tucked into his dinner.

Between mouthfuls, he cautioned her. "You know you can't share anything I say to you, right?"

She wrinkled her brow and nodded. "Of course."

"I'm meeting Sharon MacDonald and her brother-in-law at the morgue at seven."

"Kyle."

He raised his eyebrows. "That's right. Kyle."

"They will provide the formal identification, but it's hard to imagine it will be anyone other than Adam MacDonald."

Vanessa chewed on her lip before asking: "And based on what I sensed from your earlier comments, are you thinking it was something other than an accident?"

He shrugged. "We won't know until the autopsy."

"But?"

"But yes. I will be surprised if it's ruled an accident."

"Why?"

"It's too soon to get into any of that. Right now, it's just my gut feeling." He scraped the last of the stew off the plate. "And by the way, my gut feels a whole lot better than it did. Thank you for this."

She nodded. "You're welcome. So, what am I allowed to say?"

He frowned. "Why say anything at all?"

"Because tomorrow I'm going to meet Lynn in Port Hood. I'm making a lasagna tonight and promised I'd bring it up."

MacLean sighed. "I'd rather you not be too involved in that community until we know more about what's going on."

Vanessa sat back in her chair. "Rather me not be involved? What does that mean? I'm the one who involved you, remember?"

"Fair enough, but just let things settle a few days until we know more."

"Well, I'm sorry if it doesn't suit you, but the lasagna is going into the oven right now and tomorrow morning it's going to Port Hood." She stood and walked into the kitchen and a moment later, Gordie heard the oven door slam shut.

Gordie sighed, stood and picked up his plate, carrying it into the kitchen. He spoke to her back as she stood at the kitchen sink, looking out the window. "I'm sorry. I've annoyed you, but you have to understand my position. For all we know, there's a murderer in Port Hood and you're too important to me to let you put yourself at risk."

She turned to face him. "I get it. I do, really. But you've just done it again."

He frowned. "Done what?"

"You said 'to let me'. Gordie, I'm a grown woman and somehow, I've managed to survive to the great age of fifty-six figuring things out for myself."

He shoved his hands in his trouser pockets. "I'm not allowed to care and want to keep you from harm?"

"Of course. And I appreciate that, but caring doesn't mean controlling."

He felt himself flush. *Dad controlled Mom. I don't do that.* "Fine. Have it your way." He knew he sounded surly and defensive, but couldn't help himself. "Look, I better get moving to get to my appointment for seven. Thank you for supper. I appreciate it. And thanks for looking after Taz all afternoon."

She nodded. "Do you want to leave her here until after your appointment?"

He shook his head. "No, thank you. She'll be fine in the car. I'm sure it won't be for long."

"Right, then. Keep in touch."

Gordie hesitated and then leaned in to kiss Vanessa on the cheek. "Thanks again."

"No problem."

***

The identification was now positive. The body was that of forty-year-old Adam MacDonald. Sharon had been pale and quiet, simply nodding when MacLean asked if this was her husband. MacLean had glanced at Kyle, standing with his arms straight at his sides, fists clenched and at the look Kyle spoke the words. "That's him. That's Adam."

Now MacLean was on the way home, back to Isle Madame and the peace of his house. His stomach churned as if the stew he'd consumed for supper wasn't sitting well. He wondered if that was brought on by the stress of the unexplained death of the fisherman, or the disagreement with Vanessa. *I'm just not great at relationships. I'm better off on my own. Taz never makes me feel this way.*

CHAPTER 7

MACLEAN HUNG HIS JACKET on the back of the chair in his workstation. He had left home early to drive the hour and a half to the office in Sydney and now missed his usual morning walk with Taz. As well as serving to blow away the morning cobwebs in the brisk sea breeze, he usually spoke aloud to the dog. Granted, Taz didn't do more than cock an ear or tilt her head at him during these conversations, assuming there wasn't a dead fish or other distraction to draw her away from his side, but the act of talking out loud always helped him to think. Without that release, he was out of sorts.

He walked down the hall to Sergeant Arsenault's office and rapped his knuckle on the doorframe of the open door.

The muscular man in his form-fitting shirt gestured for Gordie to come in. "I see that the formal identification confirmed that this body is indeed MacDonald."

It did not surprise MacLean that Arsenault already knew the latest information. He was curt, often sarcastic and critical, but he stayed on top of things. "Yes. Both Mrs. MacDonald and the brother, Kyle MacDonald, were there to confirm the identity."

"Right. Do you have any theories?"

MacLean raised his eyebrows. "Still gathering information, so it's a bit too soon to say."

Arsenault nodded. "Yeah. Fair enough."

MacLean waited, but when Arsenault stared at his computer reading an email or report, he was forced to speak. "Where do you want to go from here, Sergeant? Yesterday, Albright and I went to the scene before we really knew it would be an active case. Do you want us to carry on, or did you want to assign it to someone else?"

His boss turned his attention back to Gordie. "Remind me about what else you're working on right now?"

MacLean went through the files he had on the go, including a domestic violence case that looked like it might close soon because the woman wanted to withdraw her complaint against her common-law boyfriend, and a few other reports and follow-ups.

"Right, right. Okay, hand that one over to Norris, and keep the others going when you aren't actively working on this MacDonald case."

MacLean nodded. *Yes!* "And Albright? Is she on this with me?"

"Yes, go ahead, but MacLean?"

Gordie knew what was coming. On his previous case, Gordie had neglected to communicate with his partner, endangering her life. Sergeant Arsenault didn't take any formal action at the time, but he never missed an opportunity to remind MacLean about his mistake.

"Sergeant?"

"Let's not have another situation like the last time. Make sure you keep tabs on what your partner is up to."

MacLean stood. "Right, Sergeant." *Dammit, will you ever let that go?* "We'll set up the briefing room and give a general update at ten o'clock. By then, we may have some preliminary post-mortem results to share."

His supervisor nodded, already focussed again on his computer screen.

MacLean walked back down the hall to the open plan area where the detectives had their workstations. He moved to Roxanne Albright's desk and when she looked up; he grinned.

Her eyes widened.

He nodded. "I need a coffee. Ready for a green tea?"

She stood up. "Let's go."

They made their way out to Gordie's Santa Fe and drove the few minutes along Grand Lake Road to the Tim Hortons coffee shop nestled in the corner of the mall. Gordie had a quick cigarette as they walked across the parking lot and then nicked it before both of them put on their navy blue masks emblazoned with a small crest of the CBPS. He led the way into the coffee shop. "I'm buying. Want anything to go with the tea?"

Roxanne shook her head and left him to get the drinks while she snagged the table in the far corner. There were only three tables available as the others had small signs instructing people not to sit at them, in keeping with the rule of allowing only fifty percent capacity for in-restaurant dining. In fact, the signs read: "Donut Sit Here', which made the instruction at least a little humorous, and it was difficult enough to find any humour during a pandemic.

He carried over a tray with the glass cup of her tea and his white mug of coffee.

When he settled, they both took out their notebooks and, as he read from his, she made notes in hers.

"It's official. Sarge agreed that you and I are on this and I'm to offload the domestic I'm working on over to Norris." He looked up. "What have you got pending? Anything that should be reassigned?"

Roxanne grimaced. "I've been doing some analysis on victim services. Identifying possible gaps, quantifying usage of existing services, that sort of thing."

"Are you on a deadline?"

"Not really. I've been at it for a couple of months, liaising with Victim Services, conducting interviews, putting it all together into a database in order to run reports against it."

"Jesus. Rather you than me. Is that something you can put on the back burner?"

"I'm sure I can. I'll take the morning to contact a couple people and explain the situation, cancel a couple of meetings I've got on the schedule and share out my work so far in case anyone wants to review it so far. It's probably not a bad time to get some stakeholder input, anyway. By this afternoon, I should be clear."

"OK. that sounds good. We've got a briefing at ten with the rest of the Major Crimes gang, so as soon as we get back, I'll check in on how the post-mortem is going, so please make yourself available for that. This afternoon we'll go and start tracking down people to interview. We'll put together a list of names that we need to start with. We'll also want to check in with the Mounties because they should have the boat in their shop by now." He made a note in his book. "I need to see if Sarge wants John Allen to take over the forensics examination of that or leave it where it is."

Roxanne nodded and referred to John Allen, the Cape Breton Police Services head of forensics. "Maybe Allen's team can go and just help out? That way, we've got our own eyes on it without stepping on toes."

"Good thinking. I'll check with John first to see how he feels about that."

Gordie drained his mug. "Ready?"

She stood. "Lots to do before ten. I'll go in a few minutes early to make sure the meeting room isn't a pit."

"Great, thanks." They both knew that the large meeting room was used as a lunchroom as often as it was for meetings.

They drove back to the office, and each got to work with an energy they hadn't felt for a while. Not since they closed the cold case of a murdered teenage girl months ago.

Rather than telephone John Allen, he trotted down the steps to the forensics lab in the basement. The bright white lighting reflected harshly off the tiled walls and made Gordie blink. He made his way over to the small office of the head of forensics. "Hey, John. Can I interrupt you?"

The tall, thin man swivelled his chair away from the computer to face Gordie. He removed his glasses and rubbed his eyes. "Think you already have."

Gordie grinned and lowered himself into the empty chair at the side of Allen's desk. "I might as well carry on, then."

Replacing his glasses, John Allen waved at Gordie to go ahead.

"Don't know if you've heard about the fisherman who was found dead on his boat yesterday?"

"I heard something about it."

"The boat's been taken by the RCMP to Inverness. Their forensics team is going to take a look at it, but you know I'd feel better if it was your team doing the processing. Albright had a good suggestion. Are you willing to have your guys go up there and work with the Mounties?"

Allen frowned. "Why? Is there an issue with their forensics team?"

MacLean was quiet for a moment. He didn't want to admit that, because a young Mountie had irritated him, he had negative thoughts about the entire team. "Nothing that I know of."

John Allen shook his head. "In that case, I'd rather spend their budget than ours. I'll be copied on the report and if anything looks off, or if you think there's anything missing, I can dive into it, but otherwise, let's play nice, Gordie."

MacLean felt a flush rising to his face. "Sure. No worries."

In the long narrow briefing room, Roxanne had straightened the chairs to face the whiteboard at the front of the room and was busy making notes in red marker. A photo of the victim was attached to the board with a magnet, and under it she had written:

• Victim: Adam MacDonald, 40 yrs. of age - fisherman

- Family:
- Sharon MacDonald, widow (1 daughter, 10 yrs. old Izzie)
- Kyle MacDonald, brother
- Danny MacDonald, father
- Location of death? LFA 27 (not 26B)

Gordie's partner turned to him as he sat down on a chair in the front row. "What else should I put up?"

"That's enough for now. It's all we really know."

She put down the marker. "How did it go with John Allen?"

He grimaced. "He rightly told me to let the Mounties do the forensics on the boat, if they're willing."

Roxanne raised an eyebrow. "What's bothering you?"

Gordie shook his head. "Just being territorial, I suppose."

She walked across the room and started a pot of coffee. The meeting would start in ten minutes. After pouring water in from the large bottle that stood by the machine, she turned back to him. "Let it be."

He held up his hands. "Done."

The coffee was ready by the time the rest of the Major Crimes team arrived. Some brought their own beverages, but a couple got fresh coffee before taking a seat. Detective Norris filled his cup and held it up in the air in the direction of Roxanne. "I love briefings when Detective Albright is in charge."

There was laughter around the room. Getting anyone else to make a pot of coffee was generally a challenge.

When Sergeant Arsenault walked into the room, everyone quieted down and Gordie began. He gave a summary of the events as they knew it about the *Sea Child* with its deceased fisherman on board. He then turned the briefing over to Roxanne, who took the group through the interviews they had conducted so far.

One detective asked what the significance of LFA 27 was, and she responded with a small shrug. "It just means that he was found, anchored, outside of his own assigned Lobster Fishing Area. That may or may not have anything to do with his death, but it's strange. As you probably know, the fishing season is pretty short, so these guys are very focussed on their own areas and maximizing their catch every day without wandering around sightseeing."

MacLean took over again. "Next steps are to go back and interview anyone and everyone we can find that may know what he was up to, who his enemies were and what his state of mind has been. We'll also take a look at his finances, of course, and check his phone records to see who he's been talking to."

Arsenault stepped forward then. "Norris – I've instructed MacLean to hand off that domestic to you."

Detective Norris nodded. "I'm just finishing the report for the prosecution on the Keane sexual assault case, so that's no problem. If you need any other help, let me know."

MacLean gave a thumbs up sign. "May take you up on that. We'll see how the interviews go, but I may get you to run his phone records."

"No problem. Let me know."

MacLean looked around the room. "That's about it. then." He glanced at his boss. "Albright is clearing off her desk, and I'll start setting up interviews. After that we're gone."

Sergeant Arsenault gave a curt nod. "Make sure you stay in contact."

MacLean gave a mock salute. Arsenault frowned, turned without another word, and left. The rest of the room emptied slowly, some stopping to gather around the coffee pot to speculate and fill up their cups.

"Think this is another lobster-stealing incident?"

"Maybe he had a girlfriend in that neighbourhood."

"Took the boat for a run and got lost in the fog."

MacLean shook his head. "No shortage of imagination in this

group, anyway." The others grinned and moved on to other topics, and MacLean and Albright left the room.

At Albright's desk, Gordie stopped for a moment. "OK, you finish what you need to do and I'm going to work on a list, starting with the other crew member. What's his name again?"

Roxanne flipped open her notebook. "Dab Haan."

"Right. You didn't get a phone number for him, did you?"

"No. Kyle would have it, though. Or Dannymac will for sure because they were old buddies, apparently. It sounded like Adam and Kyle only kept him on under sufferance because the old man demanded it."

Gordie nodded. "I'll call MacDonald Senior. Find out what the story is there."

"Should we meet with those friends of Sharon MacDonald's to get a picture of their relationship?"

"I'll definitely put them on the list." He stood. "Come over when you're ready and we'll make our plans."

CHAPTER 8

THEY ARRANGED, AS USUAL, to meet at the Tim Hortons in St. Peter's, where Roxanne left her car parked. They travelled the rest of the way together in Gordie's car.

"You know, I don't mind driving once in a while. You could always leave your car parked."

Gordie glanced at his partner and made a face. "Sure. We could do that." He turned up the music on the sixties station and hummed along off-key with an old Supremes song.

Roxanne laughed. "OK. I get the message. Did you actually get a hold of Mr. Haan or are we just taking a chance?"

"Nope."

"What if he isn't there?"

"We may check in on forensics or go to Lynn Duggan's place."

"Ah yes. The protective friend."

Gordie nodded. "They seem very close, so she should have a good idea of what the MacDonald's home life was like. Let's see how our time goes."

They drove in comfortable silence for a bit and then Gordie turned down the music. "What did you think of the wife?"

Roxanne frowned. "I didn't form much of an opinion so far, but my initial impression is that she was very worried yesterday morning and then, when we were there in the afternoon, she genuinely seemed in shock. Why? What did you think?"

He nodded. "I agree, but there was something lurking there. Something she didn't talk about. Yet."

"What makes you say that?"

"Partly the whole exchange with the daughter."

She nodded. "Right. I didn't read too much into that. Seemed like a natural reaction from the child. You always blame the person who's handy, don't you? I know I always adored my father as a kid and automatically blamed Mom when there was some kind of dispute between them, or I didn't get my way, but I know now that it was because my dad was often away so my mother had to be the one to say no."

"How come your father was away?"

She shrugged. "The usual maritime complaint. No work around here, so Dad went out to Alberta to work on the oil sands."

He nodded. "A month out there and a week or so back home?"

"Something like that. I don't remember now. He finally got work as a heavy machinery mechanic in Truro, so after that he was home, and we were all glad of it, other than it meant we had to leave Nana and move to Truro."

"And that's where your folks still live?"

"Yup. I came back to live with Nana in Big Pond when I got the job with the Police Service, and I'm so happy being back."

"It's a different sort of life, isn't it?"

She grinned. "For sure. What about you? I never hear you mention your father."

MacLean hesitated, a sudden image of his drunken father lifting his hand to his mother. "Let's just say I wish my father had gone to the oil sands and stayed there."

Gordie felt Roxanne study him but was grateful when she didn't press for more information.

He slowed down as they approached Port Hood. "Sounds like this place may be tricky to find. I know we go through town and turn right on Court Street. After that, we continue on for a while on Old Rocky Ridge Road."

"Seems straightforward enough."

"That's the easy part. After that we look for an unmarked laneway on the left which will take us into the woods and his cabin."

"How far along Old Rocky Ridge?"

"About six kilometers. A little past the junction with New Rocky Ridge Road."

Gordie slowed down to forty once they came to a junction and then almost immediately a second junction. "Jeez. Old Rocky, New Rocky and now Old Rocky goes off to the right. I'm not sure if we follow New or Old."

Roxanne pointed. "There's a laneway going off to the left. Think that's it?"

"One way to find out."

He turned into the rutted driveway, creeping along for several moments. He stopped outside an old cabin. "This must be it."

Roxanne nodded to the red pickup truck parked outside the cabin. "Looks like someone's home, anyway."

CHAPTER 9

THE HOUSE WAS LITTLE more than a cabin. Worn cedar shingle siding on the small one-story structure may have been red once, but was now mostly a weathered grey colour, with remnants of the original red paint only visible under the eaves where it was protected from the maritime storms. Broken items littered the yard that, in Gordie's view, should have gone to the dump long ago. Old lobster traps with the netting frayed and torn, floats with their colour long washed away by sea churn, and metal mechanical pieces of mysterious origin all lay submerged in long brown winter-dead grass and weeds.

Roxanne grimaced at Gordie at the sight of the place and followed behind him to the door. Gordie made a fist and knocked hard on the door. "Mr. Haan? Detectives MacLean and Albright from the Cape Breton Police Services here."

They waited and heard only the wind in the trees. He tried again. "Mr. Haan. Open the door."

When there was still no response, Gordie tried the old latch handle on the door and found it to be unlocked. He pushed it open and called out again. "Mr. Haan! Police. I'm coming in."

Gordie went inside and stopped to allow his eyes to adjust to the dim light. The interior of the cabin was surprisingly tidy. It was small, with everything contained in the one room with a door at the back of the room, suggesting either a bathroom or a back exit to an outhouse. An old, stained table had two wooden ladder-back chairs drawn to it, but was clear of any dirty dishes or old food. A large fireplace dominated one wall and the smell of smoke filled the room from a low fire that smoldered. The cabin was comfortably warm between the fire and the sunlight streaming in through a tall window to the left of the fireplace. An old Boston rocker with threadbare cushions sat near the fire and a faded sofa faced the fireplace. There was a single bed in one back corner and in the other corner was a kitchen of sorts with a butcher-block counter-top with a sink, a two-burner gas stove and a small bar fridge.

Gordie nodded towards the bed. "There."

"Is he alive, do you think?"

Gordie called out as he approached the bed. "Mr. Haan." When he reached the bed, he leaned over. "Oh yeah. He's alive." He touched the man's shoulder and when that didn't have any effect, he shook him.

The sleeping man started and sat up as Gordie stepped back. When the elderly man twisted to sit and then lurch to his feet, an empty rum bottle fell to the floor.

Haan kicked the bottle out of his way and blinked to focus on Gordie and Roxanne. He stood, weaving slightly. His thinning grey hair stuck out in all directions and his ill-fitting dark grey cardigan hung loosely off one shoulder, exposing a yellowed t-shirt beneath. He wore green heavy cotton work pants that were stained from years of wear. "Who the hell are you?"

Gordie pulled out his identification and explained who they were. "We need to talk to you about Adam MacDonald."

Haan shuffled to the table and leaned on it for a moment. "Now?"

"Now."

"Jesus-effen-Christ. All right. Sit down. Let me just go have a whizz and then I'll talk to you." He disappeared through the door into what was now clear to see, a bathroom tacked on to the back of the cabin.

Roxanne looked at the table with its two chairs. "I'll go sit on the rocker. I'm okay with having a bit of distance from him."

When Haan came back into the room, he stooped and picked up the empty bottle. He shook it forlornly and then looked at Gordie. "I got nothing to offer you unless you want tea."

Gordie held up his hand. "We're fine, thank you. Let's sit down, Mr. Haan."

"Dab. No one calls me Mr. Haan."

"OK. Dab. That's an interesting name. Is it short for something?"

He sighed as though he had told the story too many times. "My name's Diederik, but when we came from Holland to Canada in the 50s, people had a hard time saying it. When I was a kid, my dad had me fixing nets and one of his pals once said 'that kid's a right dab hand at fixing nets' and ever after the name stuck. Even my family used to call me that." He wound down with a final comment. "They're all gone now."

Gordie judged Dab was awake and alert enough by now to get to the matter at hand. He nodded over to Roxanne in the corner, who poised her pen over her notebook to take notes.

"Dab, you've worked for the MacDonald family for many years now, I understand."

"Yeah. Dannymac took me on probably 30 years ago. Something like that. All the years run together, and I lose track of time."

Gordie smiled. "It happens to me too sometimes. At some point Dannymac stepped back from the business and the boys took over."

Dab nodded. "Adam's OK, but neither of them is a patch on Dannymac."

"Why not?"

He grunted. "Just not. Adam's slow, so it takes longer to finish

66

every dump. And don't get me started on Kyle. You know he's not interested. He doesn't have the love for *Sea Child* like Danny-mac does."

Gordie nodded. "If I understand the arrangement, Adam basically ran the business, and you and Kyle crewed for him. Is that right?"

Dab cocked his head. "What do you mean? Ran the business?"

Gordie flushed as he realized that no one had told Dab yet about Adam. "Dab, I'm sorry. I thought you knew. They found Adam late yesterday afternoon. He's dead."

The old man rested his head in his hands and closed his eyes. His voice was low. "I thought he was missing. I thought you were trying to find him."

"I'm sorry. I should have said."

He raised his head, and his eyes were bleary and bloodshot, his voice accusatory. "I wouldn't have spoken against him if I'd a known."

"You didn't say anything wrong, and I need your complete honesty so we can figure out what happened. Dab. The Coast Guard found the *Sea Child* way up by Pleasant Bay. Do you know why Adam might have taken the boat up there on a workday?"

Dab frowned. "Pleasant Bay? That's not even in our LFA."

Gordie nodded. "That's true."

The fisherman shook his head. "Doesn't make sense. Did he have a crew with him?" Dab's voice betrayed his confusion.

"He was alone when the boat was found."

Haan picked up the empty rum bottle again and shook it hopefully before shaking his head. "I don't know why he'd be there."

"Did you notice anything different about him lately? Was he worried or happier, or any change at all?"

He shrugged. "I don't know. We didn't talk about *feelings*." The man's voice was scornful. "We worked, and it's hard work. No time for chat when you're out there hauling up three hundred traps in a day. Maybe when we sat down for a few minutes to eat our sandwich at lunch, there'd be some talk, but mostly about the weather, or boat or haul."

Gordie nodded but pushed on. "But Dab, you've been around forever. You know the community. You know the MacDonald family. Don't tell me you wouldn't spot something out of the ordinary."

He mumbled. "I keep myself to myself."

Gordie changed tack. "You're still friends with Dannymac, right?"

He nodded. "He looks after me. Sometimes brings me out some supplies if he knows I'm low on funds." Dab threw a glance at the empty bottle again.

"So Dannymac comes out to visit once in a while. Did he ever mention he was worried about Adam, or noticed any problems?"

Dab scowled. "You'd have to ask him."

Gordie sighed. "Did Adam or Kyle come out to visit as well?"

Haan sniffed. "Nope." Then he relented. "Well, Adam came a couple times when he needed something fixed like a trap or net, but nowadays, people replace things as soon as fix them."

"Had he come to see you lately?"

"No. He wouldn't come during fishing season. Off season is when we do the maintenance."

"Right, that makes sense. Tell me about yesterday. You went to work as usual."

Haan nodded. "I went out as always and got there around fifteen minutes before setting-off time."

"And the *Sea Child* was already gone?"

"Yup. I asked a couple of the other guys if they'd seen *Child* that morning, but nobody had. Adam must have left really early."

"Had he ever done that before?"

"Never."

"Had you argued about anything?"

Dab frowned. "No. I don't argue with people."

"So, what did you think when you didn't see the boat?"

Shrug. "I just thought that maybe they decided to save money and were going to work it with just the two of them."

"And then you saw Kyle?"

"Yeah. He got there just when I was thinking I might as well go back home."

"That must have surprised you."

"Sure. Then I thought maybe Adam got a whole new crew. Maybe he and Kyle had a falling-out. They don't always get on. But Kyle seemed as mystified as me and he told me to wait. He went and talked to one of the other captains who was short a hand and Kyle arranged for me to work with him for the day." Dab paused and then added. "That was good of Kyle. He didn't have to do that." He frowned as he thought further about Kyle's kindness in finding a place for him to work that day. "Kind of amazing that he did."

"Did the crew of the other boat have any thoughts on where Adam was?"

Another shrug. "If they did, they didn't tell me."

Gordie looked over at Roxanne. "Anything you want to ask?"

She shook her head and flipped her notebook closed.

Gordie stood. "Thank you for your time. Again, I apologize for the shock. If anything occurs to you, please let me know." He glanced around the cabin. "Do you have a telephone here?"

Haan shook his head. "Nope."

Roxanne stood and led the way outside. As Gordie reached the door, Haan's voice reached him. "You might want to check with Adam's new pal."

Gordie swivelled back. "New pal?"

From his seat at the table, Dab nodded. "A couple of weeks ago I saw Adam talking to a guy on a Harley out by the garbage bins behind the Canadian Tire. Never saw the guy before or since. Can't tell you anything else about him."

Gordie raised an eyebrow. "What were you doing behind the Canadian Tire?"

Dab scowled. "There's a charity bin back there as well, and sometimes I drive by and see if there are any bags there. Sometimes there are some good clothes to be had." He added defensively. "People don't want those things anymore, so I might as well have them."

MacLean agreed. "You might as well. Did Adam and his pal see you?"

"Adam didn't. He had his back to me. The other fella did."

"So, you got a good look at him. What did he look like?"

Haan shrugged. "What do they always look like? When those fellas buy a Harley, they lose their razors. Long hair. Long grey beard."

Gordie didn't remark on Dab's own want of a razor based on the stubble on his chin. "That's been helpful. Thank you. If anything else occurs to you, like maybe a license plate number, let me know."

Haan snorted. "When do I go back to work? I need the money. A guy can't live on air, you know."

"I'm sure one of the MacDonalds will be in touch." Gordie closed the door behind him before he became embroiled in a discussion about work. Gordie knew he'd be tempted to tell the fisherman that if Haan just tidied himself up and went to the wharf early in the morning, he'd probably get taken on by someone.

He sucked in a deep breath of fresh air and shuddered as the close contact with the alcoholic fisherman seeped away from him once he was out of the stuffy little cabin. It was always the same. Gordie suffered flashbacks of his childhood whenever he came near someone whose pores exuded alcohol like those of Dab Haan.

He shook his head to rid himself of the memories and strode to the car where Roxanne patiently waited.

He climbed in and as he started the car, he brought her up to speed on Haan's last-minute revelation.

Roxanne waited until they had bumped their way down the rutted laneway to the main road before pulling out her notebook and updating her notes from the interview. "A guy on a Harley. Not much to go on."

"No. And for all we know, it was someone just asking directions. Could be nothing."

"But it might be something."

Gordie grinned at his partner. "Yes. It might be something."

"Where to now, boss?"

"I think it will be worth going back to talk to Dannymac again. I want to understand more about the relationship between all these men."

"Including Haan? You think he might have something to do with this?"

"Probably not, but I just want more information."

CHAPTER 10

MACLEAN DECIDED TO LET Roxanne take the lead with Dannymac this time. Maybe a gentler touch would work better. He explained his reasoning to Roxanne as they drove the few minutes back to the MacDonald home.

They drove up and parked beside the well-kept house. Gordie led the way and knocked on the door, but when MacDonald Senior opened the door, he stepped back to have Roxanne lead the way.

They were led again to the kitchen, and again Gordie was impressed with how neat and clean everything was. He knew that his own kitchen would not compare favourably with this one, and he himself was in perfect health, unlike Dannymac.

MacDonald filled and clicked on the kettle without asking if they wanted anything. He pulled out three mugs and set them on the table beside the sugar bowl, that was obviously a permanent fixture.

Roxanne moved towards the refrigerator. "Shall I get the milk? Why don't you sit down, Mr. MacDonald, and when the kettle boils, I'll make the tea if you just point me to where I'll find the tea bags."

He didn't argue but waved his hand towards the canister set

on the counter, and then sat down at the table while Gordie took another chair, leaving the one directly opposite from MacDonald for Roxanne.

Gordie glanced around the kitchen. "Is Kyle at his own place today?"

MacDonald nodded. "I needed some peace and quiet. He'll be over with some lunch later."

The kettle boiled, and the two men watched in silence for a moment as Roxanne made the tea. She put the pot on the table and then joined them.

Gordie pulled out his own notebook and pen and pushed himself back from the table a little.

Roxanne poured some milk in a cup, swirled the teapot a bit and then poured out some tea. "My Nana always told me that a polite person will take the first cup of tea and the last cup of coffee from a pot." She put the tea by her own spot and then waited as MacDonald put some milk in his own mug before she filled up his cup. Gordie nodded to her to set the pot down. He'd get his own in a minute.

She began. "Mr. MacDonald, now that we have confirmation that the deceased is definitely Adam, we need to gather as much information as possible. We understand that this may feel intrusive at a time when you want, as you said, 'peace and quiet', but we need to get answers while things are still fresh in the minds and memories of those who knew Adam best. I hope you can understand that."

He nodded. "You have a job to do. I get that. It won't bring Adam back, but I get it."

She smiled. "Thank you for understanding. Let's start with the relationship between Kyle and Adam. We know they worked together day after day in close proximity. There must have been times they disagreed." Her voice lifted at the end, making the statement a question.

"Well, sure. They were grown men as well as brothers, so of course there were times they argued. Never seriously, though. Adam was strong-minded and felt he had the experience and know-how to run the business best. Sometimes Kyle had ideas for doing things differently."

"What happened in those cases? Did you have to intervene and pick a side? That might have made the loser of the argument unhappy."

"No. Mostly, I stayed out of it and let them sort it out. I didn't have the energy to get in the middle of it, and besides, I trusted Adam. He usually had a good head on his shoulders."

"Did Kyle resent that way of working?"

"No, why would he? He's not a child who expects to get his own way all the time."

"Tell me a bit about Dab Haan. We were there earlier and met with him."

"What do you want to know?"

Roxanne glanced at Gordie, who gave a small nod. She went on. "He seems an unlikely crew member, between his age and his fondness for rum."

MacDonald reached for the teapot and topped up his cup, the tea a dark, strong brew. "He wasn't always like that. When he worked for me, there were days we'd go out, just the two of us, and we'd haul traps for hours and run my dumps in the same time as a crew of three. Hard work, but we were a good team." The frail-looking man smiled at the memory.

Roxanne pushed on. "But those days are behind him now, aren't they? Did Adam just keep him on out of pity?"

Dannymac scowled. "He can still pull his weight, I assure you. What Dab doesn't know about fishing and equipment maintenance doesn't bear knowing."

"OK, fair enough. Did Adam appreciate Dab's experience? Or did he just put up with him, do you think?"

"Adam knew Dab's worth."

"You two went back a long way, I think?"

He smiled. "I knew him from school when we were kids, so yes, a long way."

"How did Dab feel about working for Adam, and working with Kyle?"

"I guess you'd have to ask him."

"I'm asking you, Mr. MacDonald."

He shrugged. "He wished it was me and him, I guess. It's hard fitting in with young people."

"Did they argue?"

"Who?"

Gordie saw her clench her jaw. "Did Dab Haan argue with either of your sons?"

His voice was grudging. "Not like a regular thing. Adam told me that Dab wanted more money but there wasn't more to be had, and that's what he told Dab. Far as I know, that was an end to it."

"When was this?"

"A couple of weeks ago."

"Did Adam tell you how Dab reacted to the situation?"

"Said Dab wasn't happy about it. Adam told him he was a free man and if he wanted to find another boat to crew on, he wouldn't hold him back."

"Did Dab try to find another boat?"

"Not that I know of."

"Dab must have complained to you. Did you try to intervene?"

"Dab wasn't happy, but I told him there was nothing I could do. I'm not managing the business anymore. Adam is. Was."

Roxanne nodded. "You try to help Dab out, though, don't you?"

MacDonald folded his arms across his chest. "No harm in that. If I want to help an old friend once in a while, it's allowed."

"Yes, of course. In fact, I think you found the perfect way to ease the problem away."

Dannymac remained silent, staring into his mug.

"How does Kyle get on with Dab?"

"Fine. Kyle doesn't make the decisions, so there'd be no complaints between them. They aren't friends, like, but Kyle respects Dab and they just get on with their work."

"When we met with Dab Haan, he mentioned he was grateful to Kyle for getting one of the other boats to take him out to crew yesterday when it was clear that they wouldn't be going out on *Sea Child* to work."

Dannymac nodded. "Dab'd be grateful for the work. Every day he doesn't fish is a day with no money coming in."

"Yes. It just seemed to me that Dab was surprised that Kyle would take the trouble."

He shrugged. "I guess with everything going on, Dab wouldn't have expected Kyle to give him a thought, but that's Kyle. He does kind things. He looks after me."

"One last thing, Mr. MacDonald, and then I think we can leave you alone. Dab mentioned he saw Adam not long ago talking to a man who rode a Harley-Davidson. Do you have any idea who that is?"

Gordie saw the older man blink, and it seemed that he paled.

"No. No idea. I don't know all the friends that Adam or even Kyle have. Maybe Sharon knows."

She nodded. "Have you ever seen Adam with someone matching that description?"

"No."

"All right. We'll check with Sharon. Detective MacLean, did you have any other questions?"

Gordie put his book away and stood up. "No. Thank you for your time, Dannymac. I know this is very hard on you. We may have more questions in the future as we discover more facts surrounding Adam's death, but that's it for now."

"When are you releasing the boat? This is a critical time for us and Kyle's arranged for someone else to haul our traps today, but no one's going to do two runs a day ongoing."

Gordie bit his lip. "I'll check on that for you, but I suggest that you and Kyle try to rent a boat for tomorrow. It may be a day or two yet before we can release her."

MacDonald shook his head. "Well, I hope you get on with whatever you have to do. Time is money."

They got back in the car, and as Gordie started the vehicle, he turned to Roxanne. "Ready for another tea?"

"Sure. I didn't see a Tim Hortons though. Whatever will you do?"

He laughed. "I'm getting adventurous in my old age. There's a bakery coffee shop just down by the Shore Rd."

"Right. I remember passing it. Funny name on it."

"Apparently made by adding his and her names together. Sandeannie's."

The one-story grey building was busy with cars coming and going. They went in and studied the menu.

Roxanne turned to Gordie. "Don't tell me you're having an oat cake. Even you must be ready for a change."

"I *am* ready for a change as it happens. I'm having a beaver tail."

"Wow. You surprise me. I figured that would be too sweet for you with all that cinnamon and sugar."

"As long as you don't dip it, it's good. Haven't had one in ages. Want to share it?"

She grinned. "Why not? I need something nice after some of the places we've been today." She didn't mention Dab Haan's little cabin, but Gordie knew that was what she was talking about.

Gordie ordered for both and paid while Roxanne found a table in the corner.

When they had their drinks and half the beaver tail pastry in front of them, they made their plans.

Gordie sipped his coffee while he flipped open his notebook. "I'd say it's a bit late to go see how the forensics are making out with the boat. I think what we'll do is head home and from there, I'll call them and see what they know or don't know. You head home and type up the notes from today. Do you need mine from the MacDonald interview?"

She shook her head. "I think I recall the important points, so I'll write it up in my own book first and then, when I've got the reports done, I'll email them to you to look over. You can add in anything I've missed."

"Sounds good. We'll go into the office tomorrow unless I tell you differently after I talk to forensics."

Roxanne wiped her fingers after finishing the sticky baked dough. "Are you expecting anything much from the forensics of *Sea Child*?"

"I am, actually. I am."

CHAPTER 11

A FTER MACLEAN DROPPED HIS partner at her car in St. Peter's, he debated with himself about what he should do later. The debate had nothing to do with forensics or interviews. He decided that the best thing was to go home, make his phone call to his RCMP colleagues about *Sea Child* and then take Taz out for a walk to clear the cobwebs. It was a nice late afternoon spring day, and he knew the fresh air was just what he needed.

He got home, greeted Taz with a good rub down of the big dog's head and in turn was greeted by her with a firm poke, despite his best effort to dodge her. "We'll go out in a bit. Let me just get this call out of the way and then we'll go for a good walk."

Taz seemed to understand and settled on her bed in the corner of the kitchen while Gordie sat at the table with his notebook open and phone in hand.

As much as he loathed the idea, he started with a call to the constable he had met yesterday. "Hello, Constable Jeffreys. Detective MacLean here. I just wanted to connect to see what progress your forensics team has made with the *Sea Child*. Is there a report yet?"

He listened to the tension in the Mountie's voice as he explained no reports were complete and available yet. "The team is still processing the fishing boat."

Gordie knew that if it were up to Jeffreys, the report would be a long time coming before it was shared with him. "The family are keen to get the boat back as soon as possible, as you can imagine. Every day they can't fish is a significant financial loss."

He listened to the standard 'it takes what it takes' response. "I understand that, of course. They need to take the time to process it thoroughly, and at the same time, it's useful to remember that this is a necessary tool for the family's livelihood."

Before Jeffreys could add anything further, Gordie cut him off. "Please keep me informed, then. You have my number." He hung up, knowing full well that the constable wouldn't go out of his way to contact him.

"Come on, Taz. Let's get out of here."

Gordie drove to one of his favourite spots. This rocky stretch of coastline on Isle Madame, where he lived, was accessed via an old, rutted road. Taz leapt from the back of the car and galloped along the short, wooded trail towards the shore. When Gordie caught up to the dog, he stopped for a moment and breathed in deeply. Seagulls screeched as Taz ran towards a flock that had settled to pick sea snails from a clump of seaweed. The mild fish and salt scent cleared Gordie's sinuses, and he felt better than he had felt all day.

"Come on, Taz, we'll go this way first." He headed into the wind and the fresh breeze blew into his face and sent his thick white hair streaming. His eyes watered, but Gordie rejoiced and felt invigorated.

His dog walked sedately beside him, having gotten the first excited shot of adrenalin out of her system. "Well, Taz. What am I going to do about Vanessa? I know she's pretty annoyed with me, but was it wrong for me to worry about her and warn her off getting too involved?" Gordie glanced down and smiled to see the quizzical look his dog gave him; one ear pricked and the other flopped down.

"Do I call her and apologize? Is that what a fellow does, even though I didn't do anything wrong?"

Taz, bored with the conversation, trotted off to sniff at a piece of lobster shell.

Gordie was stumped. *And this is why I'm not good at relationships.* He thought of his sister. *Maybe I should call Jeannie. Jeez. A guy in his fifties shouldn't need to call his sister for romance advice.* He abandoned the idea.

He let his mind wander, considering how simple life had been when it had just been his dog and him. He played the positive and negative elements of a relationship. *OK Gordie, admit it. It's nice having the company, and if I'm honest, a physical relationship. It's been a long time since I've enjoyed that. And she's a splendid cook.* He felt himself frowning. *But what the heck? Why should I apologize for just doing the right thing? That makes little sense. But if I don't apologize, where do we go from here?*

He sighed. *Is this worth it?*

Gordie realized Taz had roamed quite far ahead now, and he shouted for her to come back. The wind lifted her long white hair, just as it had for his, but on her it was lovely. "Come on, my girl. Let's go home. I've got another tough phone call to make."

***

Her phone was picked up on the second ring. "Vanessa?"

"Hi Gordie. I hoped you'd call."

This was a good omen.

"Vanessa, I think I came across as telling you what to do, and that really wasn't my intention." Before he knew it, the words were out of his mouth. "I'm sorry and didn't mean to make it sound like you aren't a responsible adult." He hesitated and ended by adding "I just worry."

"I get that, Gordie, and I'm sorry too. I probably reacted too strongly. I'm sensitive to men that tell me what to do. Throughout my career in the educational field in Ontario, it seemed like men were in charge and often it looked like they made their career by stepping on a woman."

"Hard to imagine anyone, man or woman, getting the better of you."

He heard the smile in her voice when she responded. "I wish I were as tough as you think of me. Let's call a truce. You work at not telling me what to do, and I'll work at not taking it personally when you do. How's that?"

"Seems fair."

"Does that mean you'll come over later?"

"I've got some reports to work on, but after supper, I'll bring Taz and I'll come for a cup of tea."

"I've got an apple crumble in the oven to go with it."

"I guess I shouldn't have had half a beaver tail earlier."

She laughed. "You stopped at the bakery in Port Hood."

"'Fraid so."

"By the time you get here, you'll be ready for the apple crumble."

He laughed as well. "That's what I'm afraid of. I'll see you later."

After he hung up, Gordie felt a load lifted from his shoulders and was glad he had called, even though he hadn't been sure which way the conversation might have gone. He stroked his dog's head. "Always best to get it over with, Taz. Remember that for the future." He nudged her towards her bed and pulled his laptop computer forward to get started on his reports.

***

On the hour and a half drive next morning to his office, Gordie used the time to make a couple of hands-free phone calls. First, he called John Allan, the head of their own forensics department.

Allan answered just as Gordie thought it would switch to voicemail. "Allan."

"John. Good morning. Gordie here. If I lose you, I'll come in and see you when I get there."

"You must be on that stretch north of Big Pond, are you?"

"I am indeed. I just passed Irish Cove and I can tell you Bras d'Or Lake is some beautiful. A little mist rising off the water, and I just saw an eagle sweep past on the way to look for his breakfast."

"I guess that helps make up for the crazy drive you're willing to do."

Gordie chuckled. "You should try it. Some great real estate deals to be had in West Arichat right now." He became serious then. "John, have you heard anything from the forensics team of your RCMP colleagues?"

"About the boat, you mean?"

"You got it."

"Not a word. They may still be processing."

"That's what the constable told me yesterday afternoon, but I don't necessarily trust what he tells me. I'd love to take a trip up to Inverness just to go in and talk to them myself. How do you think they'd feel about that?"

"You mean you want me to call them?"

"You know me so well."

"Well, I can call them, but if they sound at all unhappy about it, I'll tell them you won't go, right?"

Gordie held back the sigh. "Yes, all right. But be persuasive, John. Use your charm."

Allan snorted and disengaged the phone.

MacLean dialed Albright, but by then he was in an area with no service. When he did finally get through to her, he was almost at the office. "Good morning, Roxanne."

"Hi, Gordie."

"Do you need a tea or anything?"

"No, I'm good, thanks. I saw you sent out a note about a unit briefing this morning, though. Did you want to pick up anything for that?"

"No. I'll save the bribes for when I need something from the team. It'll be a pretty short briefing, but can you go in and set things up? Whiteboard with the key names, dates and times of what we know so far. The usual."

"Sure. I'll get in there now."

***

Gordie's first stop when he got into headquarters was his boss' office. Sergeant Arsenault looked up as Gordie approached.

"Morning, Sergeant. Did you want a briefing before the meeting, or are you ok to wait?"

"Any surprises so far?"

"Not really. It's very early in the investigation still. No obvious suspects or motives yet."

Arsenault rolled his shoulders, making his pectoral muscle and triceps flex and press against his tight short uniform sleeves. "I'll wait, then."

Gordie waited until he was well away from sight of his supervisor before shaking his head.

When the half-dozen members of the Major Crimes Unit team were assembled half an hour later in the briefing room, Gordie stood in front and introduced the case. "This is the MacDonald case; a fisherman out of Port Hood, who went missing on his boat, the *Sea Child*, two days ago. Detective Albright will take you through what we know so far."

Roxanne took Gordie's place as he went and sat down in one of the new ergonomic chairs spaced out in rows of three. He settled into the comfortable chair and adjusted the seat height to accommodate his shorter legs. His five foot and eight inches represented one of the shortest members of the team. He recalled the grey plastic, one-size-fits-all chairs that had been in the room previously. With the onset of Covid-19, they had received these new rolling chairs that allowed people to space themselves out for safe distancing.

After Roxanne had explained who all the names belonged to, what they knew about the location of the boat and what their interviews had revealed so far, Gordie stepped back up to the board.

"Next steps will be to continue our interviews. As Detective Albright mentioned, we are interested to find out more about the possible friend with the Harley-Davidson. Also, we want to dig into some of the finances of the people we've met so far. We need to understand if there is a financial motive here somewhere. We knew that the crew member, Dab Haan, wanted a raise and didn't get one. The MacDonald family's financial situation needs to be determined. Fishing can be lucrative, but it isn't always reliable, so there's a lot of work to be done to get a picture of the situation. When we narrow down the avenues of investigation, I may call on some of you for help, but in the meantime, Detective Albright and I will just carry on."

Gordie took some questions.

"What about the autopsy? Anything from that?"

MacLean shook his head. "We don't have it yet. It's on our list to follow up on today. I wish this was all within our own four walls, but our Mountie colleagues have their teams working on the forensics, so I need to be patient."

One of the detectives called out: "good luck with that."

There was laughter around the room, and then when the questions petered out, Sergeant Arsenault stood up. "What's everyone hanging around here for? Party's over."

Roxanne and Gordie stayed behind after everyone else left. Gordie stared at the board before turning to his partner. "The picture isn't big enough. We need to get a fuller list of people who were a part of Adam MacDonald's life or at least came in contact with him, even if they weren't friends."

"The other fishermen?"

He nodded. "That's a start. I also want to know if anyone up in Pleasant Bay saw *Sea Child*. Was she a familiar sight to the folks there?"

"You think Adam had been there before?"

Gordie shrugged. "Something took him there. Maybe it was a one-off, but maybe it wasn't. Did you get Constable Jeffreys' number?

Roxanne smiled. "I have it. Sure you wouldn't rather call him yourself?"

"I'll leave that pleasure to you. See if he talked to any of the locals about this. Maybe he himself has seen *Child* there before. It's his patch. If he doesn't know anything, we may need to go back up there and do some scouting around ourselves, but I'd rather avoid that if possible."

"Sure, I'll call him. What about you? You staying around here for the day?"

"I think so. I've asked John Allan to see if the forensics team in Inverness will let me come and see them in person, but even if they say yes, we'll look at doing that tomorrow. Today we'll work the phones. I'm going to check in with Sharon MacDonald, and I may also call that friend of hers, Lynn."

"What about Kyle?"

"He should be out fishing right now. I'll wait with him until I have a bit more background. We don't have enough to ask for financial records from the bank, so we'll have to see what we can dig out, just by nosing around."

They each went back to their workstations and got busy.

Sharon MacDonald answered the phone on the second ring. "Mrs. MacDonald, Detective MacLean here. I just want to check in with you. How are you holding up?"

Her voice sounded surprisingly strong. "I'm adjusting to the shock, I suppose. My mother is coming to stay for a few days, so that will help."

"That's good. I'm glad you aren't on your own. Has Kyle come by, or Dannymac?"

"I spoke with Kyle on the phone. They rented a boat for today, but he wanted to know if I heard anything about when they'd get *Sea Child* back."

"I'm following up with the forensics team today, so by the end of the day, I'll call you to let you know what the status is. Sharon, have you given any more thought to why Adam might be up in the Pleasant Bay area?"

"I have thought about it, but can't think of any reason."

"All right. I'm sure we'll figure it out sooner or later. We met with Dab Haan yesterday."

Gordie raised his eyebrows to hear her chuckle before abruptly stopping. "That must have been an experience."

"He's an interesting character. He said a couple of things that I hoped you could shed some light on."

"Oh?"

"First of all, Dab mentioned he had asked Adam for a raise a couple of weeks ago, but that he was turned down. Were you aware of that?"

"No, but it doesn't really surprise me. The time to negotiate a raise would have been at the beginning of the season, not partway through, unless they were having a great season, but it hasn't been *that* good. Not bad, but not good enough to warrant a raise. I don't know why Dab would ask all of a sudden like that."

"The other thing he mentioned was that he had recently seen Adam talking to a man who rode a Harley- Davidson. Does that sound like anyone you know? A friend of Adam's?"

"No. I don't know anyone like that. A couple of friends of his have dirt bikes, but I'm sure Dab wouldn't mistake a dirt bike for a Harley."

"No, I agree. That seems unlikely."

"We'll leave it at that for now then, Mrs. MacDonald."

"Please call me Sharon."

"Sharon, then. I'll be in touch later in the day."

Her voice changed. For the first time in the conversation, he heard tears in her voice. "Detective? When will Adam's body be released? We want to plan the funeral. I've been in touch with the funeral home, but until I know when I can have Adam, we can't make any arrangements."

"I understand. I'll find out what I can before I call you back later."

He hung up the phone and sat at his desk, fingers steepled together as he mused over the conversation.

You sounded a lot more cheerful than I expected, Sharon. And it took you long enough to ask about getting your husband's body back.

CHAPTER 12

SHARON MACDONALD HUNG THE phone up after speaking with Detective MacLean and chewed on her bottom lip for a moment. She felt the sweat prickling under her arms and knew she hadn't handled the call very well.

It doesn't matter. What does he expect? I'm upset about the loss of my husband, so if I seem a bit scattered, it's no wonder.

After the call, she went back to what she had been doing. She signed the cheque for a year's worth of school fees for Izzie's music school and sealed it into an envelope. She affixed a stamp and carefully wrote out the address.

I think I may just move to Halifax when this is all over. I'll be closer to the school and Mom. The real estate market is booming, so I should get a good price for the house.

Sharon missed Adam. She closed her eyes for a moment and imagined his arms around her. Keeping her safe. Loving her and looking after her.

Yes, she missed him, but still. Now all things were possible.

CHAPTER 13

JOHN ALLAN DID HIS magic and Gordie was given the go-ahead to take a look at the *Sea Child*, along with the RCMP forensics. He arranged with Roxanne that she would come to his house in the morning at ten o'clock and they would go together. Now he was studying the autopsy report which had been sent to him. He decided to consult with his forensics lead and took the report down to the basement lab where John Allan worked.

He entered the bright and gleaming room and shivered in the chill. He saw Allan at his computer in his small office and waved to the technician, who asked if she could help him. "No thanks, I just want a word with the boss."

She nodded and went back to studying the slide on her microscope, and Gordie entered Allan's office.

Allan had already swivelled his chair and sat with his glasses pushed to the top of his head. He looked just as a science wizard should: thinning hair, glasses, and a long, serious face. Gordie knew Allan had a wicked sense of humour, but he wasn't one to use what some called 'dark humour' when dealing with the dead. With them, he was always solemn and respectful.

"What brings you down here, MacLean? Didn't I do everything you wanted by getting you in to see the boat?"

"You did, and I'm grateful. I'm here to thank you."

John smirked. "Why am I suspicious?"

"OK. I'm also here to go over the autopsy with you."

Allan slid the glasses off his head and back into position and reached for the file Gordie proffered.

Gordie sat back and waited while Allan flipped through the pages.

"Seems pretty straightforward. He received a blow to the temple which caused a minor fracture. That, in turn, lacerated the middle meningeal artery." He stood up and led Gordie out to a large diagram of a human skull in various colours to show the bones and arteries of the face and scalp.

"See here? This is where the four skull bones come together to meet at the pterion. It's the thinnest part of the skull and the weakest. Your man took a blow here to the temple, and that caused a tiny but deadly laceration to this large artery. That caused an epidural hematoma, which is a buildup of blood around the brain. He suffered severe bleeding, and that caused his brain tissue to swell, resulting in death."

Gordie frowned at the image in front of him and then turned to John. "Is it possible he just fell down? Maybe a big wave struck the boat, and he lost his balance?"

"It's possible..."

"But you don't think so?"

Allan led MacLean back to his office. "Let's just say I'd want to understand more about these bruises." He opened the file again and flipped to some photographs with close-up shots of bruises on both upper arms. "It appears to me someone gave this man a hard, sharp shove. I believe someone grasped him by the upper arms and pushed, hard. It's difficult to say if that happened at the same time as the blow to the temple, but it's likely."

"You're saying that someone gave him a strong shove and then he fell and hit something on the way down, causing the blow to the temple?"

"That's what it looks like to me. And then there is this." He pulled out an 8 by 10 photo of Adam's left hand, which had a deep, dark cut curving around the edge and palm.

"Could that be accidental?"

"Sure. Anything is possible, but it happened pretty close to when he died. And the cut looks like a defensive wound to me. Possibly some sort of curved weapon made it."

"Like a gaff hook?"

He titled his head in thought. "Maybe, but I'd expect that to deliver more of a puncture that a slash like this. Definitely possible, though."

"We're talking homicide then?"

"Ah. Now you're asking me for manner of death."

Gordie held up his hand. "I know. You don't need to remind me. You can't call it."

Allan reminded him, despite MacLean's comment. "Exactly right. That isn't for me to say. Only the Medical Examiner can pronounce on the official cause and manner of death."

"I'm not asking for something official, but am I chasing a killer or is it likely to have been an accident, in *your* opinion?"

"Based on what I'm seeing in the file, I think someone caused this person's death. I don't think he just fell of his own accord."

MacLean nodded, recalling the last case he worked on. "The M.E. in Dartmouth just looks at the file, though, right? Any idea how long it'll take for him to decide?"

Allan rolled his eyes. "That depends on more things than I can predict." He ticked them off on his fingers. "Depends on their workload, or if they want to see tissue samples etc, etc." He relented then. "I would suggest you carry on investigating as if it were a homicide, and if it gets ruled accidental, well, you've wasted a bit of time. If you wait, you may lose valuable time."

MacLean stood. "You read my mind. Thanks for the input, John." He picked up the file and left to bring his partner up to date.

When he reached Albright's desk, he set the file down in front of her, but before she opened it, he asked: "Ready for a tea?"

She stood and opened her locker for her jacket. "Always."

They took her car and Gordie smiled to think that a year ago, he wouldn't have allowed it. He liked to be in control, he could now admit, at least to himself.

As if she read his thoughts. "Nice of you to let me drive."

He shrugged. "Once in a while, it's nice to be chauffeured around."

She laughed. "To the coffee shop, at least."

"If you play your cards right, I'll even let you buy this time."

He went to their favourite table in the corner while Roxanne ordered and paid. She brought it over to him and set down his coffee, as well as a small plate with an oatcake with a pat of butter on the side.

He sniffed. "You call this service? Usually the oatcake is already buttered."

"You'll have to talk to the staff about that. They're training someone new."

"Ah well. I'll let it go this time." He spread the butter in a thick layer on the crisp oat biscuit and then settled back.

Roxanne took a sip of her green tea. "What's the latest, then? Did you talk to John Allan?"

"It's a homicide."

Her eyes widened. "Is it? Did he say that?"

"Not definitively, but that's his opinion. We need to wait for the Medical Examiner in Dartmouth to say so officially." He took a sip before adding, "and the M.E. may not agree."

Her shoulders slumped. "Maybe an accident, after all?"

MacLean went through his notes, giving Roxanne the full story as Allan had given it, ending with: "We're going to proceed as if it was a homicide."

"Will Sarge agree?"

Gordie liked that she now abbreviated their boss's title as he did. "Hopefully. I'll let you know after I meet with him."

He closed his notebook and then nodded to his partner. "Any luck with the Boy Mountie?"

"I think you're a little hard on him. He's keen and wants to make a name for himself. No harm in that."

"Right. So, what did he have to say? Did he do any interviews?"

"He did, as it happens."

"And?"

"And, first of all, he thinks he remembers seeing *Sea Child* himself before. It's quite distinctive with the red and white."

Gordie raised his eyebrows.

"He may have seen it a couple of weeks ago for the first time. Jeffreys knows most of the boats that fish out of Pleasant Bay and there isn't one that colour, but there is one that's a darker, deeper red and it may have been that one that he saw." Roxanne shrugged. "Our constable can't be certain. He talked to a few of the locals after they towed *Sea Child* in and while they were waiting for the recovery team to come and take the body away. Apparently, no one knew the crew of the *Sea Child* personally, but a couple of fishermen had spotted the boat earlier in the day. Naturally enough, there was talk about whose boat it was because if anyone were fishing, they were encroaching on the Pleasant Bay lobster fishing area."

"No one went out to challenge the *Child*?"

"It sounds like a couple of different crews studied the boat through binoculars, but when they didn't see any fishing activities, they figured it was some tourist and didn't worry too much about it."

"They didn't worry that they didn't see activity of any kind?"

"Sounds like they're too busy with their own work, although eventually, someone did call it in."

"True."

"Did no one else see the same boat there a couple of weeks ago when Jeffreys claims he saw it?"

"If they did, no one's saying."

"And no one saw any other boat near the *Child*?"

"Nope."

Gordie stood and collected his plate and mug. "Let's get back. I better fill Sarge in. Tomorrow we'll go get a close look at *Sea Child* ourselves. I'll have to find out when the M.E. will release the body as well. I told Sharon I'd let her know. The family is anxious for both the body and the boat to be released."

"I can understand that."

Roxanne drove them back to the office and Gordie went immediately down the hall to Sergeant Arsenault's office.

His sergeant waved him in and gestured him to sit. "I just got off the phone with John Allan. Sounds like he sees the fisherman as a suspicious death."

Gordie nodded. "I plan to continue the investigation as if it is a homicide."

"Fair enough, but don't come down too hard on anyone until we get the call from the M.E."

MacLean shook his head. "I don't know enough to come down hard on anyone. Right now, it's just about asking questions."

"All right, and MacLean?"

"Sergeant?"

"I don't need to remind you to keep your partner informed, do I?"

Gordie felt the heat rise on the back of his neck. His failure to communicate in his last case, which put Detective Albright in serious danger, would never be forgotten. "No, Sergeant. You don't need to remind me." *But of course, now you have, and that's the point.*

MacLean went back to his office, having received the blessing of his sergeant to go ahead with the direction of the investigation.

He spent the rest of the afternoon making calls and writing up his notes. When he left the office for the drive home, he spent some time mulling over the last call, which was again to the widow. He broke the news to her that he wasn't yet able to give a solid date for the release of either her husband's body or the boat.

Sharon had seemed almost disinterested. The one thing he noticed, was she became anxious about was how the news, or lack of news, would be communicated to Dannymac and Kyle. Gordie agreed that he would call Dannymac.

Maybe it's just that the little girl is home from school, and she didn't want to talk.

He pulled over in a parking spot overlooking the view, but instead of admiring the shimmering water and low forested mountains, he looked up and dialed the number for Dannymac.

"Mr. MacDonald? Detective MacLean here." Gordie always erred on the side of formality when calling someone.

He waited to hear MacDonald's acknowledgement and then continued. "I've spoken with your daughter-in-law, and I wanted to call you personally as well to give you an update. I'm afraid we can't release your son's body yet. The autopsy has been conducted, but it's now up to the Medical Examiner to review the report and then determine if the death is suspicious or accidental. He may need further tests to make this determination, so we have to wait until he's completed his review and provides his decision."

MacDonald sighed and asked about the boat.

"I hope to have more information on that tomorrow. As I understand it, tomorrow should be the last day of processing the *Sea Child*. In fact, my partner and I will be going to Inverness to meet with the forensics team ourselves. After that, I'll be in a better position to tell you next steps. I recognize that this is costing money as well as adding to the stress of the whole situation. I'll do everything in my power to move things along for you. Will you relay this to Kyle?"

Gordie disengaged and pulled out of the scenic lookout spot.

He felt that Dannymac's reaction had been in keeping with what he had expected. Grief and frustration were both evident in his voice. And weariness. *The poor man sounds exhausted.*

When he reached St. Peter's, he called Vanessa. Last night had gone well, and they had avoided any discussion about the case. He had mixed feelings because he'd love to talk things over with her. Vanessa was clever and had great insight. She had been a teacher, and she had a good read on people. At the same time, he wanted to avoid any more conflict with her.

Maybe I better just stick to talking to Taz.

He called Vanessa to say he had work to do that evening, but since he'd be in Inverness tomorrow, perhaps they could have dinner together. He invited her out to Port Mulroy to the local inn, which served good, plentiful home-cooking style meals, and he smiled when she agreed. All was well again. At least for the moment.

CHAPTER 14

ROXANNE DROVE TO MACLEAN'S house early the next day. Gordie let Taz out to greet his partner and grinned to see Albright try to dodge the dog's probing nose. "I told you before. It's best just to let her poke you and then it'll be over. The more you try to avoid her, the more she'll pursue you."

Roxanne shook her head. "I can't just let someone, even Taz, goose me without protest. Sheba doesn't do that."

Gordie nodded. "I think it's a Great Pyr thing. I don't know any golden retrievers that do it. How is that rescue of yours settling in anyway? Is your Nana happy with the new addition to the family?"

She smiled. "Nana loves Sheba. For all her initial protests against getting a dog, I know she missed going out to all her pre-Covid clubs, and it was getting her down. Sheba has been a godsend and because she's almost three years old, she's calm enough that Nana can handle walking her. Having her has helped bring the sparkle back to Nana."

He led her into the kitchen of his small one and a half story house. "That's great to hear. Tea?"

"I better not. As it is, I better make a pit stop before we head out."

He waved down the hall. "You know your way by now."

By the time Roxanne returned to the kitchen, Gordie had finished his own morning cup of tea and rinsed out the mug. He took out a dog biscuit and handed it to Taz, who took it from his fingers delicately before taking the treat to her bed in the corner of the kitchen.

"Right. Let's head off, then."

Albright stopped to stroke the big white dog's head. "Another day on your own, Taz."

"She's fine. She just goes to sleep, and today will be a good day for her because Vanessa has said she'd come and get her. Taz will love that."

When they were settled in Gordie's car, Roxanne grinned at her partner. "Things must be getting serious with Vanessa that she's allowed to come and take your precious dog away for the day."

"It's good for Taz. The neighbour sometimes stops in to look after her as well."

Roxanne chuckled. "You aren't trying to say that Vanessa and your neighbour lady are in the same league?"

"Maybe not." He admitted.

Albright left the subject alone and turned the conversation to the day ahead. "What do you think we're going to learn from the *Sea Child*?"

Gordie swallowed his initial reaction. which would normally be 'Let's wait and see'. Instead, since their last case together, he made more of an effort to share his thinking with his partner. "I think we'll have confirmation that another boat recently bumped up against *Sea Child*. With a bit of luck, we may get an indication of the type of boat to give us some direction."

"Really? Is that even possible?"

"I'm not sure. I know that there is a database for identifying paint chips from cars, called PDQ, Paint Data Query, but honestly, I don't know if we can use it for boat paint. But we'll find out."

"Interesting. You're a wealth of information, MacLean."

"Well, I'm not sure it will be helpful. Even if it's possible, I somehow doubt our budget will run to that kind of analysis unless we knew it was critical to catch a killer."

"Still. It's interesting."

"Speaking of interesting, I had an email note from John Allan, who got a call from the lead forensics guy. Apparently, they found something that will be of great interest. That's all I know. Allan either knew nothing more, or he was being cagey with me. I called him but got his voicemail. I suspect he just sent me that to wind me up."

"Now I'm intrigued. John Allan doesn't strike me as someone who would just say something to wind a person up."

"No, you're right, but he could have been more explicit in his note to me."

Albright returned to talk about the boat. "Let's say another boat did bump *Child*. Let's say someone boarded her and attacked Adam. In my mind, the big question is still why? Why was he up in that area when he should have been in Port Hood getting ready for a day of fishing?"

Gordie nodded. "Maybe he was up there to poach from someone else's traps. That's something he'd do alone and maybe overnight, right? He wouldn't want to be seen."

"And it just happened that the owner of those traps was also out in the middle of the night or pre-dawn anyway, and caught him? If that was the case, wouldn't the other fisherman just call the police?"

"Maybe not. Don't forget that terrible case of Phillip Boudreau back in 2013. Where I live in Isle Madame, there are still families torn apart by it. People who thought one side was right, and some who thought the other side was."

She nodded. "I remember that." Roxanne put up her hands as if to say, 'that proves my point.' "Wouldn't people have learned from that experience? If someone is poaching from you, let the authorities deal with it."

"There are many who still believe they can deal with things themselves. Calling the cops is a sign of weakness."

Soon after passing the bakery where they had shared a beaver tail pastry the other day, Highway 19 turned inland. Gordie remembered the treat and felt his stomach rumble, but knew it would be a long while before he would have another one. He must have consumed a week's worth of calories on that one snack.

Roxanne settled back, and they drove in companionable quiet, listening to the radio until they arrived at the outskirts of Inverness.

Gordie turned into the parking lot of the two-story brown brick building. Behind the main office building there was a long barn-like structure that housed garages and the forensics lab for vehicles, or in this case, a boat.

They each put on their masks and went into the front reception area to sign in and receive visitor identity badges. After a moment, a female sergeant came out to meet them.

"I'm Sergeant Ada Benoit. Call me Ada, please." She leaned in, bumping elbows with Gordie and then Roxanne. She stepped back again to enforce the required social distance space between them.

What a difference from our sergeant. Gordie smiled and nodded. "Nice to meet you. I'm Gordie MacLean and this is Roxanne Albright."

"Do you need a coffee or a bio break?" Ada waved towards the washrooms.

Gordie nodded. "I'll say yes to both."

The RCMP sergeant in her summer uniform led them through the locked barrier, slowing down at the washrooms. She pointed down the hall. "Come down to the canteen, first door on the left, when you're ready."

When Gordie joined Ada Benoit in the canteen, she directed him to the self-serve coffee machine where he helped himself to a cup of coffee, dropping a loonie, a dollar coin, into the empty coffee tin beneath the sign that showed that the price of a coffee or tea was 50 cents each. He nodded to Roxanne as she came over. "I paid for yours."

They sat at a large table in the sun, overlooking the garage in the back. It was a relief to remove their masks temporarily. Gordie held up his cup of coffee. "Pretty cheap cup of coffee."

Ada smiled. "Don't celebrate yet. It's pretty cheap coffee."

He took a sip and shrugged. "I've had worse."

Roxanne had made a tea for herself. "And that's why I drink tea. It's hard to make a bad cup of tea, as long as the water's hot enough."

The sergeant looked out the window and nodded towards the building which held the boat. "I'll let Dr. Ingram, our Forensics Specialist, take you through the findings, but I will say that while I respect you are lead on the case, we will want to work in partnership with you on this."

Gordie raised his eyebrows. "That's interesting. Is that because young Constable Jeffreys is putting pressure on you?"

She frowned. "I don't assign resources based on their individual desires, but on the needs of the case."

Gordie felt his face heat up. "Of course. I apologize."

Benoit smiled. "No problem. I know where you're coming from. He can be overly enthusiastic at times. Now, if you're ready, let's get out there and see what we've got."

Albright and MacLean followed Sergeant Benoit out through a rear door of the building and into the big, grey-sided building to the rear. She led them along a hallway and then entered a large open room, bright with various light sources, from standard ceiling fluorescent tubes to LED lights on portable stands. In the middle of the space *Sea Child* stood, her red hull and keel looking dull encased in dried-on seaweed.

A young man with a mop of shaggy brown hair, wearing a white coat, came forward to greet them. Benoit made the introductions. "Dr. Mike Ingram, Detectives MacLean and Albright from the CBPS."

God, he's just a kid. Gordie nodded. "Thank you for meeting with us. I always prefer to see things with my own eyes rather than just read the report."

Ingram held up his clipboard. "I understand. Let's get started, then." He led them around to the side where Gordie had already noticed the scrape. He felt his heart quicken. *I knew this was something.*

Ingram pulled out a small LED flashlight and shone it on the scrape. "I believe you had noted this already, Detective MacLean?"

"I did. I wondered if it was important."

"It may, or it may not be. It's definitely a scrape of paint from another boat. No question there."

"But?"

"But a couple of things. We can't be sure when the contact was made between the two boats. We can tell that it was recent because the weather didn't have time to blow away the loose flakes yet. Likewise, there's no sign that water has washed anything away, so neither weather nor waves have had a chance at it, leaving us to conclude that this happened within about 18 hours of us collecting our sample."

Gordie chewed his bottom lip. "That's good news. The next question is, what about the paint? Can you tell much from it? Like what sort of boat, it came from?"

"I'm afraid not."

Gordie gave an involuntary 'tsk' with his tongue. "I thought you folks have a database that identifies paint chips?"

"Ah, yes. Our PDQ program. You're right. We have a Paint Data Query program that runs queries against an international database, but unfortunately, it's just for vehicles. It can tell us the make, model, year range and even manufacturing plant of an automobile. Marine paint is an entirely different kettle of fish." The young scientist smiled at the metaphor.

Roxanne shook her head. "Isn't paint, paint?"

"Not at all. While they primarily designed automotive paint for appearance and to protect against weather, marine paint also needs to protect against the corrosion of sea water and the growth of marine organisms."

Albright looked as deflated as Gordie felt. "Ah. I see. So, the paint chip you collected can't help us then?"

"I wouldn't say that. We have it analyzed now, so if you find a boat that you suspect may have been the one to rub against the *Sea Child*, we can collect a sample from that and compare it as a known sample against this one."

Gordie nodded. "Right. That might be important if we want to prove someone from that other boat had close contact with the *Child*."

Dr. Ingram smiled. "Exactly. Well, almost exactly. We can place the boat there, but we didn't have any DNA as part of the paint chip, so the boat and people are two different things."

Gordie felt he might as well have simply read the report instead of making the trip out. "Was there anything else of any use? The blood stain maybe?"

Ingram led the way up a set of movable steps placed to give access to the deck of the *Sea Child*. Sergeant Benoit left to talk to one of the other forensic specialists, leaving Ingram, MacLean, and Albright squatting down around the stain on the deck. "We took samples of the blood here" he circled the stain on the deck boards, "here" he pointed to a corner of the steel storage chest that holds the catch in seawater, "and there" shining his flashlight on the washboard, the wide rim of the boat where the traps rest while being unloaded and rebaited.

"And?" Gordie wished the thorough scientist would cut to the chase.

"All samples proved to be from the victim, Adam MacDonald."

Disappointed again, Gordie stifled a sigh.

Albright frowned. "He must have bounced around a lot."

They all stood to take a closer look at the three spots. Ingram stepped over to the steel fish box. "He hit his head here. There were hairs and scalp skin on the corner here, as well as blood. Head wounds are tricky. Even a sharp knock to the head may have taken several minutes to take effect. He may have talked and even walked the distance between the storage chest and here before collapsing. Then, internal bleeding would have become more profuse, leading to his ultimate death."

Roxanne moved across to the washboard. "And what do you think happened here?"

"I think that was the first injury. We found blood on the gaff hook as well. I believe that for some reason, he grabbed the hook, not by the wooden handle as one would expect, but by the hook itself. If he reached for it quickly, as for example, because it was about to fall overboard, the injury would have been more of a puncture."

Gordie nodded. "That's what our forensics man said as well."

Ingram continued. "I believe the hook was in motion and it lacerated the victim's hand as he tried to defend himself or as he tried to wrestle it away from whoever had hold of the handle end. The hook slashed his hand. I believe that caused him to jump back."

Albright envisioned the scene. "And he fell against the steel tub."

Ingram shook his head. "If he had just stumbled, I don't think the injury would have been as serious. In fact, I suspect he would have reached back his hand to catch himself. No. He was pushed."

Gordie nodded. "Yes, that's what the autopsy showed. Someone shoved him and essentially threw him against the tub."

Ingram nodded. "Which led to his death."

Albright persisted. "But if you say he may have walked even after the knock to his head, it's possible the person who pushed him left and didn't even know how serious it was."

Ingram smiled. "That's beyond my scope. I can tell you that after he collapsed, he bled for some time, so yes, it's possible the assailant left the victim, not knowing what he or she had done."

"Or they were just heartless." Gordie murmured. "Well, you've given us a solid picture of what happened. What about fingerprints on the gaff hook? Anything?"

"There were a couple that were usable. A full set from the victim, on the wooden shaft. There were a couple of others on the handle, so if you get me something to compare them to, I might be able to help you, but there were lots of smudges which would come from gloves."

MacLean nodded. "That's everything, I guess, is it?"

"I have one more thing to show you. Let's go to my office."

They followed Ingram down the steps and to the rear of the garage space where there were large tables, similar to the forensics lab at MacLean's own building, along with two offices. Ada Benoit was already sitting in Ingram's office, waiting for them.

Ingram opened his filing cabinet and pulled out a plastic evidence bag sealed with red evidence identification tape. Mike Ingram held up the bag in the light to clearly show his prize to the audience.

Albright gasped and Gordie muttered, "oh my."

CHAPTER 15

THE PLASTIC BAG WAS bulky with the box it contained. On the front, on an orange background, the large black letters stated '32 AUTO' with smaller lettering giving specifics of the box of pistol cartridges. Detailed proudly on the ammunition box was *32 ACP 71 Grain Jacket Hollow Point Ammunition Box of 50.*

Gordie took the evidence bag from Dr. Ingram and hefted it. "Is the box full?"

"Not quite."

"Where did you find it?"

"In the cabin beside the steering, there's a plate that can be removed to access the workings of the steering. It was held on loosely with two bolts, rather than the ten, which seemed strange. It made me wonder if there had been problems with the mechanics, which might have meant that the boat wasn't drivable."

Albright nodded, "meaning you thought he might have broken down."

Ingram nodded. "Instead of just the usual mechanical cables and whatnot, we discovered they had created a large cavern back there. Deep in the back of that hidden storage place, we found this box."

Gordie bit his lip. "Maybe it's been there for a long time? I assume you didn't find a gun, or even you, a master of suspense, would have mentioned it by now?"

"No gun. But plenty of space for guns. I don't think this has been sitting in that cubby for a long time. The carton would deteriorate over time, getting damp and mouldy. No. This box is pristine, so I'm guessing no more than a few weeks. And before you ask, only one person's prints are on it; those of the victim, although there are smudged prints, probably from someone wearing gloves."

"Show us this cubby."

Ingram let the way back up the steps to the boat and into the cabin. To the left of the steering wheel, a metal plate was bolted to the wall of a lower cabin. Above the steering wheel, the wall created a countertop, so the entire area looked much like a kitchen counter. On the countertop were miscellaneous items, a rag, a paper coffee cup, a small portable radio. The face plate was deceptively innocuous, easily hidden, especially if someone draped a towel or jacket from the counter over the plate to hide it from view.

The forensics lead pulled a screwdriver from the pocket of his white coat and hunched over to remove the screws and plate. He shone the light into the dark space, and Gordie and Roxanne peered inside.

Gordie straightened up. "A 32 isn't much bigger than my hand."

Sergeant Benoit spoke up from behind them. "That's right. A Beretta Alleycat, as an example, isn't even as big as your hand. It has a short barrel and I've seen one in a pocket holster that's designed to look like a wallet. Easy to hide, which makes them a popular gun, even though some reports say that it's fallen out of favour lately."

Both Roxanne and Gordie turned to look at Benoit as she went on. "I spoke with one of my colleagues in Halifax. He used to work with the Firearms and Toolmark Identification team out of Quebec. He tells me that aside from the small size of a .32 pistol, making it easy to hide, it's also popular because it has a reduced recoil."

MacLean looked back at the hidden cavern. "That space might house at least 20 guns, along with that many boxes of ammo or more."

Benoit nodded. "Now you understand why we want to stay connected to the case."

"Yes. I understand." He paused. "I always thought that smuggling guns was something that happened more commonly at the road border crossings, like in Ontario. It just doesn't seem very practical to me to bring guns by water from...where? Florida?"

She shook her head. "They may have come from Florida originally, but with the U.S. Canada land borders having been closed for so long now because of the pandemic, my friend in Halifax thinks there's enough money in it to bring them by water up from Maine or elsewhere. It seems convoluted to come all the way around through the Canso Straight, but if the returns are high enough, people will do the most improbable things."

Benoit turned, and the two detectives followed her, leaving Ingram to fasten the faceplate back in place.

They waited at the bottom of the steps for Ingram to rejoin them.

Gordie held his hands up in a questioning gesture. "Where do we go from here with the *Sea Child*? Can she be released, given this information?"

Benoit nodded. "We've discussed that. Dr. Ingram and his team have completed their forensics analysis. Having found prohibited ammunition, we could technically impound the boat, but we've decided to release her. I'd like to have you continue your investigation. Given what you know so far, do you believe Adam MacDonald was working alone?"

"It's impossible to know at this point, but the actual owner of the boat, MacDonald Sr. seemed as mystified as we were as to why Adam would be so far outside of his own assigned LFA. Both he and the other son, Kyle, seem keen on getting back to fishing."

"We'll release the boat, but I'll be assigning Constable Jeffreys to keep a sharp eye open to see if she comes back to the area where we found her."

Gordie nodded. "Makes sense."

They thanked Ingram for his time and headed back to the main building.

Benoit escorted them back to the front reception. "You'll contact the owner, then?"

"Yes. Any chance the boat can be trailered back to Port Hood today still?"

"It's only a half hour away. I'm sure I can make that happen."

"Great. It'll be ready for them to go fishing tomorrow, then. Let me know what time you figure the boat will be at the harbour, and I'll let Danny MacDonald know to be there to sign the paperwork. We'll keep in touch, Ada, and let you know how we're progressing. This certainly puts a whole different slant on things. I honestly thought we'd find this was a case of lobster poaching."

Gordie and Roxanne went back to the car and sat there for a moment. Her eyes were wide when she looked at him. "Are we really talking about gun running?"

"So it seems. Where in the world would the weapons go from here? Let's assume we're right that MacDonald meets up with a boat coming in from the U.S. and his job is to move it on. It still seems strange that he'd go up to Pleasant Bay." He started the car. "We have lots of questions to answer, Detective Albright."

After bringing Sergeant Arsenault up to speed, they called Dannymac. "Danny? MacLean and Albright here. We're on our way to see you. We'll be there in about twenty minutes."

MacDonald's voice sounded weary. "Do you want Kyle here as well?"

"That's unnecessary. The boat is being released, Danny, so it's good news."

His voice lifted. "That's great news. All right. I'll see you soon."

Albright looked at Gordie. "Shouldn't we talk to Kyle as well? I assume you want to talk to him about the guns?"

"Yes, but I'd like to gauge Dannymac's reaction first. As far as we can see, he's been an honest, hard-working fisherman all his life. I can't imagine he'd go along with a scheme like this. I'm not sure we can say the same for Kyle."

"He may end up calling Kyle over, anyway. At least he'll want to give him the news about the release of *Sea Child*."

"That's true, and then it may be even more interesting."

***

Dannymac was alone when they arrived. He led them into the now familiar kitchen.

Gordie sat across from the older man. "I'm waiting for a call from the Mounties to let me know when *Sea Child* will arrive back to the harbour and then you'll need to go down to meet them to sign the paperwork confirming they are releasing her to you in good order."

"It's good of them to bring her home. Kyle figured he'd have to arrange to pick her up."

"Everyone recognizes how hard this has been for you, Danny, and we want to help as much as we can."

Dannymac narrowed his eyes. "You could have told me this on the phone."

"Danny, the forensics team found something that we have trouble explaining. Detective Albright, can you please show him the photos you took?"

Gordie watched his face pale.

Danny handed the phone with its photos of the box of ammo back to Albright. "Where'd you find that?"

Albright swiped her phone to reveal a close-up photo of the cubbyhole in the front console of the boat and held it for him to see. "The space behind the steering has been enlarged to create a storage area. This is where they found the box of ammo."

Danny shrugged. "Probably been there for years."

111

Gordie watched the man's face go from grey to red. *He's shocked but doing his best to cover it.*

MacLean shook his head. "Forensics don't believe so, and I trust they know what they're talking about. And by the way, Adam's fingerprints were on the box."

Danny remained silent, and Gordie continued. "However long it's been there, the question remains. This is ammunition for a prohibited weapon. Does Adam, or anyone else in your family, own a .32 gun?"

Danny glared at Gordie, his face a deep enraged brick-red colour. "Certainly not. I don't know what you are accusing us of, but we are just honest, hard-working, fisherman."

"How do you explain the ammo, then, Danny?"

"I don't have an explanation. Sometimes in the off season, we charter the boat for tourists. Adam captains it, and he takes half a dozen people out for a tour along the coast. Most of them are Americans, so maybe one of those dropped a box of ammo, Adam found it later and threw it back there to keep it safe and out of the way. How do I know? He never mentioned it. I doubt he gave it another thought."

"Yes, that's possible." Gordie's phone rang, and he walked into the hall to take the call.

When he returned, he heard Albright's voice calming the old man, explaining about the autopsy. "We need to wait for the Medical Examiner in Halifax to give us the word. It's out of our hands, I'm afraid, but I'll give them a call later to see if I can get any estimate of when that might be."

MacLean nodded to Dannymac. "The *Sea Child* should arrive at the wharf at 4:30 to release her to you. We'll leave you now, Danny. We'll circle back to talk to Kyle at a later time, but we will need both of you to go in to Port Mulroy to have your fingerprints taken. The Mounties have agreed to do that, so you don't need to come all the way to our offices in Sydney."

Dannymac frowned. "Our fingerprints? Why? My prints, Kyle's

and Dab's will be all over the place. I don't go out fishing anymore, but I often go down and help tidy up the boat when I feel up to it."

Again, Roxanne was soothing. "This is just basic procedure, Danny. We understand what you are saying. We expect to find the prints of all three of you, so when we find a print that doesn't match one of you, we can follow that up."

"All right. I'm tired now. I'll call Kyle and have him get me to go meet the Mounties, but right now I need to rest."

MacLean gestured to him to stay seated. "Thank you for your time, Danny."

When Gordie and Roxanne were back in the car, they agreed to go back to the coffee shop for a late lunch.

Roxanne grinned. "Having a beaver tail?"

"Good Lord, no. A sandwich and coffee will do me."

It was busy, so they took takeout to eat in the car. A turkey-pesto on an Italian roll for her and a black forest ham on home -baked brown bread for him. They settled themselves in the car with their drinks and sandwiches and between bites, they talked about what they had learned.

"You don't think the family is involved in Adam's death, do you, Gordie?"

He shrugged. "It's too soon to know, but no. I don't in fact think so. If someone in the family did this, why would they go all the way to Pleasant Bay? Doesn't make sense."

"So, if we put aside the family, what do we have so far? Dab Haan told us he saw Adam talking to an unknown man on a Harley. That's not much to go by."

"You got that right. If that person and Adam were in some kind of arrangement, more people knew about it than just Dab Haan, who stumbled upon them. We go back to the wife; we talk to some of their other friends. We know that Lynn is a friend of Sharon's, but what about friends of Adam's? Who are they?"

She nodded. "Do we start with Sharon?"

"Right after we finish lunch, that's where we are headed. Tomorrow we'll spend in the office and plan our strategy going forward. We need to check Adam's finances. If he's been taking in more money than what can be accounted for with the fishing, we need to chase that down. Dannymac is right. One box of illegal ammo doesn't a criminal make. There could be a somewhat reasonable explanation for it, but we still have the question of 'what took him to Pleasant Bay?'"

Roxanne wiped her fingers off and drained her cup of tea, stuffing the napkins and paper cup into the paper bag her sandwich came in. "Do you think it's worth another trip up to Pleasant Bay?"

"Absolutely. We need to tread with care there, but yes."

"You mean, don't step on Constable Jeffreys' toes?"

"Exactly. You have a way about you. He'll be on your list to contact tomorrow to let him know that we'll be in the area. Use your magic to smooth his feathers."

She laughed. "He may surprise you, now that he's officially on the team. This could be a big case for him, and I think he'll be fine."

Gordie gathered the trash together and opened the car door. "Fingers crossed."

He walked over and deposited the garbage in the can and paused to light a cigarette. He took his time to come back to the car, stopping to cough and then dropping half the cigarette unsmoked to grind under his foot.

Roxanne waited for his return. When he climbed back in, she raised her eyebrows as he shook his head. "What's wrong?"

"I get closer to quitting every day."

"That's a good thing."

He started the car. "Ready to take on the wife?"

"Let's get at it."

CHAPTER 16

SHARON'S EYES WIDENED WHEN she opened the door to Gordie and Roxanne. Her face paled, and then she turned away from them to lead them into the house. Gordie glanced at his partner who raised an eyebrow. He hadn't imagined it. Sharon MacDonald was flustered to see them.

They sat in the living room, Sharon on the sofa and Gordie and Roxanne each in one of the floral-patterned easy chairs. It was a bright, airy room and the furniture was in good condition. *There must be decent money in fishing.*

Roxanne took the lead. "Sharon, we just wanted to bring you up to date on where things stand."

"Are you releasing Adam's body?"

"No, I'm afraid not yet, but the *Sea Child* is being released back to Dannymac today."

The widow gave a little shrug. "I'm more interested in when I can arrange the funeral. It's not right to take so long about this. People keep asking me."

"I understand your frustration. It's out of our hands, so we all need to be patient."

"Is that it, then?"

"No. The forensics team found some puzzling things about the boat, which have raised questions."

Sharon shook her head. "I really can't help you with anything about the boat."

Gordie studied her. *She didn't even ask what we found.*

Roxanne continued. "We found a box of ammunition on the boat. Did Adam have a gun?"

Her face flushed. "God, no. What a notion. Adam was the most peace-loving, kind man you'd ever want to meet. He would never have a reason to have a gun. Lots of people we know go moose hunting in the fall. Not Adam. Never."

"This wasn't ammunition that would be typical for moose hunting, Sharon. This was the sort that fits a small handgun."

She straightened up. "Well, it wasn't Adam's. Maybe you should be talking to Kyle."

"Does Kyle own a gun?"

"I'm not saying that. I've never seen him with one, and I never heard Adam mention it. Since it wasn't Adam's, the ammunition might have belonged to Kyle. That's all I'm saying."

Albright pulled out her notebook. "Aside from Kyle, who were Adam's closest friends?"

Sharon frowned. "Why? They're all just ordinary guys. They didn't do anything to Adam."

As Roxanne flipped open her book, Gordie took over. "Sharon, right now, we don't know what happened to Adam. We need to talk to everyone who had interactions with him to figure this out. You want that too, right?"

"Of course." She rose. "I'll get our phone book. Do you want a cup of tea?"

Gordie nodded. "I'd love one, thank you."

Roxanne shook her head. "I'm fine for now, thank you."

They heard the tap run, the click of the kettle, and then a drawer opening and closing. Sharon MacDonald came back in carrying an old-fashioned brown leather-bound phone book. There were slips of paper, torn envelopes with return addresses, and sticky notes stuffed into the book, making it thick with names and numbers.

She flipped through the pages. "His best buddy is Andy LeBlanc." She read out his phone number. "They were in school together."

Gordie encouraged her. "That's great. Anyone else we could talk to?"

She flipped through the book again. "There's Johnny McMaster. They coached hockey together for girls under nine for a couple of years. That's when Izzie was playing hockey, but she gave it up for music." Sharon smiled for an instant. "That was a good choice." She looked up. "We didn't force her, you know. She just took an interest in the fiddle and now, well, we're just so proud of her. Did I already tell you she's been accepted into the Maritime Conservatory for Music?"

Gordie smiled. "You're right to be proud. It must take a lot of practice."

"Yes." She looked back down at the address book on her lap. "Right. Friends. Here's Johnny's number." She read it out. "Well, those two are his closest. Anyone else are just buddies he knows down at the sports centre or from the Port Mulroy Legion. Not really close friends."

Gordie nodded. "Do either of those men ride a motorcycle, do you know?"

"No. I've only ever seen Johnny with an SUV and Andy with a blue pickup truck."

Roxanne closed her book.

"I think that's everything for now. Thank you for this and we'll let you know the moment we have more information from the Medical Examiner."

They all rose, but Gordie held up a hand to stop Sharon. "We can find our way out. Thank you for your time."

As they walked back to the car, Roxanne noted, "You didn't get your tea."

"I know. Oh well, probably just as well."

Albright checked her watch. "Did you want to track Kyle down?"

"Let's leave it at this for today. I need to let things mull for now. Tomorrow, we'll brief the team and decide where we go next. What do you think?"

"Sounds good to me. I'll write up the notes when I get back to Big Pond and I'll fire them over to you to look over."

"Great, thanks." After a few moments of thoughtful silence, Gordie glanced at his partner. "What was your sense of Sharon? She seemed edgy to me. Something a little off about her, but I don't know what or why."

"You mean when we first got there?"

"Yeah. She recovered, but when she first saw us, I swear she wanted to slam the door in our faces."

Roxanne laughed. "She was frazzled. No question about it. I think she has a guilty conscience, but it could be about anything. It doesn't mean she's involved in any crime."

"I know. I was a little quick to jump to that conclusion once before," Gordie alluded to their last case before he continued "so I agree, but even when we were telling her about the forensics report, she didn't seem entirely surprised to me."

"You're right. There's something not quite right there, but for some reason, I just feel that she's authentic."

Gordie knew that some of their colleagues would scoff at Albright's feelings, but he wasn't one of them. He set great store by instinct and gut feeling.

"We'll need to probe a little further with her, but for now, we'll leave it."

His partner refused his invitation to come in, choosing instead to get straight into her car when they reached his house. With a cheery wave, she drove off, and he turned to go into the house. Taz acted as though he'd been away for a week, bumping her nose against him and circling him, her tail waving enthusiastically.

Taz led him to the back door and together they did a couple of circuits of the fenced-in yard, Gordie smoking and the dog sniffing every spot where a squirrel may have crossed during the day. Gordie spoke out loud to the dog as they walked. "I like working with that girl, Taz. Haven't I come a long way?" The big white dog looked up at him and Gordie patted her head. "Was it only a year ago that I thought I'd never be able to work with a partner? You were all the partner I needed back then." They reached the far corner of the large yard and turned to follow the side fence back towards the house. "Don't worry, you haven't been replaced, but I guess it's not a bad thing that I can work with someone else without getting all pissed off. Is that yours, Roxanne's or Vanessa's influence, I wonder?"

Gordie finished his cigarette and butted it into the can of sand he kept beside the white plastic chair placed by the kitchen door. "Ready to go back in?" He held the door open and followed the proud white plume of Taz's tail inside.

He made himself the cup of tea he had missed out on at Sharon MacDonald's house and then settled into his easy chair in the living room to call Vanessa.

"Hiya. I'm home now, so I'll be in good time to pick you up for dinner. You're not getting all dressed up, are you?"

He smiled to hear her laugh and when she assured him she was just going comfortably tidy; he agreed. "I'm not sure what that is, but as long as I can go in my usual black jeans and a shirt, I'm happy."

He hung up, looked at the time, and decided he had enough time to check his emails, make some notes, and still have a shower.

As he thought back through the day, he wondered if people just naturally looked guilty when they talked to the police, or was it that both Dannymac and Sharon MacDonald had been hiding something?

***

Vanessa looked lovely in a high-necked lilac sweater and slim black pants. Her blond hair rested on her shoulders, and her freckled face, devoid of any make-up, was sun-flushed from her afternoon's work in the garden.

Gordie's breath caught, and he wondered, not for the first time, why she was going out with him. He leaned in to kiss her lightly on the lips, and she grasped his hand at the same time.

She stepped back. "Did you want anything before we go? A cup of tea?"

"No, not for me. I'm starving. What about you? Are you ready?"

Vanessa nodded. "I'll just get my bag."

He led the way to the car and opened the passenger door for her.

"You're such an old-fashioned guy, Gordie MacLean."

"Something wrong with that?"

She smiled, and he closed the door.

At the restaurant, Vanessa opened the car door herself before he had a chance to go around to her side. She led the way, chatting as she went. "I took a peek at the menu on the internet today, so I think I know what I want already."

"I didn't look at the menu, but I think I know what I'm having as well."

They waited for the hostess to come to seat them. "Steak?"

"And fries."

When they were seated, Vanessa asked for a glass of the house merlot and Gordie had a bottle of Alexander Keith's beer.

He glanced at the menu and then closed it. "Yes, it's confirmed. Steak and fries with a house salad on the side."

Vanessa took another minute before closing her menu. "Seafood linguini for me, which comes with a salad."

They ordered and sat back to enjoy the view of the Canso Straight as the sky turned from red and orange to purple and grey; the deepening colours of the dusk reflecting off the water.

She picked up her glass for a sip of wine. "Am I allowed to ask how the case is going?"

"Sure. I know I can trust you not to share what I say with anyone." He hoped his voice didn't hold too much of a questioning tone.

"Of course you can."

He lowered his voice and they naturally both leaned closer across the table. "We met with the forensics team in Inverness today. They found a box of prohibited ammunition on the boat."

Vanessa tilted her head. "Is that important?"

Gordie shrugged. "It could be."

Her eyes widened then. "Was he shot?"

"No, no. He fell against the steel storage locker and the blow to the head ultimately caused his death."

"Ah, OK. It was an accident then?"

"We'll have to wait for the M.E. to pronounce the official cause of death." Gordie hedged.

"Well, that seems like good news to me." She studied his face. "But you aren't convinced."

"We need to continue our investigation. I need a lot of convincing, I'm afraid."

She nodded, satisfied. "Lynn came over this morning for a visit."

"Oh?"

"We're getting ready for the summer quilting festival. There's so much to do, aside from just getting our quilts ready. There will be lessons and demonstrations, and then just the food and associated vendors, of course."

"I wouldn't commit to anything in a hurry."

"You think we may need to cancel because of the pandemic?"

"It's a crazy time. Just look at us here. Restaurants are only allowed to work at half capacity. I don't know what it'll be like come summer."

"It'll be outside, so hopefully it will go forward. It would be so disappointing to have to cancel."

"I know. I think you should continue, but don't spend any money yet to book anything. That would be my advice."

The meals arrived and Gordie was content to tuck into his food and continue to listen as Vanessa chatted about the festival and the sorts of things they were planning, including fiddle music.

"Mmm. Music?"

She gestured with her fork. "Yes. In fact, Lynn suggested that we ask young Izzie, you know, the daughter of Adam and Sharon Mac-Donald, to perform. She's apparently very talented. Perhaps she's the next Natalie McMaster. It's no wonder that she's been accepted at the Conservatory." She took another mouthful of linguini.

"That's a pretty fancy school, isn't it? Must be pretty pricey."

Vanessa shrugged as she swallowed. "She may have received a scholarship. I think there are several of those available from different arts organizations."

"True."

The conversation turned as darkness fell. "Look how beautiful the darkness is on the water. I want to do a quilt using those colours. Black and the deep green and blue of the water, with just a flash of the last bit of red from the sun."

"I'm sure it will be beautiful."

His thoughts were not on quilt making, and Vanessa dropped the subject. "Lynn mentioned that Dab Haan's been on a bit of a bender. He must be pretty torn up about losing his friend."

Gordie focussed again. "I think he likes his drink at the best of times."

She tsked. "I know. It's sad, isn't it? I think it may be worse this time. Lynn said that she dropped by to see Sharon yesterday evening and Dab was there when she arrived. It seemed like he was harassing Sharon about money, but of course Sharon has nothing to do with the business. She told him to go talk to Dannymac or Kyle."

"Is that right?"

"Poor man must have thought Sharon might have been a soft touch to help him out."

"Did Lynn hear anything else?"

"I don't think so. When Dab saw Lynn, he grumbled a lot but left right away. I wish there was something we could do to help him."

Gordie stifled a sigh. "You can only help a person who wants to be helped."

"I know, I know. I don't mean I want to get him into rehab. Maybe there are some little things to make life easier for him." She put up her hands. "I don't know. I'll have to think on it a bit."

Again, he bit back his words to tell her to leave it alone, not wanting to ruin this nice evening. *What harm can she do? He's not like my father. Haan isn't a mean drunk.*

He drove her home, and it was late when he left the comfort of her cozy house to head back to Taz, waiting patiently on Isle Madame for him.

CHAPTER 17

GORDIE ARRIVED EARLY AT the office the next morning. His mind had been busy on the hour and a half drive in with things to do, but first, he went to do his morning penance in the form of briefing Sergeant Arsenault, who was always the first one in.

His skin glowing as if he had just come from the gym, Arsenault waved Gordie in. "It sounds like your adventures yesterday raised some interesting questions."

Gordie felt his muscles tense. *Why does he always make it sound like I'm out there playing around, doing nothing?* "True. After we met with the forensics, which you know all about, we went to talk to MacDonald Senior and Mrs. MacDonald. Senior seemed shocked at the find by forensics, but hid it well. Mrs. MacDonald seemed more flustered by our appearance at her door than by the information about the ammunition. She clearly didn't believe it was connected to her husband and didn't seem too disturbed by the find."

"The appearance of cops at the door always fluster some people. Natural reaction. You think she's in the clear?"

"I'm not ready to say that yet. She's given us a couple of contact details for friends of Adam's, which we need to follow up. I want a better understanding of the dynamics of the family."

Arsenault leaned back in his swivel chair and linked his hands behind his head. "Surely just the logistics of the whole thing would take her out of the frame. The boat way up in Pleasant Bay while she's at home with their daughter?"

"That doesn't mean she didn't pay someone."

Arsenault snorted. "You read too many spy novels, MacLean."

MacLean shrugged. "We are already looking at weapons trafficking. Is it such a stretch to believe a hired assassin is a possibility? Let us just do the investigation step by step."

His sergeant leaned forward and put his hands flat on the desk. "I'm not suggesting anything else, MacLean. Now if there's nothing else?"

Gordie stood. "All right if I have one of the team help with chasing down phone records and financials?"

"Take Norris. I'll send him a note to tell him to put everything else on the back burner."

"Great, thanks."

MacLean went back to the detective work area and found Albright at her desk checking her email. "Good morning. Thanks for those reports last night. Great work."

"I started to set up the briefing room, but wasn't sure how much you wanted to put up on the board."

"Let's go do that now and I'll tell you how it went with Sarge."

She followed him to the briefing room, and they stood in front of the large white board. Albright had added a heading 'forensics' and put a bullet point for '.32 ammo' and one for 'blood on gaff hook'.

Gordie picked up a blue marker and added a new heading. 'Interviews to be done' and below that listed Adam's two friends: Andy LeBlanc and Johnny McMaster, along with the widow's closest friend, Lynn Duggan and the other friend Yvonne. "Anyone I'm missing?"

Roxanne furrowed her brows. "What about people up in Pleasant Bay?"

He nodded and added 'witnesses in Pleasant Bay.' "OK, we've also got to get a warrant for the MacDonald finances. I want both the business and personal records."

She took up the green marker to indicate documents versus people and made the note. "You want the records of Kyle and Dannymac as well?"

"I'd love it, but we won't get them. No, we can justify the victim's especially given the ammo find, but anything more would be a fishing expedition."

Roxanne groaned to acknowledge his little joke and then continued. "Phone records?"

"For Adam, yes. I want both his mobile and the home phone."

She poised the pen to add more. "What else?"

"I want someone to check for CCTV out back of the Canadian Tire. There are a few stores there and maybe one of them will have a camera looking out at the parking lot."

Albright added it to the list. "Right. You're looking for the guy on the motorbike that met with Adam."

"Allegedly."

She nodded. "True. I'm not sure how reliable Dab Haan's information is."

"Let's think positive for the time being. We'll have to get on that quick because even if someone does have CCTV, the meeting took place a couple of weeks ago and by now may be erased."

Gordie continued. "Let's also start a list of follow-up interviews. Kyle MacDonald is on the top of that list. I want to talk to Dab Haan again as well." He hesitated and then gestured to Roxanne to sit down. "I had dinner with Vanessa last night."

Albright put the marker on the ledge of the whiteboard and sat down in one of the chairs in the front row. Her voice, puzzled at the sudden departure from talking about the case. "That sounds nice. Go somewhere good?"

Gordie frowned. "Never mind all that. You know she's friends with both Lynn and Sharon MacDonald?"

"Right. I had almost forgotten that, but that's how we got this case in the first place."

"Yes, well, Vanessa was talking to Lynn yesterday, who claims that Dab Haan visited Sharon MacDonald."

Roxanne's face cleared as she made the connection between the dinner date and the case. "Ah. That's not a big surprise, I guess. Haan worked for Adam, so I can see that he'd want to visit the widow."

"Yes, but according to Lynn, Haan was pressuring Sharon for money."

"That's a bit odd, but drinkers can be unpredictable."

Gordie muttered. "Don't I know it?" He ignored her glance and went on. "Why would Haan hit Sharon up for money instead of his old buddy, Dannymac?"

She shrugged. "Maybe he was just trying to take advantage of her when she's vulnerable?"

"It's possible. Anyway, I want to take another run at him, preferably when he's sober. With the *Sea Child* back in business, I think we'll time a visit for when the fishing is done for the day and he hasn't had a chance yet to fuel up."

"Talk to him at the wharf instead of at home. Makes sense."

"We'll spend the day here and then tomorrow we'll both drive up to Port Hood to meet the boats coming in. I'd say around ten just to be sure."

"Sounds good."

"Sarge is giving us Rob Norris to help, so I plan to get him on tracking down the records. How do you feel about taking a trip up to Pleasant Bay to meet with your new best friend, Constable Jeffreys? That's why I'm saying you take your own vehicle, because after we meet with Haan, I'll arrange to talk to Kyle, and you carry on up to Pleasant Bay."

"And try to track down a witness or two, I assume."

"Yes, that's the main thing. There may be some protest that you're covering the same ground he's already done, but just blame it on me. If you think you could get away with it, I'd be fine with you just going straight to Pleasant Bay and talk to the locals without involving Jeffreys at all."

"I'll think about it, but I think that would just make things worse with him, and you never know when we may need him."

Gordie sighed. "You're right, of course. I'll leave it to you to figure out. OK, we've got things ready here and have half an hour before the briefing. I'll run over and get some doughnuts. You want a tea while I'm out?"

"Sure. Want some money?"

He rolled his eyes. "I hope I can spring for some doughnuts and a couple of drinks."

She grinned and left him to the doughnut run while she went back to her desk.

***

The briefing went well, and Detective Norris sat with Gordie after everyone else had left the room.

Rob Norris was an easygoing detective, taller than Gordie, but with his perpetual slouch and shaggy-looking chestnut hair, he didn't immediately strike a person as someone who had the experience and skills that he, in fact, possessed. Perhaps because he was so laid back, he wasn't prone to debate with their sergeant, unlike Gordie, who at times couldn't help himself. This made Detective Norris a favourite with Staff Sergeant Arsenault, but Gordie liked him despite that flaw.

MacLean closed the file and handed it to Norris. "You're all set, then? You'll chase down the warrants and get stuck into digging out the financials?"

"Yup. No problem. Now that I'm done with going to court, I'm glad to have some time to relax around the office. It's a perfect little holiday for me."

Gordie shook his head. "When I spend too many hours inside this building, I want to explode."

Norris laughed. "You're too much like your dog. You need the wind blowing through your white hair to be happy. I'm more like a cat. I'm content to curl up here in my familiar surroundings."

They stood, and Norris waved the file at Gordie. "Go on and let me get at this."

"Thanks, Rob. I appreciate the help."

Gordie went back to his desk and spent the rest of the morning and into the afternoon reviewing all the reports from the beginning. He also contacted the Medical Examiner's office. The assistant there assured MacLean that the M.E., Doctor Creighton, would return his call later in the day. She believed he had completed his report but wouldn't share anything further.

It was after two o'clock when Dr. Creighton called. It was a brief call. The M.E. was crisp and not given to long, drawn-out discussions.

When Gordie hung up, he gave fist pump in the air. "Yes."

Roxanne looked up and rolled her chair over to his desk. "OK, spill. What's the good news?"

"That was the M.E. He's reviewed all the evidence and has called it a homicide. The finger marks on Adam's arms confirm he was grabbed with force and shoved. The shove caused him to slam his head against the steel storage locker and that led to his death."

"Murder."

"No, he can't go so far as to say that. It might end up being manslaughter. It depends on what we find out about the motive. Did someone meet with Adam with malice in mind? Or was it an argument that got out of control? That's what we need to figure out. But definitely a homicide of some sort. Knowing that, we can go at this with more vigour now."

"That's great. I've arranged with Gerry to meet him in Pleasant Bay tomorrow at noon."

"Gerry?"

"Constable Jeffreys."

"His parents called him Gerry Jeffreys? No wonder he's uptight."

Roxanne shook her head and rolled back to her own desk and Gordie got up and walked down the hall to Arsenault's office, stopping only to let Rob Norris know the news.

"Sergeant?"

Arsenault looked up from his computer. "Yes, what is it?"

"Just thought you'd want to know. The M.E. has determined the manner of death as a homicide, so we are good to go full speed ahead."

"OK, good news. That'll make it easier to get the warrants we need. You and Albright will be out of the office tomorrow, then."

MacLean tried to keep the joy from his voice. "Yes. Boots on the ground. It's always better talking to people in person, I find."

"All right. Carry on. I suppose the body can be released now?"

"Yes, I'm about to contact the widow to find out which funeral home she'll be using so we can have the remains released to them."

"That's progress, anyway."

Arsenault turned back to his computer and Gordie returned to his desk to make the calls to Sharon MacDonald and Adam's father.

The afternoon drew to a close and Gordie rolled his shoulders as he waited for his computer to shut down. His cell phone rang, and he saw it was Vanessa.

He leaned back comfortably in his chair and answered with a cheery, "Hi there."

Before he got any further, it horrified him to hear the sobbing of his girlfriend through the phone. He leaned forward. "Vanessa? What's wrong? Talk to me! What's going on?"

Roxanne had already put her jacket on but hearing Gordie's stressed voice, she came over and hovered nearby.

Gordie tried again to make sense of what Vanessa was saying. "Slow down. Take a deep breath and talk to me."

He listened, the furrow on his forehead deepening. "OK. I'm calling the Mounties right now. Don't touch anything. Are you in your car? Good. Stay there. Lock the doors. In fact, no. Don't stay there. Drive out on to the main road so you can direct the Mounties when they get there, and you'll be more out in the open. Got that? Good girl. I'm on my way, but the Mounties will be there soon. Deep breaths, Vanessa. Deep breaths."

Roxanne waited for her partner to make the phone call, biting her bottom lip as she tried to contain her questions.

MacLean called the number in Inverness and took a deep breath. "Sergeant Benoit? This is Detective MacLean. Someone has killed one of the witnesses in the Adam MacDonald case and my friend, Vanessa Hunt is on the scene. She's the one who discovered the body. The victim's name is Dab Haan."

CHAPTER 18

A FTER HE WAS SATISFIED that the RCMP were en route, he hung up and started gathering his jacket and laptop bag, chucking the laptop, mouse, and files in the bag and then frustrated when the bag didn't close, pulling them out again to shove them in once more. All the while, he ranted. "I told her to stay away from it all. I told her she shouldn't be involved, but no, she felt sorry for Haan and I'm sure she was out there taking food or God knows what." He glared at Roxanne. "Why alone? Why in the world was she alone?"

Albright shook her head. "I hope you aren't going to blast Vanessa like this. It's the last thing she needs."

Gordie finally got the bag to close and threw the strap over his shoulder. "Of course not. That's why I'm blasting you. To get it out of my system."

She swivelled and grabbed her own jacket. Wearing it, she sat to log out of her computer. "Go on. I'll be right behind you."

He nodded. "I'll just stop in to tell Sarge."

Gordie hustled down the hall again and, without knocking,

stepped into his supervisor's office. He brought his surprised sergeant up to date, who waved him off. "Go on. Let me know what you find out. Call me on my cell any time."

Gordie pulled out of the lot and dialed Vanessa's number. When she answered, he heard voices in the background. "Vanessa? Are the Mounties there?"

Vanessa's voice was calmer now. The tears had stopped. "Yes. I'm sitting in the back of one of their cars with a blanket and a cup of tea."

God love them. "Are you all right?"

"I'm fine, Gordie. It was just the shock. I should have called them myself, but all I could think of was to call you."

"You did the right thing. Absolutely right. Can you talk about it, or do you want to wait until I get there?"

"I can talk." Gordie heard the tears in her voice again. "It was awful, Gordie. I shouldn't have come on my own and I did hesitate but then I told myself I was being silly."

He tried to keep his voice neutral. "Why *did* you go there alone?"

"I made some shepherd's pie and put it in individual containers for the freezer, and Lynn had baked some rolls, but then when I got to her place, I found out that she had a dental appointment this afternoon. I said I could just run the food over while it was still fresh. It didn't seem like a crazy thing to do, Gordie."

"Of course not. I can understand that you were just trying to be nice."

"He was down on his luck, you know?"

"I know. Listen, I may lose you. There are parts along here where the service is crap. If I do, I'll call you back as soon as I can, OK?"

"I understand. In fact, I'm all right now and I see one of the Mounties coming this way. Maybe we just wait, and I tell you the whole thing when I see you?"

He heard the car door open and Vanessa's voice saying, "Yes,

Constable Jeffreys. I'm fine now. Gordie, I have to go." The phone disengaged and music came on over his radio.

He gripped the steering wheel. *Jeffreys is there talking to Vanessa. It should be me. Damn it. I should be out there in the field and not in the office so much. It's a bloody ridiculous way to run a case.*

Since he couldn't talk to Vanessa, he called his partner. "The Mounties are there now. They better not give us a hard time about looking at the scene."

"Why would they? It's your case."

"Your pal Jeffreys is there talking to Vanessa now."

"That makes sense. He was probably not far when Sergeant Benoit put out the call. That's his area, right?"

Gordie grumbled. "I know, but I don't have to like it."

"You like the fact that they came to her aid right away, don't you?"

"Don't be so bloody reasonable."

She laughed. "Sounds like she's fine anyway, so you can relax. I left right after you and I can't see you anywhere ahead of me. Slow down and get there in one piece. That's the best thing you can do for Vanessa."

"Yeah, yeah. OK." He eased up on the gas a fraction. "What do you figure happened? Who would be after Haan, do you think?"

"It's got to be something to do with the guns, right? Who else would want him dead?"

"He was arguing with Sharon MacDonald."

"True. Maybe he.."

The phone cut out, and the radio came on again. *No service.*

He took a few deep breaths, settled back, and let his mind wander as he drove the familiar route.

He was startled out of his reverie when his phone rang. *Vanessa.* "Vanessa, hi. How are you doing? I'm about 35 minutes away."

"I'm on my way home, Gordie. Constable Jeffreys took my statement and then told me I should go home."

"Good. Yes, that was the right thing. Shall I stop by for a few minutes? I will need to go to the scene."

"No, you go and do what you need to do. Right now, I just want a long hot shower and a cup of camomile tea."

"All right. That sounds like just the thing. I'll go, but I'll come after I'm done. How about I pick up a pizza or something on the way?"

"Yes, that would be good. I don't think I'd be able to produce much of a dinner, but what about Taz?"

"I'll call the neighbour to go in."

"If you're sure."

"I'm sure. Now drive carefully, and I'll see you as soon as I can."

He hung up, feeling a little better knowing that Vanessa would be away from the scene when he arrived. *If I could just keep her away altogether, I'll really be happy.*

He drove past the exit for Isle Madame, considering for a moment, doing a detour to pick up his dog, but decided against it. *Can't have Albright arrive at the scene ahead of me.* Instead, he called his neighbour and asked her to go in to let Taz out and feed her. He knew that secretly, the elderly widow was happy to do it. Taz always gave her a warm welcome, knowing she'd get extra treats from the caring woman.

Gordie arrived at the scene. Vehicles filled the muddy yard. The Medical Examiner's van loomed darkly against the backdrop of the green trees. An RCMP cruiser and forensics van crowded to the side of the yard, giving access to the men getting ready to transport Haan's remains to the morgue. Gordie parked in the laneway, scraping against the bushes as he clambered out of his car. Yellow scene of crime tape was fastened to bushes and rusting machinery to create a wide circle around the cabin. As Gordie moved towards the scene, Constable Jeffreys strode towards him.

Gordie nodded. "Constable Jeffreys. Good job of securing the scene."

Jeffreys frowned, and ignoring the comment, handed Gordie a pair of blue crime scene shoe covers. He recorded Gordie's name in his book and the time he arrived. "Follow the yellow flags. Don't step anywhere else."

Gordie nodded. "Got it."

He stepped with care, following the path laid out by the forensics team. The door of the cabin stood open, and he entered, stopping just at the threshold. The quiet little place where he had so recently been looked like a carnival now. White-clad forensics technicians worked without speaking; photographing, dusting for fingerprints, laying out yellow plastic markers with numbers to identify evidence for photography, and taking measurements.

A figure enshrouded in a white scene of crime suit approached Gordie. "Detective MacLean. I didn't expect to meet you again so soon."

"Dr. Ingram. No, neither did I."

Ingram held a clipboard with graph paper on which he had completed a rough sketch of the scene. Since Haan's body had already been removed, MacLean peered at the sketch to see if he could get a sense of what had happened. Ingram nodded and held up the sketch, preparing to step Gordie through it, when Roxanne arrived. She stopped to put on a set of booties and then joined Gordie and Ingram at the entrance to the cabin.

Ingram shifted to allow both Gordie and Roxanne a view of the sketch. "The victim was found here, lying on his back." He pointed out the stick figure of a man near the table at the rear of the cabin. "It looks like he was sitting at the table when someone entered the home. He stood, but before he could step away from the table, he was shot."

Both MacLean and his partner echoed the word at the same time. "Shot?"

The lead forensics investigator nodded. "We found a casing here by the door." Ingram pointed at the sketch first and then they all swivelled to look to the left of where they stood. Beside a small brass casing, a yellow marker with the number 3 highlighted the spot.

"Can you tell what size the round was?"

"A .32."

Gordie nodded. "Like the box we found on *Sea Child*."

"Yes."

Ingram went on. "Haan took a couple of steps forward. People can survive being shot by a .32, depending upon where they've been hit. He may not have even been aware of what was happening at first and I won't know until the autopsy is done, but it looks to me like he was hit in the chest, but not the heart. I'm guessing the round hit bone, fragmented, and that was that. The loss of blood would have meant the end within a few minutes. I think he just crumpled, lay back, and died."

Roxanne shook her head. "God. I know he annoyed some people, but he didn't deserve that."

Gordie frowned. "He did have at least one friend. Dannymac.."

She nodded. "That's true. He may know who his next of kin was."

Ingram held up his clipboard. "That's all I can give you right now. I need to get back at it."

MacLean nodded. "Thanks for this. Your team will do the autopsy, or do you want to send the remains down to us?"

"No worries. We'll do it."

Ingram turned back to the crime scene and Albright led the way back towards the perimeter and Constable Jeffreys.

They stooped below the yellow tape and then stood to talk to the RCMP constable.

Gordie pulled out his notebook and pen. "Constable Jeffreys, you were first on the scene, I understand."

"That's right."

"This has been a busy couple of weeks for you."

Jeffreys remained silent.

Gordie persevered. "Can you please tell me in detail what you observed when you arrived?"

Now Jeffreys pulled his notebook out of his top pocket. "At the end of the lane, a dark grey 2016 Kia Forte Sedan was parked on the shoulder of the road, license plate CHP 750. The registered owner, Miss Vanessa Hunt, got out of the car as I approached and waved me down. I got out of my vehicle to speak with her, at which time she told me that she had been to the home here, attempting to deliver some food parcels for the homeowner, a man known as Dab Haan."

Gordie felt his jaw clench as he willed the man to pick up the pace, but he calmly jotted down a note or two as Jeffreys continued.

"Miss Hunt was quite distraught, and I didn't want to leave her on her own, so I had her get into my car and I provided her with a blanket. I drove up the lane to where you see my car now and, as I had tea in a thermos, I poured her a cup to settle her nerves while I went to see the scene. Once I ascertained it was as she described, and the victim was deceased and beyond medical intervention, I taped off the perimeter." At this point Jeffreys flushed, perhaps recalling the scene that he had attempted to secure.

Gordie looked up from his notes. "When you were still out at the end of the lane, did you notice any vehicles in the area? Anyone slow down to go past you, perhaps?"

"Nothing. No vehicles came by while I was there. There were no clear tracks from any vehicles in the laneway. As you can see, it is quite rutted and stony, and although I walked the length of it while I was waiting for forensics, I did not see anything that would be helpful."

"When you took Miss Hunt's statement, did she mention seeing anything or anyone in the area?"

Gordie glanced up when Jeffreys hesitated for a breath's length. "I don't have any notes to that effect. No."

Roxanne frowned at Gordie, but neither one asked Jeffreys to explain his hesitation. They both knew that Gordie would be talking to Vanessa as well, but it didn't seem obvious that Jeffreys knew about the connection.

He continued on hurriedly. "I didn't feel that there was anything further that the witness could provide, so, after checking with Sergeant Benoit, I told the witness she could go home. I informed her that someone would contact her for a formal statement and confirmed she had not touched anything other than the door, which was ajar when she arrived, so she pushed it open."

MacLean snapped his book closed. "All right, thank you, Constable. I'll liaise with Doctor Ingram about the post-mortem and other reports."

Jeffreys nodded and returned his notebook to his pocket.

Gordie walked Roxanne to her car. "I'm going to see Vanessa now, but I suspect everything is as we heard. I doubt she'll have anything further to add. Did you notice the hesitation, though, when I asked if the witness had seen anything or anyone?"

"I did. Seems like there's something there, but if so, why wouldn't he have written it down?"

"Maybe it's so negligible that he didn't think it was important. Anyway, I'll find out and shoot you a note later."

"This changes the whole scope of the investigation into the Mac-Donald case. They have to be connected."

"Oh yes. I can't imagine that they aren't. OK, I'll be in touch after I've spoken with Vanessa."

"Don't give her a hard time."

Gordie scowled. "I'm not an ogre."

She looked at his face and laughed. "Oh?"

CHAPTER 19

H E CALLED VANESSA WHEN he was on the way. "I'm on the way, but how would you feel if I went home first and picked up a couple of things, including Taz? I'd like to leave her with you for a couple of days if you wouldn't mind."

Her voice sounded less frantic. "Oh, Gordie, yes on both counts. I'm better now. The hot shower and tea helped, but still, it would be a great comfort to have you both here."

"Right, then. You relax, and we'll be there before you know it. I'll pick up some food on the way, so all you need to do is take it easy. Watch TV or something. One of those home renovation shows you like so much."

He disconnected the phone to the sound of her light laughter. Remembering how he first met Vanessa when bones were discovered in her garden, he shook his head. *She's a tough cookie. First, she finds a skeleton in her garden and now this.*

He drove faster than he should have and when he arrived home, he hustled around throwing a few things into an overnight bag, along with some dog treats. Gordie took the half bag of kibble for

Taz, making a mental note to pick up some more food in the next couple of days. Since he intended to leave Taz there to look after Vanessa for several days, he needed to stock up. He spoke to his dog as he gathered things together. "She'll think she's looking after you, Taz, because I'll be so busy. We both know the truth, though. I trust you to keep her safe, right, girl?" The big white dog nudged Gordie as if to agree that she understood.

Within ten minutes, Gordie was back in the car with Taz settling in the back.

***

Vanessa flung the house door open and came out to meet them at the car. Taz ran circles around her friend, bumping her, front and back, before finally loping off to sniff around the yard. Gordie handed Vanessa a pizza and the carryall bag while he himself took the dog food and other dog accessories, arms loaded with bed, food dish, and favourite ball.

As soon as the door closed behind them, Gordie dropped everything in the mudroom and reached for Vanessa to give her a hug. She set the pizza and his bag on a bench below the coat hooks.

Vanessa was the same height as Gordie, and she murmured into his ear. "This is just what I needed."

After a moment of simply holding each other, she slipped away to pick up his bag and food and he gathered the rest of the things. "Where do you want all this stuff?"

Vanessa called from the stairs on her way to the bedroom. "Put Taz's bed under the living room window. That seems to be her favourite spot. Put everything else on the kitchen table. I'll stash it somewhere."

They ate pizza and Gordie finally broached the subject of what had happened. "So, tell me everything from start to finish."

Wiping her fingers, Vanessa took a sip from her glass of red wine and then leaned back. "I made a shepherd's pie and divided it up into four single dinner portions and had those in plastic containers.

Lynn had baked a couple of small sourdough loaves of bread and the plan was that we would go together to bring them to Dab."

She frowned at Gordie, almost daring him to criticize her for her actions, but when he said nothing, she continued. "When I got to Lynn's place, she apologized, but she broke a tooth and had an emergency dental appointment, so I said it was no problem and I would go on my own. Lynn asked if I was sure I didn't mind. And I didn't. Not really."

Her blue eyes swam as she glanced at him again. "I knew you wouldn't be happy about it, but I intended to tell you after the fact when I could show you that delivering some food to a person in need isn't such a big deal." Vanessa took a gulp of wine. "I guess I was wrong."

Gordie took her hand. "You weren't to know it would go so wrong. No one could predict that a simple act of kindness would end like this."

Vanessa nodded. "I'm sure you heard all this from that Mountie already. But anyway." She took a deep breath, keeping one hand clasped with Gordie's and the other wrapped around her glass of wine. "I found the laneway. Lynn had given me directions. I drove up, parked, and only then did I get a bit nervous. What if he took it amiss? You know, bringing this virtual stranger food. It suddenly seemed presumptuous to me, so I just took a loaf of Lynn's bread and walked up to the door." She chewed on her bottom lip and then went on. "He knows Lynn, so I planned to explain that the bread was from Lynn and if he seemed pleased, I'd see if he wanted the shepherd's pie as well."

He nodded, encouraging her to go on.

"The door was just a bit ajar, so when I knocked, it opened. I called out. 'Mr. Haan? Mr. Haan, are you here?' Obviously, no one answered, but by then the door had swung open most of the way and I looked inside. That's when I saw him on the floor." She shook her head. "There was so much blood. It was obvious to me that he was dead. I didn't go inside. Part of me thought 'I should check in case he's still alive' but I just knew he wasn't. It was too quiet. So, I backed up and ran back to the car to call you. It was the only thing I could think of. I probably should have called 911 instead, but I just couldn't think."

"You did exactly the right thing. You're so level-headed. If you had gone inside, you would have contaminated the scene. By calling me first, I was able to get to the people who I knew would respond the fastest. You did everything right."

Vanessa's glass was empty, and Gordie released her hand to top up her wine.

"When you think back on the entire afternoon, your drive up Old Rocky Ridge Road, then on to New Rocky Ridge, then turn left into the laneway and park in front of the cabin, think about that whole journey. Did you see anyone along there at all?"

She frowned in concentration. "I recall a black pickup came from New Rocky Ridge, turning left onto Old Rocky Ridge because it turned in front of me to pass me going the other way. Towards town, you know?"

He nodded. "Why did you notice that truck?"

She shrugged. "It's such a sharp turn that a driver needs to be halfway into the intersection to see if they can make the turn."

"Good. That junction is before Haan's place, so it's unlikely they were anywhere near the house. Anyone else?"

"There was a motorbike that passed by, going towards town as well."

Gordie kept his voice neutral. "A motorcycle?"

"Yes, a big one. You don't often see them alone, do you? It seems like where there's one, there's often three or four. Tourists or bike clubs or whatever. I suppose that's why I noticed him."

"And whereabouts along the road did you pass the bike?"

"It was right after I passed that junction, so first the truck made the left in front of me and then the bike came from straight ahead. I was slowing down to look for the laneway, but it was still a ways away."

"Good. That's great. Can you remember anything about the bike or the rider?"

Vanessa wrinkled her brow in concentration. "I only saw it for an instant and I was focussed on looking for Dab's laneway."

Gordie nodded. "Close your eyes and imagine yourself there driving. You can see the bike. Is it black or another colour? Low handlebars or high? The rider – is he wearing a full visor helmet or a half helmet that looks more like a hat?"

Eyes closed, she sat in silence for a moment and then she opened them wide. "I remember! I *did* notice him. It was a split second, but I remember smiling because he reminded me of the guy who used to mow my lawn in Ontario."

"Why?"

"My guy in Ontario rode a bike too and when he pulled up to my house, the first couple of times to work on the yard, I know the neighbours wondered because he looked like he just came from a bike club meeting. He had long, grey hair in a ponytail and a long, grey beard. His helmet was one of those half helmets like you said, and he wore dark sunglasses."

"And the man you saw today looked like that?"

"It's hard to say if he had the ponytail or not, but yes. I know that all those guys of a certain age that grow their hair and stop shaving look alike once they put on a helmet and sunglasses, and I'm sure if they stood side by side, they probably aren't the same, but I saw him, he registered with me and immediately my mind went to Henry, and I smiled."

Gordie tried to lighten the mood. "I better not grow that beard after all. You may think of Henry, the lawn guy, instead."

She smiled. "No, you better not. A beard and long hair would just not suit you, Gordie MacLean."

"You're doing great. Anyone else?"

"No, that's all I remember."

"Did you mention these two vehicles to Constable Jeffreys?"

"I said nothing about the truck, but I think I mentioned the bike, but it was so inconsequential, I can't be certain now."

"Of course. I get that."

Vanessa yawned. "God, I'm sorry. I shouldn't have had so much wine."

"It's the shock more than the wine. Come on. Let's get you tucked into bed for a good night's sleep. You don't mind looking after Taz for a few days while I'm running around?"

"Of course not. I'll be glad for her company. And if Taz is here, I know you'll be back every night."

Gordie nudged towards the stairs. "You go on up. I'll tidy up here and then come up in a bit."

Once he had wrapped the remaining pizza in plastic and put it into the fridge, thrown out the box and put the dishes into the dishwasher, Gordie opened his laptop to create the witness statement, noting that he had interviewed the witness in her home. Once he completed that, he sent it off to his partner with an email note:

I don't want to derail our investigation on the MacDonald case. Go ahead up to Pleasant Bay tomorrow, as planned. Since I suspect they will tie Jeffreys up with the Haan case and it gives you a good excuse to go it alone. I'm going to Dannymac tomorrow first thing, and then when the fishing is done for the day, I'll track down Kyle. I'll let Sarge know what we're doing.

Her response came a few moments later. *A motorbike in the area. Curious. Did J. hold back this info on purpose or did he really not know?! I'll talk to you tomorrow after my trek around P.B. How's Vanessa?*

Coping amazingly well. Helped by half a bottle of merlot. ☺

LOL. OK, till tomorrow. R

He logged out and closed the computer. When he stood up, Taz trotted over from her spot on the dog bed under the living room window.

"You want to go out, don't you?"

The white plumed tail beat against his leg.

"Let's go, then. Sorry, girl, but you're going on the leash." Gordie knew from experience that Great Pyrenees dogs were independent creatures and if she took it in her head to trot off to follow a scent, he'd be powerless to bring her back until she was ready. On the other hand, this same independence was why Gordie trusted her so much as a protector.

The night wrapped itself around them in a black, misty shroud. The stars and moon were obscured by the clouds, and the damp enhanced the odours in the air. Gordie breathed deep as he wandered around the yard. Tangy salt mingled with smells of decaying seaweed and fish. An almost undetectable undernote from the pulp mill in Port Mulroy complicated the sea scents. Sounds were muffled in the misty night, creating an eerie sense of isolation, and Gordie felt a chill run up his spine.

"Well, girl, let's head in." He had to give Taz a tug to convince her to come along back to the house, as she stood, feet firmly planted, staring and sniffing at dangers in the velvety darkness that were invisible to Gordie.

CHAPTER 20

GORDIE CHECKED HIS EMAIL at Vanessa's kitchen table and then started on the phone. His first call in the morning was to his sergeant as he brought him up to speed.

Arsenault sounded doubtful. "Look, I think you need to come into the office. This sounds like it's time to hand the whole thing over to the Mounties."

"With respect, Sergeant, I disagree. For one thing, I've said it before, and I'll say it again: I'm more useful here in my own patch. Coming all the way to the office is a waste of valuable time. I can communicate with the team by phone or video conference just as easily, but I can't interview witnesses that way. It needs to be face to face and hauling them all the way to Sydney from Port Hood or even further just doesn't make sense."

"And that's a good reason to hand it over to the Mounties in Inverness."

Gordie stifled a sigh. "Second, WE are the Major Case Unit. Not the RCMP. I'm not sure they would take it over even if you asked, but why are you so keen to hand it over? Is it a budget thing?"

Arsenault's tone was what Gordie thought of as 'huffy.' "No, of course not. I simply think they are better equipped, and they are in the area up there."

"I'm in the bloody area."

Now his boss's voice grew heated. "Don't take everything so personally. We need to do what's best for the case before more people die."

Gordie raised his voice, despite his best effort. "Then let me get on with the job. That's what's best for the case." He took a deep breath. "Look, I need to call Sergeant Benoit anyway about the post-mortem. I'll ask if she feels they are *better equipped* to take the case over, and I'll let you know what she says. How's that?"

"Fine. Keep in touch, MacLean. I expect a report this afternoon."

"Right." Gordie disengaged and, for an instant, missed the old days when he had the satisfaction of slamming down the receiver after a frustrating call.

Vanessa came in after the call was over to put the kettle on. "Everything OK?"

Gordie closed his eyes for an instant. "One of these days I'll do him an injury."

She smiled as she set two mugs out and added milk to both. "Your favourite sergeant, I assume?"

He nodded. "He knows how to push my buttons. Never mind. I need to put him out of my mind and concentrate on the job."

"I'll just make the tea and then leave you to it. After my tea, I'm going outside to do some gardening. I'll take Taz out with me."

Gordie smiled. "She'll like that. She may wander a bit, but during the day she won't go far. It's only at night you better keep her on the leash."

Vanessa nodded. "I'm used to her ways now. Don't worry about us."

Making notes in his book about next steps, questions to be asked, and random questions to himself for possible discussion with Roxanne, Gordie felt himself relax as Vanessa puttered around him.

When she set his mug in front of him with two home-baked oatmeal chocolate chip cookies on a plate, he smiled at her. "I can get used to this."

"Thank you for being here last night. I was a bit frazzled, but I'm fine again now."

He pushed out the chair across from him at the table with his foot. "Sit for a moment. I have a couple more calls to make and then I'll be off and busy for the day. I'm not sure what time I'll be back, but I'll let you know."

She sat and curled her hands around her mug. "Don't worry. You do what you need to do." She gave a weak smile. "I have shepherd's pie in the fridge that needs to be eaten. Last night I thought I'd throw it out, but now that seems silly."

"It is. We'll enjoy it and think about Dab Haan's life as we do. Not his death. Just his life."

Vanessa nodded. "That sounds good. I know so little about the man."

They finished their tea and Vanessa and Taz went out while Gordie called Sergeant Benoit.

"Sergeant Benoit? It's Detective Gordie MacLean. I believe your folks are doing the post-mortem for Haan this morning. Do you feel I should be there?"

"You're welcome to attend, but I don't see a need. The report will be ready this afternoon, and I can call you to give you the highlights after I've reviewed it."

"Thank you. That sounds good. I intend to notify MacDonald Sr. this morning. He was a lifelong friend of the victim's and I'm hoping he'll know who the next of kin is for official notification. I'll also talk to Kyle MacDonald. He'll be able to do the identification, but there's no doubt at all that the victim is the man known as Dab Haan."

"I'll leave all that to you, Detective."

He took a breath. "I was briefing my boss Sergeant Arsenault, this morning and he wants to ensure that we aren't stepping on any toes in your shop, given you are doing so much of the technical support."

"Not at all. We are always here to support the Cape Breton Police Service. I don't see any issues with the partnership we have. Do you?"

"No. If I'm perfectly honest, I believe we are the right ones to do the investigation using the findings that you provide."

"That's settled, then."

"Can I ask a favour? Would you shoot Sergeant Arsenault a note to the effect that we spoke and that you are satisfied with the working relationship and processes we have in place?"

He heard the smile in her voice. "Is he trying to dump the whole case on us?"

"I'm not sure I'd phrase it that way."

"You're a diplomat. OK. Sure, I'll send him a note and copy you."

Gordie laughed. "I'm not often called a diplomat, so thanks for that."

***

Dannymac was sitting outside on the front porch with a mug and newspaper when Gordie drove up. He folded the paper and laid it under his chair and nodded to the other chair to invite MacLean to sit. "What is it now?"

Gordie thought the old man looked thinner just in the few days since he had last seen him. "Maybe you heard the news already?"

Dannymac frowned. "I've heard nothing."

"It's about Dab Haan. I'm afraid he's dead."

His thin fingers whitened as he gripped his mug. "Dead? How?"

"I'm sorry, Danny. He was shot in his home yesterday."

The man blinked several times rapidly. His mouth gaped open, and he sucked in air until he finally repeated the word. "Shot?"

"I'm afraid so. With a .32 caliber, by the look of it."

He shifted the mug to his left hand and made a quick sign of the cross with his right. "Poor old Dab. What did he do to deserve that?"

"That's what we'd like to know too, and I'm hoping you can help."

He shook his head. "I have no idea who or why someone would

want to shoot Dab. I know he could be a nuisance and a pest when he was drunk, but that's no reason to kill him."

"You're right there. Seems like more trouble than it'd be worth to kill a man for being a drunk." Gordie remembered several times he'd wanted to kill his father, who had been a mean drunk, but even with provocation, he never acted on it.

"Danny, it's time to tell me what you know before even more people die. What was Adam mixed up in? Whatever it was, I think it got both him and Dab killed."

"Adam wasn't shot."

"No, he wasn't, but somehow these two deaths are connected, and you know how."

The elderly man leaned back against the high back of the chair and closed his eyes. The sun bathed his face, outlining the deep grooves and bony cheeks of his sallow skin. "There's nothing I can tell you. I'm sorry for Dab. I wish he had come to me and maybe I could have helped him figure out whatever was going on, but he didn't. He was once a good man. I told you that. Before the drink got a hold of him. That's the Dab I always see when I'm with him."

"What about Kyle? Who does he see? Why wasn't Haan out fishing with him yesterday?"

Dannymac opened his eyes, and the keenness of the faded blue eyes surprised Gordie. "You'll have to ask him. I haven't been well lately, and Kyle doesn't tell me everything."

Gordie nodded. "All right. I will. Do you know who Haan's next of kin is? I need to do the official notification."

"You've just done it. He had no one. He saw me as a brother and when he needed a next of kin, he always put me down. The house was a rental. His pickup is junk. I'll pay for his funeral. Let me know when his body will be released." He struggled to his feet and Gordie leaned over, picked up the paper, and handed it to him. Without another word, Dannymac turned and went back into the house, looking even older than he had half an hour earlier.

CHAPTER 21

DETECTIVE ROXANNE ALBRIGHT PARKED behind the hut that sold coffee and tickets to the whale-watching tours. The wind snapped a Canadian flag beside the building and sand blew at her like a sand-blasting machine.

There were two benches behind this building, set in the sun and out of the water-side wind. Two women sat here with travel mugs, chatting. They stopped in mid-conversation to watch Roxanne as she approached.

Roxanne pulled out her identification and held it out in front as she got close. "I'm Detective Albright of the CBPS."

One woman nodded, her short grey hair moving with her head like a helmet. "I remember you from the other day."

The second woman, a little younger, her hair a mass of red curls, smiled and moved closer to her friend to make room on the bench. "Come sit down. Give us the news."

Roxanne sat down and angled herself to face the women. "This is a nice spot."

The younger woman was the spokesperson. "On a sunny day like this, it is. We come and sit here to wait for our husbands to come back from fishing. Sometimes we come even when the season is over, but not so much during tourist time."

The older woman made a sour face. "No, not during tourist time. Too busy."

Roxanne lifted her face to the sun. "Well, it's heavenly right now."

The younger woman introduced herself. "I'm Helen and this is Mary. What brings you here today?"

"I'm following up on what happened last week with the *Sea Child*."

Helen nodded. "A real tragedy. I didn't know him, but he was a fisherman. One of us."

Roxanne nodded. "Had either of you seen the *Sea Child* around here before?"

Mary was guarded. "Hard to say."

The detective tilted her head. "Not that many boats painted that bright red. I think she'd stand out if you saw her."

They were quiet for a moment, the metallic clinking sound of the flag hardware rattling against the pole, suddenly noticeable.

Helen nodded. "I've seen it one other time, and then again, this last time. The evening before you all came."

"Here at the wharf?"

The red curls shook. "No. Out beyond the harbour. Sometimes I have my binoculars with me. I like to watch for dolphins and whales. The first time I saw it, I knew it wasn't one of ours, so I was curious what she was doing here."

Mary spoke then. "Thought she might be poaching our catch."

Albright raised her eyebrows. "And? Is that what was happening? Were they fishing in your waters?"

Helen shrugged. "No. I couldn't make out what they were doing."

"They? Could you see more than one man on board?"

"I saw a boat tied up to it. Not a fishing boat. Looked like a fancy yacht but it was behind the fishing boat, so impossible to see.

It looked like two men, but maybe someone else was in the cabin. I couldn't see. They were just standing there, talking, I think."

"Odd place to have a conversation. What time of day was this?"

"Late. Almost dusk. Which is why it was really hard to see. I didn't watch for long. Just a minute or two and then, when it was obvious they weren't fishing, I lost interest. I was just out with the dog, and I needed to get home myself to get dinner going."

"And when was this?"

"A few weeks ago."

Roxanne made a note. "Was there anyone else around that might have seen them? Someone I could go talk to?"

"No. By that time of day, everyone's gone home." Helen pointed a thumb behind her. "The coffee shack was closed up. Fishermen all done for the day and gone home."

"Did either of you know the victim? His name was Adam Mac-Donald, out of Port Hood."

Both women shook their heads.

Roxanne closed her notebook. "Anything else you can think of that might be of interest? Some little thing you noticed, no matter how insignificant it seems, either the day that MacDonald died, or that previous time you saw the *Sea Child*?"

Helen frowned. "Now you've made me think of it again. I was walking with Josie, my dog, that evening when MacDonald died, and I think I heard an outboard starting up. You know they have more of a putt-putt sound to them versus the thrumming sound of a proper 353 horse-power engine of a fishing boat. It was getting dark, and I was walking away, so I saw nothing but yes, I'm quite sure I heard an outboard engine."

"That's great. That's helpful. Thanks. Well, you two ladies have a nice day." Roxanne pulled out a business card from her inside pocket. "If you think of anything else, please call me."

As she walked away, Mary called after her. "That Mountie that was here the other day might know more. I've seen him go past the house some evenings and figure he's checking the harbour for kids making trouble. He may have seen something one of those times."

Roxanne turned back. "I'll do that. Thanks."

She chewed her bottom lip as she got back in her car.

***

Vanessa Hunt was on her knees, digging the first of the dandelions out of her flower bed. She left them alone on the lawn because the bees liked them and she didn't mind their bright yellow patches herself, but in the flower bed, they took over and choked her tender young plants, so they had to be rooted out.

When Taz began barking, she looked up to see the RCMP cruiser pull into her driveway. She pushed herself up, brushed off the knees of her denim work jeans, and pulled off her gloves. "Taz, come back here. It's OK. Don't give him a hard time now."

Her calls were in vain and the dog, who had been relaxed and snoozing in the sun moments before, now circled Constable Jeffreys with her hackles raised, making her look even larger than her actual 120 pounds.

Vanessa hustled to meet the officer who had stopped and stood staring warily at Taz. "I'm sorry. She's not usually like this. Most of the time, she's quite friendly." As suddenly as the dog's barking began, she stopped and wedged herself between them, sitting on Vanessa's feet. "Good heavens, Taz! What are you doing?" She laughed and shook her head. "Well, Constable, I won't shake your hand. I suppose we are supposed to stay six feet apart anyway, and this is Taz's way of ensuring we maintain our distance. How can I help you?"

Jeffreys glanced at the house and then back at Taz and obviously decided that staying outside was the best option. He pulled out his notebook and pen. "I just wanted to go over your statement again, now that you've had a chance to get over the shock of yesterday."

Vanessa frowned. "Oh. I went through everything already with Gordie. I mean, Detective MacLean. Wouldn't it be easier to get it from him?"

Jeffreys reddened. "He's been here already this morning?"

Now it was her turn to flush. "No, last night."

"Oh. I didn't realize he'd get to you so quickly. Yes, well. I suppose I'll just ask him for a copy of your statement, then." He closed his book and then something seemed to register with him. "You called him Gordie. Did you know Detective MacLean prior to yesterday?"

His accusatory tone made Vanessa cautious. "Yes, I met him last year when he was investigating the skeleton that was found in my garden." She waved in the direction of the flower bed and small pond.

"Right. I see. You have bad luck when it comes to finding dead bodies, don't you, Miss Hunt?"

She raised her eyebrows at his caustic words and tone. Taz stood and pressed herself against Vanessa, and she rested a hand on the dog's head. "It's not something I'm happy about, Constable. Is there anything else I can do?"

"No. Nothing. Can you please hold your dog so I can get out of here without getting covered in dog hair?"

"Of course." Vanessa gripped Taz's collar, and they stood watching as Jeffreys marched back to the car and backed out of the driveway, his tires spitting gravel in his haste.

Vanessa let Taz go. "He didn't seem best pleased to know that I had talked this all out with your dad, Taz. What was that all about, I wonder?"

She went back to her gardening, but her mind kept wandering back to the conversation. She searched her memory to identify when he had gone from friendly, if wary of Taz, to borderline rude and concluded it was when he realized she knew Gordie. He was flustered when he realized Gordie had already spoken with her, but he became frosty when he realized they knew each other.

"Strange, Taz. Definitely strange. And speaking of strange, I never saw you behave that way with someone before. You were pretty frosty yourself, madam." She smiled at the dog, who was now rolling on the sun-warmed grass a few feet away, all four feet waving in the air.

***

Gordie sat at a picnic table and watched the boats come in. He smoked a cigarette, tracking *Sea Child* as she pulled into her berth. Kyle MacDonald called out instructions to his two deck hands as they unloaded the tubs for the Co-op buyer to weigh. Half an hour previously, it was so peaceful Gordie almost nodded off, listening to the soft swish of waves against the rock breakwater. Now the air was filled with voices calling out weights, seagulls screeching, the clatter of equipment and the rumble of engines. The colours of the boats nudging into the harbour, set against the deep blue of the sea, was a painter's dream.

When the buyer finished with *Sea Child* and the deckhands had finished tidying and waved a goodbye to their skipper, Gordie went to the boat. He stood on the wharf and called out to Kyle. "All right if I come aboard?"

MacDonald poked his head out of the cabin. His short dark hair lay flat against his skull after a morning of sweat and sea mist. Kyle peered through dark-rimmed glasses that were strapped to his head with a black rubber band. He wore a heavy black sweater under orange waterproof overalls. When he saw who had called, he pursed his lips but nodded. "Yeah. Come on up."

Gordie stepped cautiously from the wharf into the boat and made his way past the steel storage locker to the cabin. In passing, he noticed they had scrubbed the deck clean of the bloodstains.

Kyle stood making notes into a logbook, but he looked up long enough to nod Gordie towards the high stool in the cabin. "Take a seat. I just want to finish this."

"Sure. Take your time."

After a minute, Kyle closed the book and then leaned back against the instrument panel, folding his arms across his chest. "What can I do for you?"

"Have you heard the news about Dab Haan?"

"Yeah." Kyle waved in the direction of the coffee shack. "The place was full of it this morning."

Not for the first time, Gordie wondered at how news travelled so widely and so fast around a small town. Kyle was stubbornly silent and Gordie prodded him. "What did you hear?"

"That someone shot Dab dead in his cabin."

Gordie nodded. "That pretty much sums it up. I told your father about it this morning."

Kyle frowned and made a tsk sound. "I was going to tell him as soon as I finished here. How'd he take it?"

"He was shocked. And I think it genuinely saddened him."

"Sure. They were like brothers. Grew up together, you know?"

"Yes. So, Kyle, now we have two deaths. Your brother and now Haan. What connected those two other than *Sea Child*?"

"I couldn't tell you."

"Can't or won't?"

"Can't. I don't know why anyone would kill Dab, other than he was going around making a nuisance of himself lately. More than usual."

"In what way?"

"He wanted a raise, but instead of proving to me he was worth more money, he was getting more wasted than usual. I had to tell him to stay home until he was ready to come to work sober. I can't risk someone that's half cut on a boat. This can be dangerous work for someone who's careless."

"Not as dangerous as staying home and getting shot."

Kyle shrugged.

"What do you think was going on with him? Why did he think he should get more money?"

"I don't know what was going on." He paused and then continued. "I might as well tell you because no doubt you'll hear about it from the gossips around here."

"Go on."

"When Dab was stumbling around drunk, he shot his mouth off. He said Adam was going to give him a raise and if I didn't give him one, maybe he'd go into a different line of work. He said that to me and he said it to other people. I have no idea what that was all about, and I told him he was welcome to go into any line he wanted to, as long as it was away from me."

"He didn't say anything else about this other job?"

"Nope." Kyle shook his head. "It was just crap. He didn't have any other job. It pissed my dad that I told Dab to take a hike. I planned to give Haan a few days to cool off, get whatever it was, grief over Adam, or whatever, out of his system, and then I was going to go and tell him to come back. When he was sober, he was good at fishing. Better than these young guys I've got now, but I'm lucky to have them. Not easy finding someone partway through the season. The buyers found them for me, and they'll pay them every week and take it off what they owe me."

"OK, let me get this straight. Adam was doing something other than fishing unless maybe it was poaching."

Kyle scowled. "Adam didn't poach. He wouldn't do that."

"Well, unless you can offer me a different explanation for what he was doing in an unassigned fishing area, I have to leave that on the table." He went on. "Haan worked with Adam every day so may have seen something or overheard something and as a result felt that he had leverage to get a raise from Adam. When Adam died, he comes to you, expecting to have the same leverage over you, but that didn't work."

Again, Kyle shrugged. "I don't know what Dab could have on Adam. I worked with him every day too and I don't know anything."

MacLean ignored the interruption. "Then Haan thinks maybe he can do whatever Adam had been doing and it would be more lucrative than fishing. How does that sound?"

"Sounds like a fairy tale to me. Dab Haan was an alcoholic that was annoying at the best of times. Someone got tired of him and that's that."

"Where did you go yesterday after you finished with the day's fishing, Kyle?"

His eyes widened. "You don't think I killed old Dab?"

"Why not? He was annoying at the best of times, right?"

"Jesus. What do you think I am? I don't go around killing people just because they annoy me."

"Where did you go?"

He sighed and closed his eyes; as if tracing his steps of the previous day. "I went to the Stop and Shop to pick up a lottery ticket and some bacon." Kyle reached under the overalls to his pants pocket and pulled out his wallet. He flipped it open and pulled out a lottery ticket and showed it to Gordie.

"And after that?"

"I went home, made myself a late lunch with the bacon, called my father to make sure he was OK and then lay down for a couple hours. When I got up, I went down to the house and told Dad I'd pick up some Chinese if he felt like it. He did, so that's what I did. We had supper together and then I went back to my place and watched TV for a bit and then bed."

MacLean opened his hands in a gesture of appeal. "OK, fair enough. I believe you, but I still think you know more than you're telling me and since I'm not getting anywhere here, I guess I'll go back to your dad, and see what he knows."

"Leave him alone. He's a sick old man, and he's been through enough. First his son and now his buddy. Just leave him alone." Kyle tilted his head back to let the sun warm his face and closed his eyes. When he opened them again, he stared at Gordie. "I wish to God I could just go back in time when it was my brother and I fishing and old Dab out there doing his bit. I never knew how good those days were before now."

MacLean studied Kyle for another moment, nodded, and made his way out of the boat.

CHAPTER 22

MACLEAN FELT THE NEED for a jolt of caffeine and a quiet smoke. He drove to the closest coffee shop and got himself a coffee and then sat outside at a table reviewing the latest conversations in his mind. *Where do I go from here? How do I prise what Kyle knows out of him? Or maybe he really knows nothing.* He took a deep drag and then had a fit of coughing. His eyes watered and he blinked to clear them as he swallowed some coffee. Gordie dropped his half-smoked cigarette on the ground and crushed it under the toe of his boot. He pictured the look Vanessa always gave him when he went out for a smoke and realized he didn't want to see that look again. *That's it. Gotta kick this habit.*

He finished his coffee, picked up the butt, and dropped his paper cup and the crushed cigarette into the garbage bin at the edge of the parking lot. Then he took the half pack of cigarettes from his pocket, felt the comforting shape of it in his hand, and then dropped that into the garbage as well.

When he settled himself in the car, he took out his notebook and called his partner. "What news, Roxanne?"

He listened with interest as she briefed him, jotting down notes as she spoke. "Good work. Did you call Jeffreys yet to question him about what he saw or heard?"

"I tried, but he didn't answer. I left a message. He may be in a bad service area."

"OK, are you on your way back from Pleasant Bay now?"

"Yes, I should be in Port Hood in about fifteen minutes."

"Right. I want to meet with Adam's friends and how about you take the two women who are friends of Sharon's? The focus is on what they noticed about the family. Any changes in their behaviour in the past month or so. Any arguments they heard about or witnessed. Any concerns they had about their friend. Things like that. I'll be asking the same questions of Adam's pals."

"Do you want to meet up when we're done?"

Gordie felt a shiver run down his back as he recalled a previous time when they were to meet up and it had all gone so terribly wrong. "Yes. Shall we try for the Tim Hortons in Port Mulroy for five o'clock?"

"Sounds good." As if she had read his mind, she added "Don't worry. I'll be there."

He laughed. "You better be. No going off somewhere without letting me know, and I'll do the same."

"Right, boss. See you then."

Once Gordie called the two men, Andy LeBlanc, and Johnny McMaster, and arranged to meet with each of them, his next call was to his colleague Detective Rob Norris.

"Norris? MacLean here. Just wanted to check in and see how you are doing with getting the financials for MacDonald."

"I was going to send you the report this afternoon. Yeah, no issue getting the warrant, so I've got everything now, both the business and the family accounts for Adam and his wife. I couldn't get the personal accounts for the extended family."

"Fair enough. See anything interesting?"

"Not in the business. It looks just as you'd expect with the revenue and the outgoings and comparing this season so far to previous years, everything is pretty consistent."

Gordie sensed Norris' excitement. "But?"

"But in the personal account, there was something. Nothing prior to MacDonald's death. Just the usual wages being paid from the business to his personal account, bills being paid, the usual. Here's the *but*. After MacDonald's death. Three days after, to be exact, a large deposit was made into the family account. Cash."

"How much are we talking?"

"Ten thousand."

MacLean whistled. "A nice round number."

"It wasn't red flagged by the bank because they look for cash deposits over ten thousand. And a few days later we see a cheque processed for the Royal Halifax Conservatory of Music in the amount of twelve thousand dollars."

"That's the place the daughter was accepted to, recently, right? Izzie. Is it life insurance? Seems pretty quick to get a payout."

"Nope. I checked that just in case. They've got two policies. One will pay off the 122,000 dollars outstanding on the house mortgage and one for a hundred thousand on his life. The missus had to wait for the final death certificate before she could put in her claim, and as you know, that took a bit of time, so she's only just submitted the paperwork."

"So, we have a source of a significant amount of money. I wonder if she went to her father-in-law to get a loan against the life insurance. That's possible if those school fees had to be in by a certain date or the child will lose her place."

"Sure, it's possible, but in cash? And why wouldn't grandpa just pay the exact amount for the school fee?"

"Good questions. OK, great work, Rob. What about phone records? Anything interesting there?"

"There are a few numbers that I'm still running down. Most are explainable local numbers, but I need more time to see if the others are anything or nothing."

"I'll let you get back to it then."

Gordie had a few more minutes before his interview with Adam's old school chum, Andy LeBlanc, so he made one last call.

He smiled to hear that Vanessa's voice was back to its cheerful tone. "Hiya. How're my two girls doing?"

She laughed. "I've been busy outside, and Taz has been busy supervising me."

"Just what I like to hear."

There was a slight hesitation, and then she continued. "That Mountie constable was here earlier."

Gordie frowned. "Oh? Why?"

"He said he wanted to review my statement again to see if there was anything to add, but when I told him I had gone over everything in detail with you already, he backed off. Not that I minded going over it again. It just surprised me he wouldn't have access to your statement. Don't you inter-police departments, or whatever you call it, share information?"

"Certainly, if he needs it, he's welcome to get a copy of my report. Did you tell him we are friends?"

"Not in so many words. He asked me if I knew you before Dab Haan's death and I told him the truth; that I met you first when you were investigating the skeleton in my garden."

"What did he say to that?"

"He didn't say much. I think he said something about following up with you, and then it seemed like he couldn't get out of here fast enough." She laughed then. "Of course, it could be that he was afraid of Taz."

"Why would he be afraid of her?"

"It was so strange. I've never seen her behave like this, but she plunked herself down right on my feet and absolutely bristled at him. She looked huge all puffed up like that."

"She was putting herself between you and what she perceived to be danger. I wonder why. Was he doing anything that seemed threatening?"

"No, of course not."

"All's well that ends well. I'm sure it was nothing. Maybe he just doesn't like dogs, and Taz picked up on that. I better run now and I'll see you both later. First, I'm meeting Albright in Port Mulroy at five, so it'll be close to six when I see you."

"We'll be here. See you later."

Gordie disengaged, and as he drove, wondered about why his dog had taken against Constable Jeffreys.

***

Andy LeBlanc managed a small building materials yard on the outskirts of Port Mulroy. His round face and prematurely balding head gleamed with a light layer of perspiration in the warm spring afternoon sun. He wore a short-sleeved red polo shirt with the company logo emblazoned in dark green on the breast pocket, and a matching dark green mask. He was the same height as Gordie himself and as Andy came forward to greet him, his forehead wrinkled and eyes wide with worry, MacLean felt he was the type of man who would be a poor poker player but an easy man to like.

Gordie displayed his identification, and Andy waved it away. "Come on into the office. Can I get you a coffee or tea?"

They passed a man wearing white ear defenders and maneuvering a small Bobcat to load topsoil from a massive hill into the back of a pickup truck. Andy waved towards the office and the driver nodded to show he understood Andy was going inside.

They stopped at a table with a coffeepot, kettle and a few mugs of different sizes and colours and Andy poured himself a coffee while Gordie shook his head to refuse the offer.

With coffee cup in hand, Andy led him to his office. The glass cubical was small. There was a desk with a computer, printer, a chair behind and two in front, along with a file cabinet that nearly filled the space.

Adam's friend sank into his seat with a small sigh, as if glad for the excuse to sit down and pulled off his mask. "How can I help you?"

Gordie slid out his notebook and pen. "You know of Adam Mac-Donald's death, of course."

Andy nodded. "God. Such a shock. His funeral is tomorrow, and it makes you think. He was the same age as me. We had our 40th birthdays together a couple months ago."

"We are working to understand exactly what happened, which is normal in any case of sudden or unexplained death. You've been friends for a long time, I think?"

"Yeah. We were kids together. Went to the same school." He smiled. "He came from a fishing family, and we were farmers, so it's a bit surprising, but there you go. Kids sort it out somehow, don't they?"

"Did you still see him regularly?"

"God, yes. My wife Janice and his Sharon hit it off and so we spent a lot of time together. Barbecues, birthdays, you know, all that kind of thing."

"Did you still spend time alone with Adam, or were the visits with the whole family most of the time?"

"Both. I have a barn out behind the house with a workshop, so sometimes we'd work on something without the girls and kids, and then sometimes we'd do family stuff."

"Had you seen Adam lately?"

"Sure. A couple of weeks ago, he came over to help me put a new engine block into a 1956 Ford F series pickup truck that I'm rebuilding." He shook his head. "That was our last day together."

"Did he talk about his work at all?"

Andy frowned. "Fishing?"

"Fishing or any side business he was doing or thinking about?"

"No. Not that I recall. What do you mean by side business? Fishing was his life. I mean, as far as work goes. Sharon and Izzie were his life. God, he adored that little girl. I remember that's what he talked about more than anything else. They were hoping to hear that Izzie was accepted at that music school in Halifax. Well, I say they were hoping, but I know at the same time he was grumbling about how to make it work if she got accepted. Izzie and Sharon were really hepped up about it, but it would have meant that from Monday to Friday Izzie and Sharon would stay at Sharon's Mom's place in Halifax and he didn't like that idea at all."

"Would he have given up fishing to move to Halifax?"

Andy's eyes widened. "Good Lord. I can't imagine it. No, I don't think so."

"Were they having any financial problems that you know of? Those school fees are steep. How did he plan to pay for it?"

Andy shrugged. "I didn't ask him about that. I suppose if I thought about it, I imagined his dad would chip in if need be."

"Did he seem worried about anything when you were together that day?"

"Not that I recall. He just seemed his normal self." He wrinkled his forehead. "Now that you mention it, though, he was a lot quieter than usual. I guess I did most of the talking when I think back. Aside from talking about Izzie and the school, he didn't have much to say for himself. He wasn't real talkative at any time, don't get me wrong." Andy nodded slowly as he thought back to his last visit with his friend. "But, yeah. He was quieter than normal. I should have asked him what was up."

"You couldn't know. When was the last time you were together with both Adam and Sharon?"

"March. Like I said, Adam and I both turned forty in the spring. What with the whole Covid thing, we didn't have a big party, but we got together for supper at their place. Adam and Sharon, Janice and me and the kids. My two boys and Izzie."

"How were Adam and Sharon together? Did you notice anything different or strained?"

"No. Nothing. I could ask Janice if you want. She'd notice

something like that more than I would, but she never mentioned it to me, and I think she would have if something seemed off to her."

Gordie tapped his pen against his book as he considered. "Can you call Janice for me and ask?"

Startled, Andy nodded. He called his wife and Gordie listened as the man gave a quick summary of the reason for his call. He asked the question and listened to a long answer. Gordie watched as Andy's face journeyed through several emotions. Raised eyebrows, then a frown, then a shake of the head. He nodded a few times, and then he ended the call.

"She said that there was nothing at all different or strained when we were together in March, but she said that a couple of weeks ago she ran into Adam, and he seemed rattled." Andy furrowed his brow. "She never said anything to me about it. Funny."

"Rattled, how?"

"She said she saw him in the parking lot behind the Canadian Tire. I don't know why she parks there, but I guess she can always get a spot to drive through back there."

Gordie nodded. "And?"

"And yeah. Janice saw him back there and called out to him to say hi, but he was in a world of his own and didn't hear her. She ran to catch up to him and when she called him again, he turned, and he looked shocked to see her. Janice said his face was white and his eyes were big like she'd scared him or something."

"Did he say anything?"

"No. Just apologized that he didn't hear her and said he had to run. He didn't even go into the store, which she thought was odd."

"Did Janice say she had seen anyone with Adam? Talking to him?"

"No, just what I told you."

"That's helpful. Thank you. I'll leave you to your work now." Gordie put his business card on the desk. "If either you or Janice think of anything else, please give me a call."

"Sure."

We need to get some CCTV from that parking lot.

"One last thing. Do you, or any other friends of Adam's that you know about, own a motorcycle?"

Andy laughed. "Nah. We're past that. I had a dirt bike twenty years ago, but now? Everyone I know drives a pickup or family car. We get our fix for speeding around, in winter, on our snow machines. Oh, and I think a couple of Adam's neighbours have ATVs, but not me."

CHAPTER 23

MACLEAN WENT FROM THE building supply yard to meet with Johnny McMaster, who owned a fitness club near the community centre in Port Mulroy. A sign posted on the door reminded people to wear masks and that appointments must be made to use the equipment. They limited capacity to no more than six patrons at a time.

Gordie went through the glass door and stopped at a reception desk where he signed in for contact tracing purposes while the college-aged receptionist called her boss to let him know MacLean had arrived.

Johnny McMaster was the opposite of Andy LeBlanc. He suited the black shorts and white t-shirt; his legs and arms, tanned and muscular. His upper body reminded Gordie of Sergeant Arsenault, with the bulging biceps stretching the fabric of his short sleeves. He had the stereotypical look of a fitness instructor.

McMaster held out his hand to shake Gordie's, but before MacLean responded, he pulled it back again. "Sorry, sometimes I forget we aren't supposed to shake hands anymore."

"Don't worry. I forget too." MacLean pulled out his identification again and McMaster gave it a cursory glance.

"Come through. Can we talk while I keep an eye on things? I've left a woman doing reps on the cable machine and I just want to supervise."

"Sure, no problem."

They stood at the back of the room filled with several large pieces of equipment that looked to Gordie's untrained eye like various instruments of torture. He pulled out his notebook. "Mr. McMaster,"

"Johnny, please."

Gordie nodded. "Johnny, I understand you were a good friend of Adam MacDonald's. How long did you know him?"

"About ten years. We used to play hockey together. Just a pickup team. Nothing serious, but we had fun."

"You didn't play hockey together anymore?"

"No, not for a few years now. Adam quit, but then we spent a couple of years coaching under 9 hockey. His daughter Izzie wanted to play so Adam was all-in." McMaster smiled. "He was a great coach. Adam loved those kids, and they loved him. Somehow, he'd always find something to compliment every single kid. And he'd have a pocket full of those expensive butterscotch candies and at the end of the game, he'd give one to each player with a comment about what made them an 'original' and great during the game, like making a good pass, demonstrated team behaviour, or good stick-handling. Whatever. Even a kid that spent most of their time on their ass on the ice, he'd find something to say, like, "I can see your skating is getting better every week." McMaster nodded as he remembered. "He didn't play favourites with Izzie, but you could see his eyes shine when he talked to her. He was so damned proud of her." McMaster paused and cleared his throat.

MacLean made a note or two, not looking at Johnny McMaster as the other man composed himself.

After a moment, McMaster took a deep breath. "So, what do you need to know?"

"Did you see him or even speak with him on the phone in the past few weeks?"

"We didn't see much of each other during fishing season, but I talked to him on the phone a couple of weeks ago. I tried to convince him to help me with the summer skills camp this year."

"How did he seem?"

McMaster tilted his head to consider his answer. "Distracted. He said he'd think about it, but he said it in that kind of way that you do when you agree to read some pamphlet that a person forces on you and you know for sure you'll throw into the closest blue box."

Gordie smiled. "I know what you mean. Did he give you any indication of what was going on in his life that had him distracted?"

"No, I'm afraid not." He paused and then continued. "After I hung up, I wondered if everything was OK at home for him."

"What made you wonder that?"

Johnny furrowed his brow. "I'm not sure. His voice was kind of low on the phone, like maybe he didn't want Sharon to hear him, even though he said nothing at all that she shouldn't hear." He shrugged. "I was probably just adding up two plus two to get five." Johnny hesitated.

"Was there some other reason you wondered about the marriage? This is a police investigation, and any information will help."

The other man sighed. "I'm sure it's nothing at all, but last year I saw Sharon having lunch in Port Mulroy with some guy I don't know. You know, I was walking past the pub on Main Street and I saw her and I almost stopped to wave but then I saw she was holding buddy's hand and I just hurried past. I didn't want to know."

"When was this, Johnny?"

"Maybe September? The weather was nice, so before winter."

"Did you ever mention it to either Adam or Sharon?"

"God, no. It might have been a relative or whatever. I don't know.

I wasn't about to cause problems. But then, because it felt like Adam wanted to get me off the phone, I remembered and wondered. I figured it's why he said he'd think about the hockey camp. He wanted to get shut of me, and I'm not used to that. If he was busy or he didn't want to do something, usually he'd just say."

"Did you ever think that Adam was having money troubles?"

McMaster shook his head. "None of us are rich, and every year the fishing business is uncertain, but no. He didn't gamble, and neither one of them was a problem drinker, as far as I know. No, I can't believe there were any real problems like that."

"Did you hear Adam died on his boat, quite a long way from his usual fishing area?"

"I heard something about that."

"Any thoughts on why that might be?"

"No idea. I don't know too much about fishing and just imagined he was out looking for a new spot."

Gordie nodded. "OK. Thank you for your time, Johnny." He handed out another card with the same advice to call him if anything occurred to him that might be helpful.

As Johnny took the card, he bit his bottom lip. "The rumour is someone killed Adam. Is that true?"

Gordie nodded. "That's how it appears. It may have been accidental, but yes. We believe that someone was with Adam just prior to his death."

"Doesn't make sense."

"That's why we're talking to everyone we can think of. To make sense of his death."

McMaster slipped the card into his shorts pocket, nodded a farewell to Gordie and went to speak with the woman who had finished her program with the cable machine and stood with a towel around her neck waiting for Johnny.

CHAPTER 24

ROXANNE ALBRIGHT CALLED LYNN Duggan first. It had appeared to Roxanne that Lynn was Sharon's closest friend, so it made sense to start with her. Lynn was home and ready to meet with Detective Albright, and in fact, was sitting out on her veranda with a glass of cola and ice when Roxanne pulled into the driveway.

The older woman stood to greet Roxanne. Her short grey hair clung to her forehead in beads of sweat. "Can I get you a cold drink, Detective?"

"That would be great, thank you."

"Cola or ginger ale. Those are your options."

"Ginger ale would be nice. Shall I come in with you?"

Lynn pointed to the other wooden deck chair. "Why not relax? I'll be back in a tick."

Roxanne sat and rested her notebook on the wide arm of the cheery, red-painted chair, with her pen at the ready.

Lynn returned and handed the detective the condensation-covered glass before returning to her own seat.

"Thank you." Roxanne took a deep sip, set the glass down on the deck beside her chair, wiped her damp hand on her pants and lifted her pen. "Lynn, I saw you with Sharon and I know she called on you to come when we gave her the news of Adam, so I believe you are a good friend to her and her family. Is that correct?"

"Oh, yes. We've been friends for years. We came together over a shared love of quilting, but our friendship grew to be so much more over time." Her eyes crinkled, and she smiled. "I was the first one she allowed to babysit Izzie."

Roxanne smiled. "That says it all, I think."

The smile slipped away from Lynn's face. "This has been such a terrible tragedy for the family. I just can't imagine how Sharon and Izzie will manage without Adam."

"Do you mean financially?"

Lynn waved her hand dismissively. "No, I know there's life insurance. Adam was far too organized to not have planned all this out. I mean emotionally."

"So, they were a close family?"

"God, yes."

"Sharon used to take Izzie down to meet Adam coming home from fishing all the time, and sometimes she'd go see him off in the morning."

Roxanne nodded. "I had heard that, but not lately as I understand it?"

"Well, now Izzie is older, and of course, during the school year Sharon had to be there for the child."

"I understand. So, you don't think that this change indicated trouble in their marriage."

Lynn frowned. "No. Absolutely not. They were rock solid."

"Did you sense anything at all from Sharon that might have been bothering her? If not with her relationship, then something else?"

"Like what?"

"I don't know. I don't know her, but you do."

"I suppose she was a bit worried about how they would pay for the school fees."

"For the music school, you mean?"

"Yes. I know it's quite expensive, but I think Sharon was checking into grants or scholarships or whatever. If anyone could find a way to make it happen, it was them."

"Was Adam as keen for Izzie to go off to the music school as Sharon? I know it means the girl will be in Halifax. That's a big change to their lives."

The woman was quiet for a moment. "I think he was very proud that she'd been accepted into the school."

"That's not the same thing, though, is it?"

Lynn drained her glass and then sighed. "I actually asked Sharon that when she put in the application last fall. Adam and Izzie were so close. They were real *pals*, you know?"

"What did Sharon say when you asked about how Adam felt?"

She pursed her lips for an instant as if trapping her answer from escaping. "She said that she thought Adam secretly hoped that Izzie wouldn't be accepted."

"Thank you for your honesty."

"But I'm sure all that changed when the child *was* accepted. And I never heard that from Adam, so for all I know, Sharon was wrong about how he had initially felt."

"Yes. Thank you."

"How did Sharon and Adam get along with his family?"

"Good, as far as I know. When Kyle first got back home from his travels to Ontario or wherever he had been, I think Adam was a bit resistant to having him on the crew. Sharon thought Adam worried Kyle would try to assert himself with decision-making in the business, but that didn't happen. Kyle seemed content to just be crew, and it wasn't long before they settled into a relaxed relationship. I saw them together many times when they got back after the day's fishing, and I saw how they were together. Kyle seemed settled, and it looked like he was happy fishing. Happy to be with his brother. And it looked like Adam felt the same. They'd be laughing or talking, and it looked very comfortable between them. I know Dannymac was pleased to have Kyle back and see the boys working together."

"Was there any jealousy that you know of when Dannymac gave Kyle the mini-home and land out at his property?"

"Nothing serious. Sharon made the occasional comment about 'it must be nice' but I reminded her that Kyle looked after his father and if he wasn't around, then she and Adam would be running out there to look after him." Lynn nodded at Roxanne. "You know he's got cancer, right?"

"Yes, I know. When you pointed that out, did Sharon agree with you?"

"Oh, yes. It was never serious grumbling, anyway. It all worked out fine and I think having Kyle crewing for Adam took some pressure off Adam.. It's easier when you don't need to be the boss every minute out there. It's hard work, but I think they used to have some fun, the three of them, Adam, Kyle, and Dab Haan."

Lynn's eyes filled with tears. "I can't believe that both Adam and Dab are gone now. Just like that. Two weeks ago, this was a sleepy little village, and now, God, it's hard to understand."

Roxanne took advantage of the change in direction of the conversation. "You knew Dab Haan quite well, didn't you?"

"The whole town knew Dab Haan. He was someone who we all tolerated, even though we didn't like his drinking. Not many people gave him money, but if there was a casserole going, or extra dinner rolls baked, they'd often end up at Dab's place. We look after our own here."

Roxanne nodded. "I'm from Big Pond. I know what smalltown life is like."

"You'll understand what a shock it was to know that someone killed Dab, and if I understand things, maybe even Adam?"

"Yes. I believe you saw Dab Haan having an argument with Sharon. Is that right?"

Lynn stiffened. "Not an argument, no."

"What then?"

"Dab was three sheets to the wind and not making a lot of sense, so that's the last thing that Sharon needed. Dab was standing there, weaving back and forth on her doorstep, and making loud declarations of some sort about money. He claimed Adam was planning to give him some, so Sharon should live up to the promise. It was all nonsense, of course. Sharon rightly told him to clear off. She just couldn't deal with him then and was probably a little harsher than she normally would be. I didn't blame her. She told him to go talk to Dannymac or Kyle."

"Did you hear Dab say why he believed Adam planned to give him money?"

"No. And I told you, it meant nothing. He was just drunk. When he saw me, he left."

"Did you hear anything more about Dab and what he was saying around town after that?"

"No. Most people don't even listen when he talks, I'm afraid."

"Fair enough. You spent a fair amount of time at the MacDonald house, I think?"

"Yes. Sharon and I, along with others often, get together there for quilting. The home has such wonderful light."

"Did you ever see any friends of Adam, when you were there? Specifically, anyone riding a motorcycle?"

"I know most of Adam's friends I think, but I don't know anyone with a motorcycle."

"All right. Thank you for your time and the drink."

Roxanne finished her drink and handed the glass back to Lynn, checking her watch as she walked back to the car. *Good timing. Yvonne Farley will be home from work now.*

She drove south to the edge of town, past a local hotel, and turned inland. It was a large, rambling house done over in clay-coloured vinyl siding with a red metal roof. An old farmhouse, it had a grandeur that new houses rarely had. Two stories with a partial wraparound covered veranda, the house had a huge old maple tree in the front yard with chairs set out in the shade below.

Roxanne parked and trotted up the wide wooden steps. She had to knock twice before she heard footsteps hastening towards her. The door opened and the woman she had met first at the harbour stood before her.

The woman, in her mid-thirties, shoved her hair behind her ear. The frosted blond pixie cut looked as though it had grown out of its original style and was now at that chin-length stage that was irritating. "Sorry. I was in the kitchen plugging in the kettle and didn't hear you knock. Always need a cup of tea when I get home from work."

Roxanne smiled. "I understand." She held up her identification. "I'm Detective Roxanne Albright."

Yvonne Farley nodded. "I remember meeting you. Come on through." She led the way down a long hallway to the kitchen, getting there in time to hear the kettle click off.

Yvonne waved Roxanne to a chair at the table as she took a mug and dropped a tea bag into it. She turned. "Do you want a cup?"

"Sure. That would be nice." *I'll be water-logged by the time I meet Gordie.*

Yvonne got out another mug, dropped in a teabag, and set it in front of Roxanne. She poured boiling water into her own tall white mug with the words 'Best Mom' emblazoned in red letters and then in the orange one with a drawing of a cat for Roxanne.

Roxanne waited until Yvonne had set out a large canister with sugar and the purple plastic milkbag pitcher, along with a saucer on which to put their teabags. She put two teaspoons down on the table and then sat down with a sigh.

Roxanne used a spoon to squeeze, then fish out the teabag. She poured some milk in and then, as Yvonne went through the same ritual, she said. "Thank you for meeting me. I know you have a busy life."

Yvonne nodded. "This is just about the only quiet time I get all day. "If my shift allows it, a few minutes in the morning down at the wharf and now. Between getting home from work at the Five-to-a-Dollar and when the kids come home from school."

Roxanne smiled. "Is there really anything that can be bought for five cents anymore?"

"Some of the sewing notions."

"There you go, now."

"But you can't buy just one of them."

They laughed together, and then Yvonne's face clouded. "You're here about Adam."

"Yes. You know the family well, I believe."

"I'm not sure I'd say well. I'm friends with Sharon but mostly because I have a daughter the same age as Izzie, and they play together. My husband is a fisherman too, so we have a lot in common."

"OK. That's good. Have you noticed any changes in Sharon lately? Before Adam died, I mean, obviously."

"No, I can't say I noticed anything."

"Did you see Sharon and Adam interact much?"

"Sure. I'd see them at the harbour, or at the Legion at dances. Things like that."

"How did they seem, as a couple?"

Yvonne tucked a stray lock of hair behind her ear again. "Happy. Sometimes I was envious. Don't get me wrong. I love each one of my four kids to bits, but it's tiring. My husband, Rob and I go to dances as well, once in a while, but by ten o'clock we're ready to pack it in and just go home to bed. Sharon and Adam are always so energetic, cruising around the room talking to people, dancing, having drinks."

"Did they usually just dance with each other, or other people as well?"

She frowned. "Everyone knows everyone at these things. They danced with other people sometimes, but if you're trying to suggest either of them had a special interest in anyone else, forget it. There was no one around here that they'd even look at."

Roxanne raised her eyebrows. "Around here? You mean there might be someone elsewhere that one of them has an interest in?"

Yvonne flushed. "I'm not saying that."

"You aren't denying it either."

She chewed her lip, took a sip of tea, and then set the mug down. "On the day that Adam disappeared, just before you came to talk to Sharon, I heard her on the phone to someone named Michael. I never heard her mention anyone by that name before, and I don't know anybody in her circle of friends by that name."

"Thank you. Did you hear what they talked about?"

"No. It was just for an instant. I thought it might be Adam, so I moved closer, but it wasn't. I just heard her say his name and then I moved away again."

"OK. Did you ever talk about money with Sharon? Was she worried?"

"We didn't talk about that."

Roxanne closed her notebook. As she tucked the book into her pocket, she remembered to ask one last question. "Did you ever see Adam away from home with anyone? Especially any friends that rode a motorbike?"

Yvonne shrugged. "I don't know if they were friends or not."

Roxanne pulled her book out again. "But?"

"Yeah. I saw him, maybe a month ago or more, down by the RV park, but the park wasn't open. There might have still been snow on the ground. I can't recall now. I was there with the kids, letting them run wild at the beach."

"Can you describe the person you saw Adam with?"

"I didn't study him or anything. He was just sitting on this big bike, and I just remember thinking that he must get cold riding a bike so early in the season. He had a beard and ponytail. That's all I can tell you."

"What colour was his hair?"

"The beard was grey. I saw him from the side. I think the ponytail was dark grey, more like black going grey, you know?"

Roxanne nodded. "If you looked at a calendar, can you figure out when this was?"

Yvonne stood and took the calendar that hung on the fridge with a suction cup hook off and returned to the table. Lesson times and events covered the calendar. She turned the page back to the previous page. "It was before swimming started, but after hockey finished. It must have been either Saturday or Sunday on this weekend." She pointed to April 17 and 18. "Just before the fishing season started."

"That's great. Is there anything else you can tell me? Did they seem friendly or angry or what?"

"I only looked at them for a second. They didn't seem to be arguing." She closed her eyes. "Adam had his hands in his jacket pockets. I think the bike guy had a bag he was rooting through. The kind you see strapped to the tank, but again, I can't be positive about that."

"Did Adam see you?"

"I don't know. Probably with the kids hollering like they were, he would have, but when I glanced in his direction, he didn't look at me or wave or anything, so who knows?"

"You've been very helpful. Thank you again. I'll let you enjoy your last few minutes in peace before the gang gets home."

Yvonne glanced at her watch. "No. Time's up. I have to get their snack ready and then start on supper."

Roxanne walked down the long hall again and as she opened the front door, the school bus stopped at the end of the driveway. The lights flashed, the bus door opened and an explosion of four children erupted and pelted along the driveway, barely giving her a look as they rushed past on the way to the house. Roxanne sat in the car for a moment and wondered at the transformation in Yvonne, who a moment ago looked worn out, but now wore a huge grin as her children vied for her attention, hugging, and clinging to her. Roxanne waved, but Yvonne was focussed on listening to the chatter of her children as they filed into the house.

CHAPTER 25

THEY MET AT TIM Hortons, as arranged. Gordie got his usual medium double-double coffee and an oatcake with a pat of butter. She got a steeped tea with milk with a plain doughnut, and they picked a table along the back wall.

Gordie stirred his coffee and nodded towards the empty tables on either side of them. "The good thing about this Covid business is that you never have people invading your space anymore. I like that."

Roxanne smiled. "Great, that you can find something positive in it."

He flipped open his notebook. "So, here's what I found out. The Reader's Digest version is that Andy LeBlanc's wife saw Adam one day behind the Canadian Tire talking to a guy on a motorbike. She didn't see enough of the guy to give any details, but afterwards, Adam seemed rattled. She spoke to him for a moment, but he couldn't get away from her fast enough. From his hockey buddy Johnny McMaster, I heard Adam seemed distracted when they were last together, but nothing more specific. What I heard was how close Adam and his daughter were, and that Johnny felt Adam would have a hard time letting her be in Halifax attending that fancy school all week while he stayed back at home."

"Enough to prevent her from going? That would frost Sharon, I'd guess."

"No, my sense is that Adam would do whatever was the right thing for his daughter, no matter what it cost him."

He paused and took a gulp of his coffee and Roxanne pulled out her book, ready to begin but then Gordie started again. "And"

"And?"

"And Johnny saw Sharon MacDonald holding the hand of a man, not Adam, across the lunch table in a restaurant in Port Mulroy a few months ago."

She sat back. "Oh, my."

Gordie smiled. "What did you hear?"

She opened her book. "Much the same basic story from Lynn Duggan." She glanced through her notes. "Lynn commented that Sharon was probably keener for Izzie to get into the school than Adam was, but it didn't sound like it was a major bone of contention. The biggest issue was around the school fees, but Sharon was checking on grants to help out."

"OK, that's interesting." Gordie explained what he had heard from Detective Norris about the payment in and out of Sharon's account.

"So maybe a grant came through?"

"Something to be checked definitely, but it's the fact that it was in cash that raises questions."

"I also met with Yvonne Farley. That was more interesting. She saw the mystery biker as well."

"Oh? In that same parking lot?"

"No. This was at the RV park down at the harbour."

"OK, that's new. When was this?"

"The weekend of April 17th."

"Did she give you a description?"

"Basically, the same as what we know already. Grey beard, pony-tail darker than the beard. Here's something, though. He had a tank bag and was *rooting through it,* according to Yvonne." Roxanne looked up. "Maybe taking something out to give to Adam? Maybe putting something away that Adam had given him?" She looked back at her notes. "Adam had his hands in his pockets, so whatever the transaction was, Adam didn't leave carrying a package, so it was either small enough to fit in a pocket, or he'd handed something over already when Yvonne saw them together."

Gordie's voice was low. "A roll of money would fit nicely in a pocket."

"I thought the same thing."

"Maybe he was just closing the bag up again rather than rooting through it. Job done."

Roxanne smiled. "And"

Gordie shook his head. "I deserve that. OK. And what?"

"And Yvonne reluctantly admitted to me she heard Sharon on the phone the morning Adam went missing, with someone called Michael. She didn't hear anything and didn't know anyone in Sharon's circle called Michael."

He nodded. "We need to talk to Sharon. Anything else?"

"I also talked to Lynn about Dab Haan. I asked about the argument that Vanessa mentioned between Dab and Sharon."

"Did she tell you what it was about?"

"Lynn denied it was an argument. She was pretty defensive. More a case of the town drunk being his usual nuisance. He was spouting off about wanting money, but Sharon was short with him and told him to go talk to Kyle or Dannymac."

"That's the common opinion, all right." He drank the rest of his coffee and set the cup on the plate to return it on the tray to the drop-off shelf.

"Where do we go from here, boss?"

"Tomorrow we'll go into the office and regroup. I've already spoken with Sarge and he's agreed that another team focus on the Dab Haan murder. We'll go over what we have and then let them run with it. We will continue to focus on MacDonald, but we stay in close contact with the Haan investigation to see where they cross paths. Tomorrow is Adam's funeral, so we'll leave them all alone for the day to get past that. I think the next step after that is to get Sharon in for a more formal interview."

"Sounds good. I'll write up my interviews and have them in the system tonight."

"Me too. Great work today, Roxanne. Follow up with Jeffreys tomorrow. I want to know more about what he's seen up in Pleasant Bay."

Albright flushed at the compliment. "Thanks." They rose to go. "Going out for a smoke?"

"I quit."

She stared at him. "What? When?"

Gordie looked at his watch. "Three hours ago."

"Whew. Thought I missed something major there. Good for you. I hope you make it."

He straightened his shoulders. "I will."

Roxanne tilted her head. "You know, I think you will."

"Just don't ask me how I feel."

"Fair enough. And I won't take it personally when you turn into a grizzly bear."

***

As Gordie drove back north to Vanessa's house, he debated with himself about whether he should announce his decision to quit smoking or just wait until she noticed on her own. He tried out the two scenarios in his mind. One in which he tells Vanessa he quit for her sake because he loved her. The other, more subtle with a quiet, triumphant smile when she realizes that he's quit, and it must be for her sake and what that means in terms of his commitment to her. He decided to go with the subtle approach. He never was one for big announcements.

Gordie drove up the long driveway and grinned to see Taz come bounding out of the house, followed by Vanessa. *My two girls.*

He climbed out of the car and stooped to ruffle the dog's long, white hair. "How's my girl?" MacLean clasped her enormous head between his hands and looked into her eyes. "Have you been good for Vanessa?"

Vanessa walked up and kissed him on the cheek as he straightened. "Of course, she's been good. As have I."

They walked around the garden for a few moments in the waning sun as she showed him the freshly turned earth, new budding plants and raked out flower beds.

"It's all beautiful. There's no doubt you have a real green thumb."

They went in the house, and he inhaled the scent of supper warming in the oven. Vanessa held up a glass of red wine she had already started. "Want one? Or maybe a beer?"

"A beer would be great, thanks."

When they were seated together in the cozy living room, he took a deep sip of his glass of Alexander Keith's. "Ahh. Nice." He set down his glass. "Tell me again about your visit from the Mountie."

She took a sip of her wine. "There isn't really anything more to tell you than what I already said on the phone. He came by wanting to go over my statement again, but when I told him I'd already given you every detail I could think of, he left."

"You said that he seemed a bit…disturbed by that?"

She shrugged. "I'm not sure *disturbed* is the right word. He was surprised and maybe a little put out. Maybe he just felt that he'd had a wasted trip. And then Taz didn't give him much of a welcome, so that may have put him off."

Gordie bent down to stroke Taz, laying at his feet. "Good thing you were here, Taz. You did your job, didn't you?"

Vanessa narrowed her eyes. "Her job?"

"Yes. Looking after you."

She drank her wine in silence for a moment and then set the

empty glass on the coffee table. "Why did you ask me to look after Taz the last couple of days, Gordie?"

He looked up. "What do you mean?"

"I thought you'd have very long days, what with two deaths to investigate, but it seems that you are just working the same number of hours that you normally do, so I guess I'm just not sure why Taz is even here."

"I didn't know what sort of days I'd be having, so yes. That's partly why I asked you to have her here. Why? Is it a problem? I thought you liked having her."

"I do. I always enjoy having her for a visit, but when she's here, I do feel obliged to stay home with her."

He crossed his arms. "Has she kept you from something important?"

She sighed. "Be honest with me. Did you ask me to have her in order to keep me at home?"

"And if I did think that home was the best place for you for a few days, what's wrong with that?"

She chewed on her bottom lip. "We've been through this. I thought you understood. I don't need you to *look after me*." She emphasized the words. "I'm an adult. I've looked after myself for a very long time now, and that was in Toronto, which is a whole lot more dangerous than anything Port Mulroy can throw at me."

"So, you're saying that having Taz here has cramped your style?"

Vanessa stood. "I don't know if you purposely misunderstand me, or you really are obtuse."

Gordie rose as well. "Obtuse? You mean stupid?"

"I've told you before. You call it looking after me. I call it control. I will. Not. Be controlled."

He shook his head. "Look, you're blowing this completely out of proportion. You went through a traumatic experience and if I care enough about you to want to give you a few worry-free days, how can that be wrong?"

"Give *me* worry-free days, or you?"

"Both of us."

She turned away to look out the window. Gordie felt his heart racing and wished he could have a smoke right now to calm himself.

Then she turned back to face him. "Gordie. I think this just isn't working. We have different ideas about what a healthy relationship looks like."

"Not working?" He raised his eyebrows. "What? You want me to pack my toothbrush and go home?"

Silence.

He sucked in a deep breath. "You do. That's what you're saying." He blinked several times, hoping to hear her deny it. "OK, fine. I'll go. But for how long? What does this all mean?"

Tears filled her eyes. The freckles across her nose and forehead stood out against her pale skin. "It means we're through, Gordie. I'm sorry."

He heard her words. Swallowed. Lost for words of his own, he turned and left the room to go upstairs and pack.

CHAPTER 26

A FTER A RESTLESS NIGHT, Gordie left early for the drive to the office. His eyes were gritty, and he had a headache. He was also starving and pulled into the drive-through at Tim Hortons in St. Peter's. Torn between the egg, cheese, and bacon or the egg, cheese, and sausage sandwich, for a fleeting moment, he considered ordering both. He settled on the bacon version but added a serving of hashbrown potatoes on the side. And of course, a coffee.

The smell of the food in his car helped to distract him from his real craving, which was for a cigarette. He had almost stopped on the way home the previous night to get a pack, but then decided to see how long he could go without a smoke. *The hell with Vanessa. I'll do it for myself. Save some money. Take a trip somewhere one day with all that extra cash.*

He ate as he drove and when he finished, he felt better, although by the time he finished his coffee he craved a smoke even more than earlier. Luckily, there weren't a lot of places to stop and get cigarettes, so he just kept driving. He called Roxanne to take his mind off it.

She answered on the first ring. "Good morning. You're bright and early."

"Sounds like you are too. You on your way already?"

"Yeah. I want to get the board updated with the interviews we've done."

"Great. We'll do the usual. I'll start the briefing and then hand it over. We'll have a separate briefing just for the team taking over the Haan investigation."

"Sounds good." Silence other than road noise coming through the speaker. "Everything OK?"

"Why wouldn't it be?"

"Don't know. Oh, wait. I just remembered. The smoking. Did Vanessa notice?"

"No."

"Oh wow. I'm surprised."

He took a breath. "She might have noticed, except we broke up last night."

"Oh God, no. What happened?"

"I'll tell you about it later. I'll probably lose you any time here."

"OK. Hang in there. You guys are good together. I'm sure whatever it is will be resolved."

"I'll see you soon." He poked at the button on his steering wheel and disengaged.

His mind was foggy as he drove. He tried to map out everything he wanted to cover in the briefing, but he kept cycling back to Vanessa. Her frown. Her tears. *Come on. Focus, focus.*

The next hour passed in a confusing sequence of images of Vanessa, a biker, the dead body of Dab Haan and the *Sea Child*. Like a waking nightmare, he tried to make sense of it all and then gave up.

He arrived at the office, passing his fellow smokers standing outside the back door. The scent of the smoke wrapped him, and he was torn between rushing through or lingering to bum a cigarette. He marched past his colleagues, mumbling 'good morning' on his way.

Gordie threw his jacket over the back of his chair and made his way to his boss's office. He knuckled the doorframe of the open door and Sergeant Arsenault waved him in and gestured to a chair.

"You look like hell. You feeling OK? If you don't feel well, you shouldn't come in."

"I'm fine."

Arsenault shrugged. "OK." Without any further preamble, he opened a file on his desk. "I've spoken with Joe Hennessy and Gabriel Doucette. They are ready to be briefed by you and Albright to take over the Haan case. Norris will continue on in the office and support both of the investigations, getting warrants, chasing down records, all that kind of thing."

"Good, thanks. I'll let Sergeant Benoit know that Hennessy and Doucette will be in contact to follow up on the autopsy for Haan, any ballistics information that they may have dug up, and any trace or prints that may be helpful from Haan's cabin."

"I've been talking to her already, so she knows to expect the new resources. It may be worth my time to take a run up there myself to meet her in person. I thought you were doing more liaising with those guys, but it sounds like you've been neglecting to communicate."

Don't mess with me today, Sarge. Gordie clenched his jaw. "I wasn't going to harass them for the results. I knew I'd hear when they had something to share."

Arsenault sighed. "You need to be more proactive, MacLean. Don't just sit and wait for information to fall in your lap." He waved towards the door. "Don't you have a briefing to prepare for?"

MacLean felt his heart pound as he walked back down the hall to his own desk.

Albright was at her desk, getting logged in for the day. She glanced up at him and raised her eyebrows when she saw his face.

"Want to take a quick run out to Tim's for a coffee before we get stuck in here?"

"Better not." He jerked his head towards the briefing room. "Let's get set up."

She followed him and closed the door behind them once inside. "You look like your blood pressure is going through the roof."

"Yeah. Feels like it too."

"What's up?"

"Just the usual. Sarge makes me crazy, and I know he knows it. Why does he always make it sound like I've been sitting around doing nothing? He's going to meet Sergeant Benoit up in Inverness. Apparently, he feels obliged to since I haven't been communicating with them."

"What is it you should have communicated?"

"According to Sarge, I should have been chasing them for reports. Never mind that Benoit said she'd let us know when she had anything." He shrugged. "Maybe he's right. And that's the problem, there's always an element of right in his criticism so it's impossible to argue. Does he do this to everyone or just me?"

She grinned. "Yeah. Just you, I think. Isn't it nice to be special?"

He sucked in a deep breath and took his time to exhale. "I can live without it. Especially right now."

"Don't let him get to you. I know that's easier said than done, but come on." She walked to the front of the room and picked up a whiteboard marker. "Let's get this done. The best way to put his crap aside is to prove you can get this solved."

Gordie smiled and nodded. "From the mouths of babes." He joined her and together they listed the key take-aways from the interviews.

***

After the general briefing, they met with the new Haan investigation team and Rob Norris. Since the biker was a person of interest in both cases, MacLean assigned Norris the task of searching out CCTV.

Norris ran through the notes he had made. "OK, so Canadian Tire and any of the other stores along there. Then down to the RV park. I know there's an office and a laundry building. Either of those may have something."

MacLean nodded. "Check with the manager of the park for contact details for some of the owners of the permanent trailers closest to the road and parking lot. They may have cameras on those units as well. Everyone and their brother have these things now that you can check from your phones while you're sitting at home."

Norris raised his eyebrows. "Look at you, Mr. Technology."

"Yeah, I'm full of surprises, aren't I?"

Gordie led the way from the room. "Roxanne, any luck getting a hold of Jeffreys about the activity up at the harbour in Pleasant Bay?"

"No. I'll try again. I left a message, but he hasn't gotten back to me."

"OK. Let's be more *proactive*, shall we?"

MacLean spent part of the day eliminating potential sources of the money that Sharon MacDonald had deposited. By the end, he knew it was not insurance, and according to the music school, it wasn't from grants or scholarships. It wasn't a loan from the bank, and it wasn't transferred from the business account. The only options he didn't eliminate were a loan from either Dannymac or Sharon's mother. He intended to get Sharon into the station the next day for a formal interview and this was one topic he would pursue then. That and the mysterious Michael. He'd call her by end of day and make the arrangement.

They ordered pizza for the three of them and ate lunch in the briefing room. Norris brought in his laptop. Roxanne pulled down the screen so he could project what he had on his computer.

MacLean took two slices of pepperoni, bacon, and mushroom pizza and took the greasy plate and a can of cola to a desk. "What have you got?"

Norris fiddled for a moment in silence while Roxanne took a

slice of vegetarian pizza and sat down. "OK, here we go. I'm waiting for Canadian Tire to get back to me, but I got a hold of the manager of the RV park. They have a camera on the office building but need to go down in person to see what they have recorded. It records over the tapes every two weeks, so I'm not holding my breath there."

MacLean took a swig of cola and then set the can down. "But?"

"But I got the name of one of the trailer owners who has a subscription on a camera. The usual length of time they, the host of the camera subscription, keep these videos is 60 days, but this owner pays extra to keep it for 120 days because they don't go down that often to check the unit. They don't want to get there, find out someone has broken into them and then not have any video to look at."

Albright shrugged. "Seems weird. Don't these things have notifications that alert you if there's something going on?"

"The owner told me they disabled the notifications because they got so many pings for foxes, kids riding their bikes, and other things like that. Anyway, who cares? They sent me the link to access the video on the cloud."

Norris selected the middle of April and began the playback while he got his lunch.

"There!" MacLean and Albright exclaimed at the same time.

Norris paused it and they all studied the frozen frame of Adam MacDonald standing waiting as a man on a motorbike approached. The video was black and white, so it was impossible to know the colour, but the distinctive Harley-Davidson crest was clearly visible. The profile of the rider showed a man wearing a round black helmet held in place with a chinstrap. In place of an integrated visor, he wore aviator sunglasses. A ragged ponytail fluttered halfway down his back and he wind pressed an unkempt grey beard against his throat and black leather jacket.

Gordie leaned forward, his pizza forgotten. "Move it ahead. We need to see the back for a license plate."

Norris advanced the video, and they watched while the bike

stopped within a couple of feet of Adam. The two men spoke, and they saw Adam shake his head in a clear motion of 'no'. The man on the bike crossed his arms across his chest, but his head kept nodding as if to persuade Adam to comply or agree. Again, Adam shook his head, but this time he held out his hand as if demanding something from the bike rider. Finally, the man on the bike seemed to give in. He zipped open the tank bag strapped in front of him and withdrew what appeared to be a roll and handed it to Adam. Adam palmed the roll and stuffed both hands in his pockets.

Norris backed the video up, and they watched again. "It's money, right?"

MacLean peered at the grainy image on the screen. "Looks like it to me."

He looked at Roxanne, who nodded. "Me too."

The video started again, and they watched in silence as the two men spoke for another moment and then, in the distance, they saw a van drive up and park. A woman and four children piled out, the children running for the beach.

"Yvonne." Roxanne muttered.

Although Yvonne had not believed Adam had seen her, it was obvious from the video that he turned his head in her direction. He abruptly turned away from the biker and strode away.

"Now, come on, buddy. Get turned around." Norris paused the video a couple of times as the bike started up and drove out of camera range. A second later, the bike came back within range as he headed out of the lot. The video froze and they looked at the retreating bike. They saw a license plate, but it was too small and fuzzy to read.

MacLean grunted. "Damn. Can you make it bigger?"

"I can't, but let's hope the tech guys can."

MacLean ate the rest of his pizza. "This is a real break, Rob. Great job. I'll need a couple of prints made from this. One of biker-guy handing over the roll. Another of a good profile of biker-guy. Someone other than Adam knows this man."

CHAPTER 27

GORDIE WAS UP AT five in the morning, reviewing all the reports from the initial forensics of *Sea Child* to the autopsy to the latest interviews. He was jumpy and hadn't been able to sleep anyway, so thought he might as well get up and use his time productively. Taz dozed in the corner of the kitchen, opening her eyes any time he stood up to pace around the kitchen or pour himself another cup of tea from the pot, keeping warm under the teacozy.

As the sky turned from grey to pink, the dog stood, stretched, and came to rest her head on Gordie's lap.

"You're right. Let's go out for a walk."

Gordie was dressed in an old sweatshirt and jeans. He'd shower and change when he got back. He drove down their favourite logging road, which led to a secluded sandy, rock-strewn beach. The June morning was cool, and a mist hung in the air, but as Gordie walked along, following the white flag of Taz's tail, he inhaled deeply and felt better than he had felt in days. Three days, to be precise. *Is this quit smoking business worth it?* He spoke aloud as Taz circled back to trot beside him for a moment. "The jury's still out on that one, Taz. Roxanne's the only one who even knows I'm quitting. No big deal if I pack it in."

The dog looked up at him, her head cocked to one side. He stroked her head. "Don't worry. I'm not giving in yet. Go on and have a run. We'll need to turn back soon."

A scent caught her attention and Taz jogged off to investigate a lump of seaweed and broken lobster shell.

When Gordie turned back, the sun was behind him. The mist lifted and his shadow, a long thin version of himself, led him eagerly back along the sand to his car, hastening him to get to work.

***

Sharon MacDonald arrived at the station at ten o'clock. Roxanne had taken her into the small interview room where Sharon sat, brows wrinkled into a deep 'v' and lips pursed, a cup of grey-coloured tea chilling untouched in front of her.

Gordie nodded to Roxanne, and she began the recording equipment.

"Thank you for making the trip here this morning, Sharon. We appreciate it."

Her voice was strident. "I don't understand why I was forced to come all the way down here. It's a terrible inconvenience."

Gordie nodded soothingly. "I understand that, but sometimes we need to be more formal. This is one of those times."

She huffed. "Well, get on with it, then. It's Izzie's first day back to school and I want to get home in case she needs to be picked up. This has all been terrible for her."

"Yes, I can only imagine. Before we begin, I just want to ensure that Detective Albright has read you your rights and that you understand them."

Sharon glared at Albright. "Yes, she did. I understand what she said, but I don't understand why you're treating me like a criminal."

"We just have our procedures to follow. Let's go back to the beginning when you first learned that Adam was missing. You told us you had been at home and while you were aware of Adam leaving home a little earlier than usual, you didn't notice the actual time. Is that correct?"

"Yes. It felt like the middle of the night to me, and I just woke up for a moment and fell asleep again."

"Was that unusual? For him to leave so early to go fishing?"

"Yes, because the crew wouldn't even be there yet, and you need daylight to see the buoys, so there'd be no point in heading out when it was so dark."

"But it didn't worry you?"

"I told you. I barely registered it."

"And you had been arguing the night before. Is that correct?"

"Yes. It wasn't anything major. All couples squabble sometimes."

"What was the argument about?"

Sharon sighed. "It was nothing. To be perfectly honest, I had been... we had been celebrating because Izzie was accepted at the Conservatory. I had a glass of wine too many and I was short-tempered over nothing. It happens."

"What were you short-tempered about, Sharon? It must have been something specific to go from celebrating to an argument."

"Fine. I was a little worried about the school fees and I took it out on Adam."

"Did he comfort you? Did he tell you he had the money situation under control?"

She flushed. "He tried to, but I didn't listen." Tears swam. "He always saw the best in a situation and just said something like 'it'll all work out'. But that's not an answer, is it? I took my drink outside and he went to bed. By the morning I had it all worked out anyway and with a clear head, I saw some options."

"What options, Sharon?"

Sharon pursed her lips. "What? You want to know every little detail of our finances? Fine. I was going to sell a big fancy quilt, I was going to talk to Dannymac, I was going to see about grants.

Those are just some of the options. Where there's a will, there's a way, right?"

Gordie looked at Roxanne, who removed the printout of the MacDonald bank account transactions. She slid it over to MacLean, who turned it around for Sharon to see.

Sharon paled as she saw the document with the ten-thousand-dollar deposit highlighted in yellow.

"Sharon, did you do all those things you mentioned? Sell the quilt, get loans and grants?"

She bit her lip and then said. "Adam had life insurance."

"Yes, we know that, but they haven't paid out yet, have they? Sharon, we spoke to Dannymac, and he tells us he has not loaned you any money."

The widow blinked rapidly and then picked up the cold tea and took a sip. Making a face of distaste, she set it down again.

MacLean spoke again. "Sharon, where did this money come from?"

Her face crumpled. "I don't know. Honestly, I don't know. I found it in Adam's shaving kit bag." She sighed. "I just wanted to smell his cologne; you know? And there it was. This money rolled up in an elastic."

"You're telling me you knew nothing about this before finding it hidden?"

Her voice was loud and pitched. "Nothing. If he had told me he had this damn money, we wouldn't have argued. He was like a child sometimes, just trusting and believing that he could make things come right, but he didn't tell me how. He probably just wanted to present me with the solution without saying a word." Tears tracked down her cheeks.

Gordie pulled the bank information back. "Sharon, if we are to believe you, you need to help us figure out where the money came from. Right now, it looks to us like Adam was up to something illegal and you knew about it. Perhaps you wanted the money but were frustrated with his ways and you killed him or had him killed."

Eyes wide. "No, no, no. I loved Adam. If he had just told me, I would have helped sort things out. I didn't know anything about it, and I certainly didn't do anything to him. I didn't even like arguing with him." Sniffling, she pulled a tissue from the sleeve of her grey sweatshirt.

Gordie leaned back in his chair and nodded to Roxanne.

Roxanne leaned closer to Sharon. "Sharon, who is Michael?"

Sharon blinked. "Who?"

"Michael. We know that you have a friend called Michael and we want to know more about him."

Wrinkling her brow, Sharon shook her head. "I have a friend called Michael, but I don't understand why you are asking about him."

Roxanne took the approach that the lunch date and Michael were one and the same. "A few months ago, you were seen having lunch with him in Port Mulroy. Tell us about that."

She flushed. "You make it sound like something it isn't. Michael was someone I worked with years ago at St. Francis Xavier University. Before I was married. Michael Fleming was an Assistant Professor, and I was an assistant to the faculty. We got on and have stayed friends. He's now down at Saint Mary's."

"None of your friends know about him. Why is that?"

She shrugged. "I don't know. We aren't that close, so I never mention him, I guess."

"You spoke with him on the day Adam disappeared." Roxanne slid a printout of the phone records across to Sharon. The same number that showed up for a thirty-second call on that fateful morning, showed up again the next day for a call of just under ten minutes. They highlighted both calls in yellow.

Sharon looked at the page and then back up at Albright with widened eyes. "You're spying on my phone calls?"

Albright shook her head. "We aren't spying, Sharon. We are

investigating your husband's murder. Please tell us more about Michael and your friendship."

She sighed. "I told you. We're just friends. OK, none of my friends around here know about him. Even Adam didn't know."

Roxanne glanced at Gordie and back at Sharon, who was biting her bottom lip. "Go on."

"He's gay, and that's the reason I didn't tell anyone about him." She put up her hands in a gesture of helplessness. "I didn't tell anybody because he hasn't come out and it's not my secret to tell. I didn't want to tell anyone anyway because so many people around here are judgemental. It was easier not to say anything. I wasn't about to say I had a friend called Michael and then not say he was gay because then people would think just what you thought. That there was something between us."

"I see. We'll leave it there for the moment and move on."

Albright pulled out a photo taken from the video in the caravan parking lot. "Do you know this man, Sharon?"

Sharon picked it up and studied it. "No. I don't know him. Is he the man who killed my Adam?"

"We don't know. Right now, he's just a person we want to talk to. You can see in this second photo that the man is handing Adam something that looks to us like money."

"Yes. That looks like the roll of money I found in his shaving bag."

"You can understand why it's so important to us we track this man down. Where would you suggest we look?"

"I have no idea. Adam never talked about anyone he knew with a bike. I gave you the names of his friends. Maybe they know?"

"No, they didn't know."

"Well, I don't know either."

"Did you ever hear Kyle or Dab Haan talk about a biker?"

"No. But I spent little time with the three of them. Especially Dab. I wasn't his biggest fan."

"You spent time with the family, though. Did it seem like Adam and Kyle were secretive or evasive?"

"Not that I noticed. When we were together, we typically had a meal together over at Dannymac's house and the talk was mostly about fishing or hockey or whatever. I never noticed them going off together, just the two of them unless it was to bring in a couple of armloads of firewood. I guess they could have had private conversations then, but it never felt like they were up to anything. If they were going to have secret discussions, it would have been on the boat. Not near me and Izzie or their father."

Roxanne nodded. "Sharon, why did Adam go to Pleasant Bay? What's there?"

She shook her head. "I told you from the beginning that I don't know. There's no reason. It's not his assigned fishing area." She reddened with emotion. "And before you suggest it, he wasn't poaching anyone else's catch. He just wouldn't."

Gordie picked up. "We believe you, Sharon. He didn't have a catch on board when we found his boat and if he had been poaching previously, he would have had to find a buyer and we don't find any evidence of him selling lobster on the side anywhere."

Sharon folded her arms. "Right. He wouldn't steal from his fellow fishermen. I knew that much anyway."

Gordie shook his head. "All right. I think we'll leave it at that. Sharon, if we find that the money you found was a result of illegal activities, you won't be able to keep it."

"But I've already used it."

"Yes, we know. You may need to pay it back from the life insurance."

She sighed. "I'll face that if it happens. Can I go home now?"

Gordie stood. "Yes, Detective Albright will see you out. I need you to think hard about what Adam may have been up to. Think back on conversations you had, or things he may have done that seemed off to you."

***

Roxanne rolled her chair over to Gordie's desk. "Well? What did you think?"

"I believed her. She found the money and used it. She obviously knew it came from illegal activity, but she wasn't looking a gift horse in the mouth. And about the mysterious Michael? I believe her there too, but let's confirm that one. Call St. Mary's. Find out what he was up to at the time. The phone records show a cell number so he could have been anywhere, including Pleasant Bay. Just because they weren't sleeping together doesn't mean he wouldn't do her a favour. Of course, we only have her word that he's gay. You'll need to check that somehow. You'll be better at that than me."

She smiled. "You mean asking some guy about his sex life? Why do you figure I'll be good at that?"

"Because you're a professional."

She shook her head. "So, you're eliminating her?"

"I can't see her going out to the boat way up in Pleasant Bay to kill him. And even if she hired or ask Michael to do it, what's the motivation? If she knew about the money and wanted to get her hands on it, she would have just taken it. Why have him killed?" He shook his head. "It just doesn't add up to me, so yes. I think we eliminate her unless something comes up to change my mind."

"I'll write it up. Do we charge her with anything for using the money?"

"Let's leave it for now. I want to focus on the murder. Tomorrow I'm going up to Inverness. I had a call from Joe Hennessy. He and Doucette are meeting with the Mountie forensics' team tomorrow to talk ballistics. They know from Rob Norris about the biker, and it sounds like our colleagues in red serge might be able to connect some dots for us. Norris is going around the area of Canadian Tire with the photo of biker guy. Check in with him to see how that's going."

"Right. I'll update the board as well."

"Did you ever hear back from Jeffreys?"

"No. I'll give him another call."

"What a guy. He wants to be in the middle of things, but he can't be bothered returning a call. Let me know if you hear from him. If not, I may ask about him tomorrow when I'm in Inverness. He may have nothing useful to tell us about Pleasant Bay, but the courtesy of a call would be nice."

"Not to worry. I'll chase him down."

"All right. We've got a lot of moving parts here, and with every day that goes by, I feel it slipping away." He looked up at Roxanne. "I'll go brief Sarge with the current state of things. He decided the drive up to Inverness wasn't worth his time after all, but I don't want to give him anything to gripe about. We need to make sure we're covering every angle here."

"Gotcha."

As she leaned down to roll her chair back to her own desk, she looked over at him. "How's the no smoking going?"

He sighed. "Still hanging in there. But it's tough. Can't sleep. One minute I'm starving, next the idea of food makes me queasy. Fresh air is about the only thing that helps."

"Good for you for sticking to it. Don't lose your cool with Sarge. Deep breaths."

"Ya, ya. Go on. Don't stand here nattering at me."

***

On the drive home much later, Gordie felt keyed up. He had waited until Rob Norris got back into the office but was disappointed to discover that the afternoon had been a bust. No remaining CCTV from the area and no one in the stores that backed on to the parking lot recognized or even remembered seeing the man on the motorbike. On the other hand, Rob expected the results from the technical team in the morning from their work to enhance the video, hoping to make out the license plate.

They would have his identity soon. If they could then show that

Adam and he had been having regular phone calls together, it would be a genuine breakthrough.

We're coming for you, buddy.

CHAPTER 28

EVERY CELL IN GORDIE MacLean's body cried out for nicotine. If he had a pack of cigarettes in the house, he knew he would have given in. Roxanne had suggested nicotine gum or a patch, but he didn't believe in that. *If I'm giving up nicotine, I'm giving it up. I'm in control of this. I can do it.*

He had a long, hot shower and made himself a breakfast of eggs and sausages. It took time to prepare it, but it helped take his mind off his craving.

Gordie shared the sausages with Taz. "No beach walk this morning, my girl. A sausage will have to do you."

He made himself a coffee in his travel mug and headed out to drive to Inverness, a trip of about an hour and forty minutes, longer than even his usual commute to the station. Gordie tuned his satellite radio to a country station and settled back to enjoy the drive. He never smoked in his car anyway, so this was easier than being at home. The route took him through Port Mulroy, which meant he went past Parish Lane, the turn to Vanessa's home. After doing the drive so many times over the past few months, he knew every bend in the road, every hill, and pothole. He knew it took forty-three minutes door to door. This was the first time he was going past since they broke up. He toyed with that notion in his mind. *Do adults in their fifties actually break up? It sounds so juvenile. Maybe we just parted ways?* He had hoped she would call, but it didn't seem like that was going to happen. There was no point in calling her. *I don't even know what I did wrong. I want to look after her.* His pulse quickened, and he gritted his teeth. *Maybe she'd prefer someone like Dad who only ever looked after himself. And expected everyone else to look after him too or take a black eye and worse.* He shook his head to rid himself of the image of his mother wearing too much makeup and long sleeves in an effort to hide the bruises.

As he drove past Parish Lane half an hour later, Vanessa was still on his mind. *I guess I better give her back her key. I left that night and never even thought of it. When I'm coming back later, I'll stop for a moment.*

***

As Gordie MacLean thought about Vanessa during his drive to the RCMP station in Inverness, Vanessa Hunt was also thinking about him. She sat at the kitchen table with a note in her shaking hand.

When she went out early in the morning carrying a cup of tea to admire her blooming tulips and grape hyacinths, she noticed the flag on her mailbox at the end of the driveway was up, indicating that she had mail.

That's strange. The mail doesn't come until around ten. Must be a flyer. She strolled down the drive and pulled out the envelope, which was blank on the front. She carried it back to the house, and stopped en route to study her lilac bush, which wasn't blooming as she'd like. *I must check the acidity of the soil.*

She came inside, refilled her mug, and then sat down at the kitchen table to open the envelope. The note was created with cut-out letters from the newspaper. Just the sight of it shook her.

Tell your boyfriend to stop looking for the biker or hell be sorry

The fact that there was no apostrophe somehow made the note even more frightening. Her first instinct was to call Gordie, but then she took a deep breath. *I told him I didn't need him to look after me. If I call him now, I'll just prove that he was right all along.*

Vanessa made up her mind. She found her purse and dug out the card of the Mountie who had been the first on the scene when she found Dab Haan. Constable Jeffreys. He was very nice to her that day and even though she may have been a little short with him when he showed up at her home, that was more because she didn't understand why she needed to go through the whole thing again. It was nothing against him. Only Taz seemed to take against him. He was quite polite to her.

When his voicemail kicked in, she left a message. "Constable Jeffreys, this is Vanessa Hunt. I received a disturbing note left in my mailbox overnight. I hope you can come and see me about it. Please call me at 902-626-9918."

She stared at the note and bit her lip. *It's a threat to Gordie. He has a right to know.* She sighed. *I'll leave it to the professionals. Maybe it's best if he doesn't know.*

Setting down the note on the table, she went into the living room to stoke up the fire in the wood stove. Straightening, she stopped and listened, thinking for a moment that she heard a motorcycle, but then shook her head, knowing it was her imagination. After she had loaded a couple of logs into the stove, she went and locked the mudroom door, though.

Vanessa tried to read but found herself reaching the bottom of the page with no memory of what she had just read. She closed the book and simply listened to the classical music on the radio as she stared at the flames in her stove.

Her mind went back to the past few days without Gordie. She had been furious with him. He didn't even seem to understand that his desire to look after her just felt like control. Vanessa had spent thirty years enjoying an independent life. She had enjoyed several relationships over the years, but for one reason or another, none had stuck. For the ten years before retiring and moving from Ontario to Nova Scotia, she had been the primary caregiver for her mom and with work and her mother, there hadn't been a lot of time for a relationship. When she had free time, she was just glad to be on her own, pursuing her quiet hobbies. Books, sewing, cooking. Lunch with a girlfriend or a night at the theatre with a group of friends. These things had been enough. Over the past few months, though, she had to admit she'd enjoyed Gordie's company. He made her laugh with his dry sense of humour. She admired how he loved his mother and sister. Vanessa knew a bit about the hard childhood he had gone through. She understood why he wanted to protect her, but she just wasn't prepared to accept the restrictions that put on her.

Vanessa jumped when the phone rang, startling her out of her reverie. "Hello?"

"This is Constable Jeffreys returning your call."

To her shame, Vanessa's voice choked with tears. "I received a threatening note this morning. It was in my mailbox and obviously hand-delivered because there was no address or stamp on it."

His voice was warm with concern. "I'm not far away. I'll come and see for myself if that's all right with you?"

"Oh, please do."

"I'll be there in fifteen minutes. Meanwhile, lock the doors and windows. You have your dog for protection, I assume."

She knew her voice was shaky. "No, the dog belongs to a friend and has gone home."

"OK. I'll be there soon. Try not to worry."

Vanessa went into the kitchen and put the kettle on again. The note blazed its message up at her and she turned and hastened down the hall to the powder room to splash water on her face. The knowledge that the police were on their way made the threat somehow more real. This frightened her more than when she had discovered a human skeleton in her garden the previous year. *Maybe this house is bad luck for me.*

The kettle had boiled, and she had made a fresh pot of tea when she saw Constable Jeffreys drive up. She unlocked the door and welcomed him inside.

***

MacLean met Hennessey and Doucette at a coffee shop in Inverness at 9:45, and from there they went on together to the RCMP headquarters.

Sergeant Benoit came out to the lobby to meet them. She nodded to each of them. "Gordie. Good to see you again."

"And you, Ada. You've met Gabriel Doucette and Joe Hennessey already, I believe?"

"Of course. Gabe, Joe, how are you this morning?"

Doucette nodded. "Keen to hear what you have for us."

"Let's go see, then. Anyone want to stop for a coffee on the way?" She had removed her mask and waved it towards the canteen.

Gordie answered for all of them. "We've just come from Robin's Donuts, so we're good." Following her lead, they removed their masks as well, stuffing them into their pockets.

Sergeant Benoit led them through the rear door as before and they went to the lab. When they entered the large room, Dr. Mike Ingram waved them over to the table where he had bullets, a gun and several 8 by 10 photos laid out.

Gordie nodded. "Dr. Ingram. Thank you for having us all here for this show and tell this morning."

Ingram nodded. "A pleasure."

Benoit smiled. "Mike likes nothing better than a show and tell."

Benoit stepped aside to let the three detectives get a better view of what Ingram was displaying.

Ingram started by holding up a gun. "You probably recognize that this is a Beretta 81FS. Some people call it a Cheetah. This size isn't hugely popular anymore with your average criminal, but you'll still find lots of them around. They're small and easy to conceal."

MacLean took the gun from Ingram and hefted it. "Pretty light." He looked up. "Are you telling us that this is the gun that killed Haan?"

"It's the *type* of gun. We don't have the actual murder weapon, but we know it's this type."

Doucette was excited. "You matched the bullet to one in the system?"

Mike Ingram held up his hand. "Slow down. Let's go through this so you thoroughly understand what we have and what we don't."

Behind Ingram, Sergeant Benoit smiled, and MacLean understood nothing was going to rush her forensics investigator.

Doucette nodded, reining in his eagerness for an answer.

"The bullet recovered from the victim was in surprisingly good condition. Based on what we were able to see and extrapolation, we could determine from the lands and grooves, and its right-hand twist that it most likely came from a Beretta 81 series. Perhaps not this exact model, but something very much like it."

MacLean realized he was still holding the gun and set it down, and Doucette immediately picked it up to study it.

Now it was Hennessey who tried to hurry the investigator on. "So that's all we know?"

Ingram placed two of the 8 by 10 photos side by side. They each showed enlargements of bullets. The first had a compressed head, nevertheless, distinctive rifling marks were visible. The second showed an intact bullet with clear rifling marks. Ingram took out a penlight from his white coat pocket and turned on a laser pointer, which he used to draw a box around one section, first on one photo and then on the other. "See here? These appear to be a match. The intact bullet is from a crime scene in Florida. The bullet is nicely preserved because it apparently went wild and landed in a sofa. Other bullets from the same scene were not in the same condition."

Hennessey frowned. "Is that really a match? It's pretty hard to see from these photos."

"Yes, the photos aren't as clear as seeing it on a computer screen, but yes, it's a high probability that it's a match."

Ingram gathered the two photos up and set them aside, pulling two others from a file folder and laying them down in their place. The two new photos were of cartridge cases. "As you probably know, just like a bullet is marked going through a barrel, so is the cartridge. The nice thing is that, even in this day and age of C.S.I., a lot of shooters don't seem to realize that the casings can tell us a lot. Not only can we compare the rifling grooves and lands, but often the firing pin impressions reveal tiny distortions, meaning that we may be able to match it to a specific weapon."

MacLean folded his arms. "OK. We know a Beretta killed Haan. We know the weapon came from Florida. Did you find anything like fingerprints anywhere that will give us the *who* is behind the weapon?"

Dr. Ingram gathered up the photos and put them back into the file folder. "One smudged print on the cartridge case recovered from the scene. Nothing that we have a match for in our system."

Gordie exhaled. "Damn. Sorry, Mike. I mean, this is all very interesting, but it doesn't actually get us to the killer, does it?"

Benoit stepped in. "What it gets us is evidence of weapons trafficking. How did a crime gun used in Florida get here to Cape Breton? We already suspected that MacDonald may be involved in something like that, but this gives us further evidence to support that theory."

MacLean nodded. "Fair enough. But do we truly believe that Dab Haan was involved in that?" He turned to Hennessey and Doucette. "Have you discovered anything that might lead us to think that?"

Doucette shook his head. "No. We're hearing the same as what you heard. A guy who drank too much but was a good fisherman and odd jobs man if he was sober."

Hennessey waved his hand at the gun now lying on the table again. "We've been tracking his movements for the last few days of his life and his behaviour was definitely off. He had more drink available somehow, so we figure someone gave him money. He was also going around talking up a storm to people with vague comments of coming into money soon. We're tracing back to when those comments began but have nothing definitive yet."

MacLean's phone rang, and he pulled it out to glance at the caller I.D. "Excuse me a moment. I need to take this."

Gordie stepped away to take the call from Rob Norris. "Hi, Rob. What's up?"

"We've identified the bike."

Gordie's heart beat faster. "Fantastic. Someone local? Who is it?"

"It's a New Brunswick plate, registered to a Ryan Jeffreys. His last known address was in a little place called Pointe des Robichaud."

"Never heard of it."

"It's on the coast up in the north end of New Brunswick."

"OK, did you check with local police there?"

"The closest force is Bathurst, and that's pretty far from Robichaud. They don't have any files on him."

"You want me to get these folks to check with their counterparts in New Brunswick?"

"That's what I'm hoping. I figure you must be great buddies with them there these days so you can sweet-talk them into doing some hunting around rather than going through the formal channels."

"OK. Will do." Just before he hung up, something occurred to Gordie. "Hey, Rob?"

"Yeah?"

"Jeffreys. I knew that name rang a bell when you said it. This guy's not related to my Mountie buddy, is he?"

Norris was silent for an instant. "You're getting paranoid in your old age, MacLean. It's a pretty common name."

"I'm sure you're right. I just hate coincidences."

"If you want to get your pals there to ferret that information out, go ahead and ask them, but I'm not going to call him up to ask.

I don't suppose that would go over real well. *Hey Mountie, are you related to this felon we've been hunting for?"*

"No, you're right. OK, I'll let you know if they come up with anything on this guy. Like a local address maybe."

Norris chuckled. "Good luck with that."

MacLean put the phone back and rejoined the others, who were waiting to return to the main building.

Benoit ushered the three detectives back into the main building. "Coffee, anyone?"

MacLean smiled. "I've had the coffee so may opt for tea, but sure, let's sit down for a minute and regroup."

The canteen was almost empty, and they each helped themselves to hot drinks and then took a large table. MacLean briefed them on the call with Norris.

Ada Benoit took out her notebook. "This is good. I'll get one of my guys on this to see what we can find out about him."

"You don't need me to fill in any paperwork to ask formally for support?"

"No, of course not. This is a joint investigation. Especially now that we are even more confident that it involves weapons trafficking. That's our bailiwick."

"Great, thanks."

They finished their drinks over a general discussion about gun smuggling, and while rare in Nova Scotia, not unheard of.

They made their way to the exit and then MacLean told Doucette and Hennessey to go ahead to the car. "I'll be out in a minute."

Benoit raised her eyebrows when he turned back to her.

"Ada, this is going to sound strange, and as Norris already said to me, paranoid, but could you assign someone other than Constable Jeffreys to do the inquiry about our man?"

"Just because their names are the same?"

"Not just that. If I was connected to every MacLean in the province, no doubt I'd be in trouble."

She smiled. "What, then?"

"Call it a gut feeling. It may be nothing more than we got off on the wrong foot, but there have been a couple of things that just don't sit well with me."

Now she frowned. "If there's something I should know about one of our members, you need to tell me."

"That's just it. It's nothing definitive. But, as an example, when Jeffreys briefed me at the scene of Haan's murder, he neglected to say that the witness mentioned seeing a motorbike coming from the direction of Haan's cabin. He had done the initial interview, and I specifically asked him if the witness had seen anyone in the area."

Benoit frowned. "You believe he intentionally left it out?"

"I can't say that. When I took the witness statement later that evening and probed thoroughly to be sure I got the full picture of what she had seen and she mentioned the bike, I asked her if she had told Jeffreys about the sighting."

"And?"

"And she didn't recall. But she mentioned it to me, so I think she mentioned it in her initial statement as well and he didn't note it. Maybe she was too vague. Maybe he didn't think it was relevant. I don't know."

Benoit nodded. "To be honest, I wouldn't have put him on it anyway because he does community policing. Investigating is not his job."

"I figured that, but I didn't want to take a chance."

She sighed. "I'm not happy about even the hint of something off. Keep me informed, please. In the meantime, I'm giving him the benefit of a doubt and won't challenge him. As far as I can see, there's nothing to challenge him about."

"Fair enough. Thank you."

Gordie left and joined the two detectives to catch a ride back to where his own vehicle was parked. When he got in the car, he breathed in the telltale smell of smoke on clothing. "You still smoking, Hennessey?"

"Sure. Sorry, did you want one?"

"God yes, but I won't, thanks."

Joe Hennessey turned in the front passenger seat to look back at MacLean. "Quitting?"

"Trying."

"You're a better man than me. I've tried a couple times. The wife's always at me, but even she seems glad when I quit the quitting. I'm like a bear with a sore paw when I'm quitting."

MacLean sighed. "I know what you mean, but I've gone this long. Seems a shame to pack it in now."

"How long?"

"Four days."

Gabe Doucette glanced in the rear-view mirror. "I haven't noticed you roaring at anyone. You must be doing OK."

"So far, so good, but that doesn't mean I haven't wanted to roar at anyone."

Gordie got out of the car and tapped on the roof of Doucette's car. "Thanks, guys. Catch you later."

Gordie looked at his watch. *Two o'clock. No wonder I'm starving. I'll have lunch here and then head back. Drop off the key with Vanessa and then home to connect with Sarge and Roxanne and then write up reports and plan next steps.*

CHAPTER 29

I T WAS CLOSE TO 3:30 by the time Gordie turned into Parish Lane. He waited to make the turn into Vanessa's driveway to allow her closest neighbour, Charlie Sanders, walk past. The tall, strapping man in his late seventies was brisk and fit. *He's in better shape than I am.* Charlie carried a plastic bag and stopped at the side of the driveway to let Gordie make his turn. Gordie rolled down the window to say hello.

"Hiya, Charlie. You're looking well. Enjoying an afternoon walk?"

"I came to bring Vanessa a piece of fish, but she's not home."

Gordie glanced up the drive to where Vanessa's car was parked. "Not home?"

"Nope. I saw her leave earlier, but thought she'd be back by now."

Gordie smiled. "Her car's here. She must be home. Maybe she didn't hear you knock."

"She's not home. A cop took her away this morning."

Gordie put his car in park. "A cop? What do mean?"

"RCMP car."

"OK, thank you, Charlie. I'll go up to the house. Maybe she left a note." Gordie would not give the neighbours more to talk about. He understood why Charlie was there with the offering of fish. He had hoped to get the story on why Vanessa left in a police car.

Gordie stretched out his hand. "How about I take the fish and put it in the fridge? Save you from carrying it back home again. I'll be sure to let her know you came by with it."

Charlie hesitated only for an instant and then handed over the bag. "OK, thanks. Hope everything's OK."

"I'm sure it's nothing to worry about."

Gordie put the bag on the passenger seat and the car back into drive. "Thanks, Charlie. Take care."

Gordie parked and went to the mudroom door. He knocked just in case Charlie had been wrong. Maybe Vanessa was just trying to avoid her neighbour for some reason. Even as he thought it, he dismissed it. *She's not like that.*

The door wasn't locked, but he would have gone in even if it meant using his key. The house welcomed him with its familiar scent of cooking aromas blended with woodstove smoke. His stomach clenched with the memory of this happy place. He pushed it aside and went in through the mudroom to stand at the entry to the living room. He felt its vacancy, but still he called out. "Vanessa? Are you here?"

In the silence of the house, he punched in her phone number and listened to the voicemail message inviting callers to leave a message. "Vanessa, it's Gordie. I'm at your place to drop off your keys, but your neighbour Charlie has me a little worried. He told me you were taken away in an RCMP car. Give me a call, please. I know you'll find this annoying but humour me. Please."

He stared at the phone, willing her to call him, but finally put it back in his pocket and walked to the kitchen. On the table, he saw the note she had received.

Dear God!

Gordie left the note where it was, not touching it without gloves.

He hurried back out to his car to make phone calls, beginning with Sergeant Benoit.

"Ada, it's Gordie." Wasting no time, he summarized what he had been told by the neighbour and described the note he had seen. He finished with his question. "Do you know where Constable Jeffreys is right now?"

"OK, slow down, Gordie. Vanessa Hunt is the witness from the Haan case, right?"

"Yes, and she's also a good friend of mine."

"Ah, yes. OK, that answers the question of why you were in her house. Is there a conflict of interest here, Gordie? Maybe you're overreacting?"

He clenched his teeth. "It's possible, but I think I have a legitimate concern. There's a note here threatening harm to me, and now Vanessa is missing. It's unlikely that she would have gone with any other member of your team, so please, can you just check where he is?"

"All right. Let me call you back."

He hung up and called Roxanne Albright to give her the same summary. "Did you ever get a hold of that guy? Maybe you know where he is?"

"I heard from him, and we made an appointment to meet up, but not until tomorrow. He wasn't available today. He said he had a commitment. Do you want me to come down there, Gordie?"

"No. Leave it for the minute. You're in the office, right?"

"Yes. But I can leave now."

"No, I'll give Doucette and Hennessey a call if need be. They should still be in the area. Meanwhile, I'll bag the note because no matter what, someone's made a threat and I want to know who."

"OK. Shall I go down and update Sarge?"

"Yeah, that would be great, thanks. And can you get Norris to give me a call? I want to see if he found anything out about a connection between Constable Jeffreys and Biker Jeffreys."

Gordie opened the back of the car and pulled a pair of latex gloves out of the box in his crime scene kit. He put the gloves on and took out two plastic evidence bags and went back into the house. After taking photos of the note and the envelope as they sat on the kitchen table, he carefully picked up the note by one corner and placed it into a bag. He repeated the process with the envelope. When the bags were sealed, he took out his black pen and marked them with his initials, the date, and the location of collection.

He was on his way back out to the car when his phone rang. "Rob. Thanks for calling. Roxanne told you?"

"Yes. There's nothing official here, but you may be right about a connection."

Gordie sucked in his breath. "I knew it. What did you find out?"

"OK, this is pretty primitive, and might be a different family completely, but I googled the name and found an obit for a man named Jeffreys out of Halifax. His fist name was Ryan as well, and he left behind a bunch of kids, including a son called Ryan. The deceased left behind a pack of siblings, including a brother called Gerard, along with several nieces and nephews, who aren't named."

"Gerard Jeffreys. Constable Gerry Jeffreys. Gotta be the same. They're cousins."

"It's not a sure thing, but it looks that way."

"Great work, Rob. Thanks. I'm waiting to hear back from Sergeant Benoit. They're tracking down the constable now. This makes the case."

He struck the steering wheel with the flat of his hand. *Come on, come on.* As if conjured by his energy, Ada Benoit phoned. "Ada? Did you locate him?"

Her voice was cool. "Yes, we did. He was patrolling not far from the station, checking into a complaint of kids kicking over garbage cans. He's on his way in right now."

MacLean chewed his lip for a moment. "Did you ask him about Vanessa Hunt?"

"Yes, Gordie, of course. He explained that *she* called *him* and yes, he saw the note and while he doesn't believe it means much of anything, he made a note of it and planned to write it up along with his other reports at shift end.",

Gordie frowned. "But he took her away."

"He took her back to the scene so she could show him where she feels she saw the motorbike. He wanted to see for himself if it was reasonable for her to have the kind of details she seems to remember based on the way the road bends and hills and whatnot." Benoit's voice was crisp. "It was a reasonable thing to do, Detective."

"And when they finished, what then? Did he bring her home?" Gordie had a sudden sickening image of Vanessa lying upstairs having a nap.

"No, she contacted a friend and since she was so close by in Port Hood, she asked Constable Jeffreys to drop her off there. Someone called Lynn Duggan."

"Jesus. OK. Thank you for tracking him down. Just one last thing, Sergeant." Gordie was very aware that they had reverted to Sergeant and Detective.

"Go on."

"There is some evidence to suggest that Ryan Jeffreys and Constable Jeffreys are cousins."

There was silence from Benoit. Then she answered crisply. "Thank you. We'll follow up on that, but even if that's the case, people aren't responsible for everything their family members get up to."

An image of Gordie's father flashed through his mind. "True."

Gordie hung up the phone and sighed. *Now what?* He had a sick feeling that Vanessa was going to be furious.

He called Roxanne and gave her the highlights. "Can you call Lynn Duggan, Roxanne? You know her. Just find out if it's all true and Vanessa is safe and sound."

"Chicken."

"I know. You got that right."

"All right. Stand by. I'll call you back as soon as I get a hold of her."

Gordie realized he hadn't put the fish in the fridge. *I'll put away the fish and leave my keys as I planned. It gives me a legit reason for being in the house in the first place.*

He went in, picked up the plastic bag of fish from the mudroom bench where he had left it, and put it on a plate and into the fridge. He took out the key to Vanessa's house and set it on the kitchen table, feeling a finality in the simple act as if turning the lock on another phase of his life.

Roxanne called when he was back in the car. "All is well. Vanessa has been there all afternoon and they are just about to leave for Lynn to drive Vanessa home."

"Did you talk to Vanessa?"

"No, but according to Lynn, Vanessa's phone died, and her charger doesn't fit Vanessa's phone."

"I better get out of here."

"Probably."

"Thanks, Roxanne. I'll call you later."

***

He was out walking with Taz when Vanessa called. He considered letting it go to voicemail but inhaled a deep breath of evening spring air, grit his teeth, and answered. "Hi, Vanessa."

"Hi, Gordie. Are you OK to talk for a minute?"

"Yeah. No problem. Taz and I are just out for a walk."

"On the beach?"

"No, just along the side of the road." He hesitated and then launched into his apology just as Vanessa started to speak. "Vanessa, I'm sorry…"

"Gordie, I'm sorry…"

They laughed, and he started again. "Let me."

"OK, go ahead."

"Look, I guess I did exactly what you have been complaining

about. I jumped to a conclusion and thought the worst. You obviously were fine and, like you've been telling me, quite able to look after yourself. I didn't mean for any of that to happen. I was just going to drop off the key. But then, when Charlie told me you'd been taken away in an RCMP car, I got worried, and from there... well, once I saw that note, there was no stopping."

"Gordie, it's all right. I understand, and honestly, I considered calling you first when I got that note this morning. I just...I guess I can be a bit stubborn."

He chuckled. "Do you think so?"

There was a smile in her voice. "Maybe just a little. It wasn't until I finally got my phone charged up enough to listen to your message that I heard the part about Charlie. I admit I was a bit conflicted until then and wondered how and why you were chasing me down at Lynn's place, but everything was clear once I heard your message. Charlie got you wound up, and then when you saw the note, you panicked."

"That pretty much sums it up. Can you forgive me?"

"There's nothing to forgive. If it was me in that circumstance, I'd have worried too."

Gordie watched Taz fling herself at a hole, digging frantically where a small animal once had a burrow, knowing that the squirrel or rabbit was nowhere near there now. "I'm a bit like Taz. I go with my gut and maybe that's not always the answer."

She hesitated and then surprised Gordie. "I'm not sure you were wrong, Gordie. About Constable Jeffreys, I mean."

He stopped walking. "Why do you say that?"

"It was obvious to me that when he drove along the road to Dab's cabin, he was doing his best to convince me that there was no way I could have seen that biker clearly. He kept pointing out reasons why I couldn't have seen anything; like the road had a slight bend and the sun must have been in my eyes. Things like that. It got to the point where I just agreed with him that I wasn't that sure about what I had seen. Gordie, he made me feel pretty uncomfortable." He heard her take a deep breath. "That's why I was at Lynn's place. I suddenly just didn't want to spend another minute alone with him, and I called Lynn and told her I was in the area and would love to drop by. She told me later that she heard in my voice that I was upset so she didn't ask any questions, but right away said, of course. *Come over.*" While she was on the phone, I said to Constable Jeffreys, 'you don't mind dropping me at Lynn Duggan's house, do you? It will save you the drive back to Port Mulroy.' He had little choice then, didn't he? He went straight over and dropped me there."

Gordie made the 'come' hand signal to Taz and turned to walk back to the house. "You handled that so well." Just then, his phone beeped to indicate another call was coming in. He glanced at the screen. "Vanessa, I have another call coming in. I'm glad everything worked out. I have to go."

"Bye, then." She disengaged to let him take his incoming call, but Gordie thought she sounded disappointed at the abrupt end to their conversation.

"MacLean."

Sergeant Ada Benoit's voice was serious. "Gordie, you better come in. Constable Jeffreys has some information to share."

"All right. I'm on my way. Have you already contacted Doucette and Hennessey?"

"No. You get whomever you need, but I'm beginning the interview in an hour."

Gordie called Doucette. "Gabe, where are you and Hennessey?"

"Hennessey's on his way home. I'm still in Port Hood, just finishing with an interview. Why?"

"Get back to Inverness. Jeffreys has something to say, and Sergeant Benoit will start the interview in an hour. I'm on my way and will be there in an hour and a half."

CHAPTER 30

H E MADE THE 120 km drive back to Inverness in record time. He had stopped long enough to feed Taz before heading off again.

He called Roxanne and his sergeant on the way and listened to his partner curse at missing what might be the break in the case. "Sorry, Roxanne. There's no point in you coming all the way from Big Pond at this stage. I promise I'll call you later."

He signed in at reception and a constable took Gordie to the viewing room to watch the interview in progress. Gabe Doucette rolled the chair he was crouched on, over to allow Gordie space to watch and listen. He saw Sergeant Ada Benoit and a corporal sitting on one side of a table and Constable Jeffreys across from the sergeant.

"Bring me up to speed. What's he said?"

"He admits Ryan Jeffreys is his cousin. He admits that he knew we were looking for him and that he was doing his best to muddy the waters to throw us off the trail."

"Did he say that Ryan did it? Did he kill MacDonald and Haan?"

Doucette shook his head. "He hasn't said that or even hinted at it."

Gordie frowned and listened as Sergeant Benoit asked questions to the constable, who was slumped down in his chair. Gone was the crisp, upright, somewhat arrogant bearing that had marked Constable Jeffreys before now.

Benoit looked up from the notes she had been making. "Constable, you haven't explained why you didn't want the Cape Breton Police Services to talk to your cousin. You knew very well that they were searching for him, and yet you didn't convince your cousin to come forward. Why not?"

His answer was mumbled. "He's simple. He doesn't always understand what he's doing."

"In relation to what?"

"In relation to everything. People use him. Manipulate him and then he gets into trouble without meaning to."

Her voice was neutral. "Come on, Gerry. People use him? What does that mean? You came in today and said that you had something to discuss. You said it was connected to gun smuggling. We've been here for more than half an hour and you still haven't said a word about that."

He straightened up. "All right. Ryan's been staying with me for a few months now. Before that, he was living in New Brunswick. When he was in New Brunswick, he met up with some gang members in a bar. I knew, without ever meeting those guys, that they were playing with him, but he thought they accepted him. Not as part of the actual gang, but as some sort of, I'll call it an associate member. He started dressing in the black leather jacket and he traded in his Honda for a Harley. He had a job working at a burger place and I think he gave away as much food to his buddies as he sold until they fired him." Jeffreys looked up at Benoit. "That's what I mean. People use him."

She nodded. "Go on."

"He went and hung out with these guys, and I guess one day someone was foolish enough to talk in front of Ryan about gun smuggling. The conversation was about how things had dried up since Covid and the borders were closed. This was one of their sources of revenue, and they were missing the money. Ryan throws out an idea and guess what? They actually thought it might work. The idea was crazy, but we live in crazy times. The conversation had been about someone bringing in guns by boat from Bar Harbour and taking them to Halifax, but they were worried because as a main border with the U.S., there were bound to be sniffer dogs and restrictions. So, Ryan says 'how about getting the boat to meet a fisherman who will take it through the Canso Straight and then hand it off to someone on the Magdalen Islands?'."

Jeffreys shook his head. "He's repeated the story to me so many times by now, I feel like I was there."

Benoit made a note. "And they recruited Adam MacDonald."

He sighed. "Eventually." Jeffreys chewed his upper lip before he continued. "First, they recruited me."

Ada Benoit blinked. "What happened?"

"Ryan called me and asked if he could stay with me. I've never been close to him, but he's my cousin. What could I say? So, Ryan showed up looking like some aging version of Easy Rider."

Doucette turned to MacLean in the viewing room. "I don't remember Peter Fonda wearing a ponytail."

MacLean smiled and shook his head before turning his attention back to the interview.

Jeffreys picked at a cuticle on his left forefinger. "The problem was that Ryan's not from here, and like I said, he's simple. He didn't have a clue how to find someone to go into this with him. Ryan was ready to just go down to the wharf and ask around. Of course, he'd have been picked up in an hour. They're ready to turn a blind eye to shady behaviour, but not actual criminal activity. Especially from a stranger. He'd either be picked up or beaten up."

"You talked him out of that and said you'd find someone?"

"Yeah. Ryan talked to one of the buddies back in New Brunswick, and before you ask me, I don't know their names. I know nothing about them. I told Ryan not to tell me. Anyway, he talked to someone and got the go-ahead and Ryan was authorized to offer me a finder's fee. I was to get two hundred dollars for every shipment that came through."

"That was the price of silence? Two hundred dollars?"

He nodded. "For each shipment."

"And how many shipments are we talking about at this point?"

"Ten."

"You've blown your career for the sake of two grand. Unbelievable."

Jeffreys closed his eyes for a moment. "It wasn't about the money. It was about taking care of Ryan."

"Sure. Okay, go on."

"I started looking around for someone who might be open to some extracurricular activity and I knew that Adam MacDonald sometimes took tourists out when it wasn't fishing season because he needed extra cash. I didn't know why, but it didn't matter. So, one morning when he was on his own tinkering with the engine, I went to him. We talked, and I asked if he felt like making some extra money, but it wasn't strictly legitimate."

"Legitimate? That's understating things."

Jeffreys took a drink of water. "We had spoken a few times, but never had a conversation, and I think he didn't know whether to trust me or not. He believed it was some kind of trap."

"But you were able to convince him."

"Yes. He told me he needed extra money because he and his wife hoped their daughter would get into some special school that would cost a lot." Jeffreys shrugged. "People will do just about anything for their kids, won't they? He wasn't that hard to convince."

"So, then you made the arrangements?"

"No. Then I introduced him to Ryan. Adam came over one day,

and I left the two of them to work it out. I told Ryan I had done my part, and I went out."

Benoit looked at her watch. "Do you need to take a break, Constable Jeffreys?"

"There's not much more to tell. Let's get on with it."

"All right. I now understand what was going on. MacDonald met up for the hand-off somewhere near Pleasant Bay?"

"Yes. That was part of my role, even though I argued at first, but Ryan made it clear to me that I was in now, and his colleagues wouldn't take kindly to me if I didn't carry on. I went and made sure there was nothing going on out of the ordinary in Pleasant Bay. No big fishing tournaments or sailing regattas or whatever. If it appeared safe, I called Ryan, and he did the rest."

"Did you stay to watch MacDonald meet up with his contact?"

"No. I made it very clear that I would not be a witness. I just checked out how busy it was and that was my part done."

"How did it go from being a background observer to murdering Adam MacDonald, Gerry?"

He widened his eyes and gaped at his sergeant. "What are you talking about? I didn't murder Adam MacDonald."

"Who did then? Ryan?"

"No. Not MacDonald."

In the viewing room, MacLean and Doucette looked at each other.

"Not MacDonald. Are you saying that your cousin, Ryan Jeffreys, murdered Dab Haan?"

He pursed his lips and nodded. "It was an accident."

"Were you there? Did you see it?"

"No. Absolutely not."

"Is your cousin still living at your house?"

"Yes."

"We're going to stop here and take a break."

Sergeant Benoit stood up as her corporal noted the time and stopped the recording.

MacLean and Doucette left the viewing room and met Sergeant Benoit in the corridor. They followed her to the room where her corporal was already standing with other RCMP staff, giving some highlights from the interview.

Benoit barked a few orders, assigning two teams to pick up Ryan Jeffreys. "Be careful. We know he's armed, and he's killed at least once already. Be prepared."

She turned to MacLean. "Do you want to go with the deployment or stay here?"

"Doucette will go along. I'll stay. I assume you plan to continue the interview?"

"Yes. All right." She waved to two of her team to catch their attention. She pointed to Doucette. "He's going with you." She nodded to Doucette. "Pick up a vest from the armourer and go along with Jenkins and Brady."

She walked over to a constable working at a computer. "Get some food ordered in. Don't care what it is. Sandwiches, pizza, whatever. Get some decent coffee in as well and get the kettle going. It's going to be a long night."

CHAPTER 31

SERGEANT BENOIT AND HER corporal returned to the interview room, taking a pizza in with them. The corporal had already asked what Jeffreys wanted to drink and had also taken him out of the interview room to use the facilities.

MacLean settled himself in the viewing room as they began again.

Benoit nodded, and the corporal started the recording. He spoke to record the date, time, and who was in the room.

Benoit took a sip of coffee and waited as Jeffreys took two slices of pizza and put them on a paper plate in front of him. "When we left off, you had just said that your cousin had accidentally killed Dab Haan. Please explain what you believe happened."

Jeffreys wiped his fingers on a napkin. "I was a bit worried because Ryan told me that the old guy that crews for MacDonald had seen him and Adam together. I stopped in and checked on Mac-Donald Senior one day and while I was there, I asked about that guy. Mr. MacDonald told me who he was, and that Haan mentioned he was going to start making big money, but that I should ignore him because he meant nothing by it. It seems that MacDonald Senior and Dab Haan were old friends, and he was concerned that I was going to investigate Haan. He wanted to keep him out of trouble. I made the mistake of telling Ryan about this, and without telling me about his intentions, he went to see Haan. Just to scare him." Jeffreys stopped talking and took another bite of pizza."

"Did you know your cousin was armed?"

He shook his head. "God, no. I would have taken it away from him if I knew he kept one of those guns."

"Ryan went to scare Mr. Haan. How did it escalate to murder?"

He sighed. "He tripped."

MacLean shook his head and spoke out loud. "Tripped?"

Benoit reacted the same way. "He tripped? And the gun went off?"

"That's what he told me. He didn't knock. He just stormed in, and I guess he was full of adrenalin and not paying attention. When he threw open the door and rushed inside, he tripped on the doorstep. He had taken the safety off and had his finger on the trigger. When he tripped, he squeezed, and it was just bad luck that Haan had gotten up from the table and was coming forward when the gun went off."

"Good God!"

"But that's Ryan all over. He isn't some clever mastermind criminal."

Benoit frowned. "You can downplay it as much as you like, but the fact is, he arranged for a gun smuggling operation and he killed a man."

"I know. God, don't I know? I'm not saying he's innocent."

"All right. That's what he told you happened with Haan. We'll be confirming all that with the forensics. Let's go back to Adam MacDonald."

Jeffreys shook his head as he finished the last of his pizza. "I told you already. I know nothing about that, and Ryan doesn't either."

"Maybe he just didn't tell you about that."

"He tells me everything. Look, he doesn't have a boat. I don't have a boat. If, for no other reason, that fact alone puts us in the clear."

"Why did you come forward today to come clean on all this, Gerry?"

Jeffreys stared up at the camera mounted in the corner of the room. "I knew that Detective MacLean was getting close to finding out about Ryan. And then when I saw the note this morning, I knew Ryan was getting panicky. That worried me."

She nodded at Jeffreys. "Tell me more about the note."

Jeffreys shrugged. "Ryan put a note in Vanessa Hunt's mailbox."

"The witness who found Haan."

"Yes. You know that she's MacLean's girlfriend, right?"

"Go on. What was in the note?"

"It was a stupid threat. *Tell your boyfriend to stop looking for the biker or he'll be sorry.* Something like that."

"What did he plan to do if MacLean didn't stop?"

"That's the thing. I just don't know, but I couldn't take a chance he might actually do something."

"Imagining you're telling the truth and that neither he nor you killed Adam MacDonald, why didn't he just leave?"

"Believe me, I kept trying to get him to go, but the whole COVID-19 thing has him off his head. He was worried he wouldn't be allowed back into New Brunswick, and he's terrified of catching it. He figured the safest thing was to stay put in my basement."

Benoit's phone buzzed with an incoming text. She read it and then gathered up her pad of paper, phone, and pen. "That will be all for tonight, Constable Jeffreys. You'll be taken to a cell, and we'll continue tomorrow."

The corporal stopped the recording and as Benoit left the room, she nodded to the two constables waiting in the hall, giving them the go-ahead to take their former colleague to a cell.

MacLean left the viewing room and joined Benoit in the main office area. "Have they got him?"

She nodded. "Bringing him in now. My corporal has put in a request for a fast-tracked search warrant, so we'll have that done first thing tomorrow." She looked up at the wall clock. "I think we'll take him straight down and get him booked in and leave the interview until tomorrow. How do you feel about that?"

Gordie nodded. "Sounds good. Are you able to keep them apart, so there's no chatting?"

"Oh, yeah. Don't worry, they won't be comparing notes during the night."

"Okay. I'll wait until they get here and then I'll talk to Doucette before heading out. I'll be back first thing tomorrow morning."

Ada Benoit nodded and then turned her attention to her team, giving instructions before going to her own office.

MacLean found a vacant chair and gave Roxanne a call. "You still awake?"

"Of course I am. I've worn my arm out throwing toys down the hallway for Sheba, as a way to keep myself from calling you. Give me the news."

MacLean gave her a summary of the interview with Constable Gerry Jeffreys.

Albright's voice was skeptical. "In other words, he's essentially done nothing wrong, other than take a few dollars bribe. Do you believe him?"

"Not on your life."

"When do we get to talk to him?"

"I want to focus my attention on Ryan. He's the weak link here. Tomorrow morning, I want you, as well as Doucette and Hennessey, to come up here. I'm putting in the paperwork tonight to have Ryan Jeffreys released into our custody, and we'll transport him to Sydney. They can keep their own guy here and do what they want with him as far as charges right now. When we have enough evidence, we'll charge him with Adam MacDonald's death."

"Okay. Eight o'clock at your place?"

"Make it 7:30. I want to get here early to talk to Benoit. I don't want a big discussion with everyone standing around listening."

"Right. I'll be there."

After disengaging from his call with Roxanne, he called Sergeant Arsenault. Despite the hour, his boss sounded as crisp as he did first thing in the morning. MacLean ran all they had discovered and breathed a sigh of relief when Arsenault agreed to MacLean's next steps. While his sergeant agreed to their working together, he wasn't about to relinquish a case that was so close to being solved.

MacLean had just hung up when Doucette came in looking for him. They had taken the prisoner straight down to the lock-up through a separate entrance into the building.

Doucette peeled off his bullet-proof vest and let it hang from his hand while he rolled his shoulders. "Well, that's done."

"How did it go? Any trouble?"

"Nah. The guy sees himself as a tough guy, but it didn't take long for him to cave when he saw the firepower surrounding him."

"Ready to head out?"

"Let me just return this thing and then I'll meet you at reception."

MacLean waited in the front foyer, craving a cigarette. When Doucette joined him, Gordie briefed him on the morning plan. "Benoit's going to spend some time interviewing Jeffreys, so you don't need to be here for that if you don't want to. Get some rest. As long as you're here when we are ready to take custody of him, that'll do. You'll get your chance to read the interview transcript and then, of course, we'll be talking to him in Sydney."

"OK. I'll let Hennessey know. We'll be here at eleven, but if you think it should be sooner, give me a call and we'll hustle."

"Sounds good."

MacLean went back to his car, exhausted, but still fired up after the events of the day. He had said his focus was on Ryan, but his target was Gerry. *You won't slide out of this so easily, buddy. I've got my sights on you.*

CHAPTER 32

TAZ LET LOOSE WITH a volley of barking at 7:15 when Roxanne Albright pulled into the driveway. Gordie opened the door to welcome his partner. He called back over his shoulder as she followed him to the kitchen. "Want a coffee or tea to take with you?"

"Do we have time?"

"Kettle's just boiled. Tea or instant coffee?"

"Tea, thanks."

Gordie got out a travel mug and tossed in a tea bag. He clicked the kettle on to bring it back to a boil.

Roxanne leaned down to rub Taz's head while the dog nudged against her. "She smells Sheba on me." Albright pulled gently on the dog's ears. "She sends her greetings to you too, Taz. One of these days, we'll get the two of you together again." Roxanne straightened when Gordie handed her the mug. "Get any sleep last night?"

"Not much. Between the quitting smoking and all of this, my mind just wouldn't stop."

"And what about Vanessa? Have you smoothed things out with her yet?"

He put his computer bag over his shoulder, gave Taz a biscuit, and waved Roxanne out the door. It wasn't until he climbed into the driver's seat and Roxanne had already fastened her seatbelt, did he finally answer. "I'm still working on the Vanessa, situation."

"Is she really pissed with you?"

He backed out of the drive and started on the familiar drive to Inverness. "It's hard to know. Every time I think I understand, I seem to get it wrong. I've decided to just leave things until after this case is done. Then I'll see where we stand."

They turned their attention to the case and Roxanne made Gordie go through the whole interview again as they drove.

He glanced over and saw that Albright tilted her head. "What's wrong?"

She turned to him. "You're still sure it was Gerry and/or Ryan that killed Adam MacDonald?"

He frowned. "Yes. You aren't?"

"I don't know. Why is Gerry so adamant about MacDonald when he's prepared to admit that his cousin killed Dab Haan?"

"He wants to keep himself well out of it, so he's giving up Ryan to deflect attention away from himself."

She nodded. "Maybe. By the way, I talked to the famous Michael yesterday. He's not our guy. It seems he's living with a partner now and is fine with people knowing he's gay. He was home with his other half who's called John, cooking dinner together and then watching a movie on Netflix on the evening of May 17th and never left the house. At eight-thirty on the morning of May 18, he gave a lecture on Zoom to his Business Administration 101 students, and just gave Sharon a quick call before that started to see if she'd heard yet about Izzie's acceptance to the Conservatory. I have John's details, but I haven't contacted him. I just don't see Michael being involved."

"I agree. He's off the list, but let's keep an open mind about the Jeffreys cousins until we've heard it all from Ryan. After that, we can see where it leads us."

"For sure." She turned up the radio. "I love this song." She started humming along to *Where Do You Go To My Lovely?*

***

They were signed in and given passes that allowed them the freedom to go through on their own. Gordie suggested Roxanne go to the canteen while he talked to Sergeant Benoit on his own. "You don't need to be in the middle of this if we have a debate."

"I don't mind going with you. Sure you don't want the backup?"

"Go on. I'll be there in a few minutes."

MacLean made his way to Benoit's office, and, as expected, found her already at her desk. He explained his expectation to take Ryan Jeffreys back to Sydney after she and her team had finished with their questions.

She nodded. "I saw the paperwork come through by email already this morning. No worries. It makes sense. We just want to know everything he can tell us about the gun smuggling, and then he's yours. I'm still figuring out what to do with Constable Jeffreys. He's suspended, of course, while we investigate further. Once we understand the full extent of his involvement in these crimes, he'll go in front of a board."

"Have you released him yet?"

"Yes. I sent him home. Now that we have Ryan in custody and we've searched the house, I didn't see any point in holding on to him any longer."

"Right. OK. Doucette and Hennessey will be back around eleven, and whenever you're done with Ryan, we'll take him. Meanwhile, Detective Albright and I will observe your interview, if you don't mind."

"No problem." She looked at her watch. "Let's get started."

Gordie went back to the canteen and crooked a finger to Roxanne to have her follow him. They went to the viewing room. Gordie introduced his partner to the technician monitoring the recording equipment, and then they settled down to watch and listen.

Albright's voice was low. "So, this is him. The tough guy we've been searching for all this time."

They both looked at Ryan Jeffreys, sunk down into the grey plastic chair. Seated beside him was a stout woman in her forties with bleached, frizzy hair and dark-rimmed glasses.

Gordie nodded. "And I guess that's his Legal Aid lawyer. I'm guessing Ryan doesn't smell very fresh, the way she's about as far away from her client as she can get."

Jeffreys wore his black leather jacket and underneath it was a grey t-shirt whose neckline was stretched and droopy, revealing a few wispy grey chest hairs. His salt and pepper- coloured ponytail was contained in a rubber band and hung limp and greasy down his back.

Across from Jeffreys, Sergeant Benoit was crisp in her grey shirt and dark tie. "Ryan...may I call you Ryan?"

He shrugged. "It's my name."

"Ryan, do you know why we brought you in here?"

"Not really."

"Then let me review things so you understand. On Tuesday, May 18th of this year, we found a fisherman named Adam MacDonald was found dead on his boat, the *Sea Child*. We have since discovered that he had been engaged in weapons trafficking and that you, Ryan Jeffreys, were the person who set that up. What do you know about that, Ryan?"

"Nothing."

"Let's move on then. On May 27th, a member of Adam Mac-Donald's crew, a man named Diederik Haan, better known as Dab Haan, was shot and killed in his home near Port Hood. What do you know about that, Ryan?"

"Nothing."

Benoit opened a file and pulled out an eight by ten photo which she first held up for the camera to record. It was a colour photo of the crime scene showing Haan's body splayed out on his back. "This is the man I'm talking about, Ryan. Did you know this man?"

"I might have seen him around, but I didn't exactly know him."

She pulled out another photo. This one showed a close-up of a spent casing lying near the door of the cabin. "Do you know what this is, Ryan?"

His already pasty face paled. "Looks like a shell casing."

"Yes. That's correct. This is a shell casing found at the scene of Dab Haan's murder. This is a casing for a .32 ACP round. When we searched the house where you were living, Ryan, we found a Beretta Alleycat. As you must know, since it is covered in your fingerprints, this weapon takes a .32 ACP caliber round. In fact, it takes a seven-round magazine and in the case of your gun, we discovered four rounds remaining in the magazine. Meaning that you have fired three rounds already. At least."

The Legal Aid lawyer made notes, and Ryan remained silent.

Benoit continued. "Let's go back to the question of weapons trafficking for a moment. We found a part box of .32 ACP rounds on the *Sea Child*. Our forensics team is now comparing those rounds to the ones we found in your gun and right now, they appear to be a match. We are also comparing the rounds from your gun to the round removed from Dab Haan and to the casing found at the murder scene."

Ryan Jeffreys leaned forward and put his elbows on the table, threading his fingers through the hair on his scalp, cradling his head in his hands. He stared at the table; his face obscured. His shoulders shook and then he moaned. "It wasn't my fault."

His lawyer reached over to clasp his shoulder. "Don't say anything."

Benoit hunched forward to look him straight in the eye. "Ryan, you were read your rights when you were first taken into custody. Let me remind you again that you do have the right to remain silent. You understand those rights?"

He straightened up. "Yeah, I understand. But I want you to understand. I hardly did anything. The gun smuggling. I never did the smuggling. It was MacDonald, and others. I don't even know the other guys. It wasn't me. And the other thing, that was an accident."

"Let's go step by step. You arranged for the guns to be brought in and handed off to Adam MacDonald. Is that right?"

He nodded.

"Please speak for the recording, Ryan."

"Yes. I just had one little piece to do. My buddies in New Brunswick knew the guy bringing them up from the States."

It was as though the floodgates had opened. Once Ryan decided to talk, he kept going with very little prompting.

Ryan leaned back in his chair and folded his arms. "All I did was talk to MacDonald. That's it. I don't know the name of the guy from the States, and I don't know the name of the guy from Quebec who took the guns off Adam."

"I see. So how did it work exactly?"

"I went along with Adam the first time. We went down through the Causeway and down to a point off Canso and met up with this boat from the U.S. It was a sailing yacht called Sunny's Freedom. That much I know. It was allwhite, somewhere around 35 feet. It was pretty. I remember the captain told Adam he took three days to get there because Adam grumbled it took him all day to get to the rendezvous place."

"How did this fellow get paid? Did you have the cash?"

"No. My buddies in New Brunswick organized something. I never knew all the details. They told me not to worry about it."

"But you paid Adam."

"Yes. I had an account set up in a different name and money would be put in there and I took it out to pay Adam in cash."

"How did you set up an account in another name? Do you have other identifications?"

He shrugged. "I didn't set it up. Someone else did. I was just given the card and pin number, so I never had to go into a bank. Just used bank machines."

Ada Benoit sighed. "We'll need the information on that bank."

"The card's in my wallet. You guys have my wallet. The pin is 2021."

"That was easy for you to remember."

"Yeah. My memory isn't always great."

"You're doing well so far. Let's continue. So that first trip, you went with Adam. You kept one weapon from that first delivery, didn't you?"

Ryan was affronted. "They said I could. I didn't steal it."

She nodded. "And you took some ammunition."

"I meant to take the box, but I forgot. I loaded it, but Adam took it away from me and said he would give it to me when we got home. I guess he was nervous or something."

"Yes. I'm sure he was. Did you go with him to deliver the shipment as well?"

He nodded. "Just that first time. I was just along for the ride. I didn't do anything."

"You didn't help unload the goods?"

"Well, yeah. I helped unload it. I just wanted to hurry up, and get home. It was the next day and again it took hours and hours."

"Where did this take place?"

"Off Pleasant Bay. Adam complained how long it took that first time, so the other captain agreed to a different spot closer to Pleasant Bay for the next time. I think Adam was ready to pack it in after that first trip, but once he got the thousand in cash from me, he was pretty happy and agreed to more trips."

"When did all that happen? The first trip?"

"Last year in July. After fishing season was over. He sometimes took tourists out for the day. Tourism was down but he still found people, even just from Halifax or wherever who wanted to go out for the day, so once in a while I guess he just told the wife he had one of those tourist gigs and he'd do the run. One day down to pick up the stuff and then the next day to hand it over."

"And you paid him a thousand dollars each time."

"Yup."

"How did you find Adam MacDonald in the first place?"

Ryan shrugged. "My cousin told me he heard of a guy who had been talking about his daughter and how great she was at music. She wanted to go to some special school, but it was expensive. I guess he made a point of running into Adam and casually mentioned that he might know if a way to make some extra cash."

"This is your cousin Gerry?"

He nodded.

"Ryan, you'll need to give us more information about the people involved in this operation. You'll need to give us the names of your buddies."

Ryan had been relaxed, but now he sat up straight. "No way. They'll kill me."

"They're a long way from where you are, Ryan."

He shook his head. "No. They'll find me. I get it. I'm going to jail. They know people. They'll get to me."

Benoit considered him for a moment. "Okay, we'll leave it at this for now. I will want to talk to you further, but for now, I'll be taking the bank card from your wallet to access the account. Do you give me permission for that?"

"Yeah, Okay, but I'm not saying anything more about my friends."

"We also have your phone, Ryan. We'll be able to get information from that. One way or another, we'll get what we need. If you cooperate, we may be able to help with sentencing."

He smirked. "Phone won't help you. My buddies haven't been answering the phone the last couple of weeks. They're probably long gone."

"Leaving you high and dry to be the scapegoat."

Jeffreys frowned. "They've been good to me, but they have to protect themselves. I don't blame them."

"And yet you're afraid they'll kill you. Great friends, Ryan."

He shrugged again. "That's how it is in this world."

Benoit shook her head. "When we are finished here, you will be handed over to the Cape Breton Police Service detectives who will take you down to Sydney for further questioning, specific to the murder of Dab Haan."

"Will I get some lunch? I'm hungry."

"It's only ten-thirty in the morning."

He shrugged. "I'm hungry."

"We'll arrange for some *brunch* to be brought in for you before you leave here."

She nodded to the corporal that the session was finished. "Can you get him a coffee and something to eat please, Corporal?"

The corporal stopped the recording equipment, rolled his eyes and nodded.

MacLean and Albright rose, and Gordie thanked the technician for allowing them to view the proceedings.

Gordie grinned as they left the room. "Looks like we have time for some refreshment ourselves before we head out. The guys will be here at eleven, so the timing's perfect."

Roxanne left to go to the canteen while Gordie went to have a word with Sergeant Benoit.

He found her in her office. "Did you get what you hoped for?"

She shrugged. "It's pretty skimpy. Those guys..."

Gordie interjected, "The friends?"

"Yeah, the friends. They knew what they're doing even if this dimwit didn't. They didn't leave much of a trail, and I'm guessing that even if Ryan eventually coughs up some names, they'll all be aliases or nicknames, but it would be a start. We'll see what we can get from the bank and phone records, but I imagine they were just burner phones, anyway."

"Still, you know they took the shipment to the Magdalen Islands. That's something."

"Absolutely. From there, I'm sure they were flown out. It's just too far to take them by water to the mainland. We've got some leads to work on. You're free to take him and obviously, if he gives you anything about the guns, you'll let me know."

"Of course. I'll send you my reports regardless, but if there's anything I think will be of interest to you, I'll shoot you an email or give you a call. Well, I better go to your fine canteen and get myself some *brunch.*" He grinned as he said it.

She smiled. "Go on. We'll be charging him, of course, once we finish our investigations."

Gordie raised his eyebrows. "What can you charge him with, given that he didn't actually do any of the smuggling himself?"

"He can be charged with weapons trafficking, even with his minor role. He had knowledge and consent of the firearms being trafficked. There's an implied control just because of his awareness of what went on. The three elements of the crime of possession are knowledge, consent, and control, so we will certainly be charging him with possession for the purpose of trafficking and importing weapons. I just want to get all the pieces put together before we lay the charges. You've got enough with the weapon, the casing at the scene and his fingerprints, along with his disclosure that he shot Haan, to lay murder charges, so I'm not worried that he's going to disappear on me before we add the firearms charges."

Gordie nodded. "Great working with you, Ada. Thank you for being so open and cooperative."

She nodded. "And you. I'm just sorry that I was so defensive over my constable." She sighed. "Him, I still need to figure out and deal with."

"It's understandable that you didn't want to think he was up to no good. Any good boss would be the same."

He nodded to her and went to get his coffee and sandwich before the drive to Sydney.

CHAPTER 33

MACLEAN AND ALBRIGHT HAD finished their snacks when Detectives Hennessey and Doucette found them in the canteen.

Gordie waved them to the table. "Can I get you a coffee or tea?"

Doucette spoke for them both. "No thanks, better not. We stopped just before we got here and had something and used the facilities. We're not planning to stop again until we get to the station."

Gordie nodded. "No trouble getting a decent company car?"

Hennessey dangled the key from his finger. "Got the Explorer. Wish I could afford one of these babies myself."

"Okay, great. Why don't you fellas go down and sign out our guest of honour then, and Albright and I will meet you outside the lock-up entrance."

The two detectives left while Roxanne and Gordie returned their tray and threw out the garbage. They both made a stop before going out to Gordie's vehicle.

Roxanne held out her hand. "Want me to drive? You're looking a bit done-in, if you don't mind me saying so."

He handed over the keys. "I am a bit. My lack of sleep seems to be catching up with me."

"I'm not surprised." She unlocked the doors to the Santa Fe, and they buckled in. She drove around to the side of the building where the lock-up entrance was, and they sat and waited. Roxanne tried a couple of radio stations before settling on one that played Beatles' music.

Gordie raised his eyebrows. "You're cheeky to change my station."

"The driver gets to choose. Didn't you know that was the rule?"

"I didn't."

She folded her arms across her chest as they sat waiting. "Now you do."

He shook his head. "Now I know why I prefer to drive."

"Ah, come on. You can't be complaining about the Beatles."

He was saved from saying anything when the door opened and Doucette and Hennessey, with Ryan Jeffreys sandwiched between them came out. They locked Ryan into the secure back seat and then Hennessey waved at Roxanne to indicate they were ready to go.

She let Hennessey pull out first and then followed a few seconds later, keeping close but with a safe stopping distance, behind. Gordie dropped the seat back a bit as he settled in for the two-hour drive back to Sydney.

He sighed and closed his eyes. "I could get used to this."

***

It was a little after one o'clock when they pulled into the parking lot at their home station in Sydney. The drive had been uneventful and to Gordie's surprise, he had dozed off for almost half the trip. When he woke up, the Beatles had given way to pop songs from the 70s and 80s. He hadn't even heard her change the station, but didn't admit it.

"Thanks for doing the driving."

"No problem. You get to drive later."

Gordie went directly to report to Sergeant Arsenault while Hennessey and Doucette got their prisoner booked in. Jeffreys would be held in the lock-up here for the rest of the day and then tomorrow he'd be remanded to the Cape Breton Correctional Centre.

MacLean knocked on Arsenault's door. "Sergeant?"

"Come in. Well, MacLean, I'd almost forgotten what you even look like."

"Missing me, were you?"

Arsenault leaned back in his chair. "Get on with it. Where do things stand?"

"Ryan Jeffreys is being processed as we speak. He's admitted to shooting Dab Haan, but we're going to start from the beginning with him. So far, the only thing we've got on his cousin is that he took a bribe to provide Adam MacDonald's name and to turn a blind eye."

"And you figure there's more to the story?"

"I do. I think Constable Gerry Jeffreys suddenly volunteered his bit of information, hoping to look like he's remorseful in the hopes of getting away lightly."

"Any hint that Ryan killed MacDonald?"

"Not so far. Why would he admit to the Haan shooting if he killed MacDonald as well? He claims he was only ever on one trip with MacDonald, and after that first one where they worked out how it all was to go, he never went on the *Sea Child* again."

"What about the shipment? I presume MacDonald was out by Pleasant Bay because he was scheduled to meet the American with another load of weapons, no?"

Gordie nodded. "I expect so."

"So, he must have fallen out with that guy and they never made the exchange."

"That's definitely possible."

"If that's the case, we'll be hard-pressed to find any sign of him."

"I know. I'm not convinced of that, though."

Arsenault's phone rang. "OK, well, see what you can get out of Jeffreys and let me know how it goes."

Gordie went down the hall and found the detectives waiting for him. Doucette sat at his desk; legs stretched out. "Are you taking this MacLean, or are we? Ryan's in Interview One, ready to go. He's been to the john, he's got a cup of our station's finest tea and I even gave him a couple of oatmeal cookies."

"What about his Legal Aid?"

"Yup, he's in there as well. The lady from Inverness called down and made arrangements for someone else to take the shooting charges."

Gordie laughed. "She didn't feel like making the trip down to our fair city?"

"Go figure."

MacLean picked up the file folder that lay on Doucette's desk. "Are you OK with Albright and I taking it?"

"You're the lead. We just joined in to help out."

Gordie looked at Roxanne. "Ready?"

She rolled her shoulders. "Ready."

MacLean led the way into the interview room and introduced himself and Detective Albright to Ryan Jeffreys and his lawyer, whose name was Joseph Burke.

MacLean and Albright sat across from Jeffreys, and Roxanne started the recording equipment.

Gordie opened his notebook. "Ryan, last night you spoke with RCMP Sergeant Benoit. You took her through the weapons smuggling process that you and your friends set up. I don't need to go through all that again, other than as those details relate to the shooting of Mr. Dab Haan."

Jeffreys slid the white foam cup half full of tea a few inches to the right. "OK."

"I want you to think about the day you went to Mr. Haan's cabin. Why did you go there?"

"I just wanted to scare him."

"Why did you want to do that?"

"Because I had heard that he was going around town talking

about how he was going to take over Adam MacDonald's business, and that would never happen, so I wanted him to shut up."

"How did you hear he was going around saying things like that?"

"My cousin told me."

"Your cousin, Gerard Jeffreys? Constable Jeffreys?"

"Yeah. Gerry."

"OK. So, he told you about Dab Haan, and you thought Haan might cause problems for you, so you went out to the cabin to find him."

"That's right. Just to talk to him."

"How did you know where to find Haan?"

"My cousin told me."

"All right. So, Gerry told you this guy could be a problem and how to find him. Why did you think Haan was going to be a problem? What did you believe he knew?"

"It sounded like he knew the whole arrangement. About the guns coming in and that MacDonald took them on to the guy in Pleasant Bay."

"But by this time, MacDonald was dead, so there were no more guns coming in, right?"

Ryan frowned. "I guess."

"Had you ever spoken to Dab Haan before that day?"

"No."

"But for some reason, you felt he was a threat to you. Is that right?"

"Yeah. Gerry said he knew too much."

"Even though Haan didn't know you, based on what Gerry said, you believed he was a threat."

"Yeah."

"OK. So, on May 27th, you went to the cabin. You wanted to scare Haan. What were you going to do to scare him?"

"I was going to show him my gun and tell him to shut his mouth or else I'd be back."

"So essentially you were going to introduce yourself to a man who previously didn't know you, and you were going to reveal that you carried an illegal weapon because of what your cousin had said to you."

Ryan shrugged.

"What happened to change your plan? You intended to threaten this man, but instead, you killed him."

"I didn't mean to. I tripped, and the gun went off."

"You went in with the safety off, and your finger on the trigger. Is that right?"

"Yeah."

"And yet you say you only intended to scare the man. Why would you take the safety off?"

"I dunno. Just seemed right."

"Did your cousin instruct you on what you should do? Like take the safety off?"

Ryan shook his head. "No. I'm not sure he even knew I was going there."

"After telling you that Haan was a problem, and after telling you where he lived, you don't think he knew you were going there?"

"Don't think so."

"When you went into Haan's cabin, did you speak to him?"

"No. No chance. I banged open the door and I guess he got up from the table or whatever. I saw him standing anyway in the second before the gun went off. When I pushed the door open, I took a step and then I tripped on the doorstep. It had like an extra piece of wood on top of the normal floor. I wasn't expecting it." Ryan shook his head. "Mom always told me to pick up my feet. I shoulda listened."

"What did you do when you realized you had shot him?"

"I took a couple of steps towards him, but it looked to me like he was dead, and I just got out of there as fast as I could."

MacLean paused. In the silence, Joseph Burke scribbled a few notes on his lined yellow pad and Ryan shifted his nearly empty tea-cup back to his left side again.

Gordie nodded to Roxanne.

Albright flipped her notebook back several pages. "Thank you for your honesty, Ryan. We want to go back now to talk about Adam MacDonald, and I hope you'll be just as open about that as you were about the shooting of Dab Haan."

Jeffreys looked surprised and pleased that Roxanne Albright had taken over the conversation. Perhaps he thought she was less severe. He smiled at her. "Can I get another cup of tea first? Milk and sugar."

Gordie stood and opened the door of the interview room. He spoke to the constable outside the door. "Please get Mr. Jeffreys another cup of tea, with milk and sugar."

He returned to his seat.

Roxanne nodded her thanks to Gordie and then began. "Ryan, you said you had been on the boat with Adam MacDonald the first time when you went through the smuggling process."

"Yes."

"Ryan, I think you also went with him that last time."

"That's not true."

She sat watching him in silence.

Ryan frowned. "That isn't true, I'm telling you. I just went the once. Truth is, I don't like boats much. I always have to take Gravol first because I get seasick."

Albright pulled out an eight by ten photo of Ryan talking to Adam near the RV park. "Ryan, I'm showing you a photo of you and Adam MacDonald. Do you recognize it?"

He picked up the photo, studied it for a moment, and then put it down and slid it back to her.

The constable came in carrying one cup of tea and set it down in front of Ryan. "Anyone else?"

The lawyer and both Gordie and Roxanne shook their heads, and the constable left again.

Ryan took a sip. "At least it's hot."

Roxanne tapped the photo. "You were about to tell us about this photo."

He shrugged. "Yeah. That's me talking to MacDonald. What's to tell?"

"What was the purpose of this meeting?"

"I paid him for the last trip he had done."

"We have video from that meeting, and it appears as though you are arguing."

"MacDonald said he didn't want to do it anymore. He said that fishing season was starting, and he didn't have time."

"That didn't please you. What did you say?"

"I told him I had to give the guys more notice. I said that there was already another deal in the works, and he couldn't just back out like that."

"And then what?"

"And then I paid him, and I told him to meet me again so I could give him the date of the next shipment. He agreed and said that one way or another, the next trip was the last trip."

"And did you meet him again?"

"Yeah. But not at the same place. He saw someone and that freaked him. He said it was too open there. I would have just talked to him on the phone, but he didn't like the phone. Always thought someone was going to overhear him or something."

"Where did you meet?"

"Behind the plaza in town."

"Behind the Canadian Tire?"

Ryan frowned. "How'd you know that?"

"There was a witness."

Ryan slapped his hand on the table, splattering the tea. "Haan. Jesus. I did see him before. When I saw him dead, I thought he looked familiar, but I didn't wait around to figure it out. He was hanging around behind the plaza, but MacDonald had his back to him and didn't see."

"How did your so-called buddies take the news that MacDonald wanted out?"

"They didn't care. It was too complicated, and they weren't making as much money as when someone just ran it across the border. They figured the border with the U.S. must have to open pretty soon, anyway."

"Were they concerned that MacDonald knew too much? Did they tell you to make sure he didn't talk?"

Jeffreys widened his eyes. "No. MacDonald knew very little, and he was in the middle of it, so why would he say anything?"

"What about your cousin? Did he know that the operation was shutting down?"

"Sure."

"Was he worried that MacDonald might somehow implicate him or cause him problems somehow?"

"I don't get what you're asking. I don't think Adam even knew that me and Gerry are cousins. MacDonald never mentioned him once."

The lawyer finally spoke, startling everyone. "I don't know where this is leading, Detective. If you have issues with my client's cousin, get him in and talk to him. Otherwise, let's move on."

She shook her head in frustration. "Fine. Ryan, how many trips did Adam MacDonald make as part of this operation?"

"Ten. He got a thousand for each trip. I didn't get that much. I only got two hundred. If I were him, I would have kept it going as long as possible."

"What about that last trip? What happened to the shipment? You must have spoken with your buddies to tell them MacDonald was dead. Did they ask about it?"

"No. They already knew that it was never handed over."

Roxanne glanced at Gordie. "Not handed over? Why not?"

Ryan rolled his eyes. "The American wasn't going to hand guns over to a dead guy, was he?"

"Are you saying that Adam MacDonald was already dead by the time the American got there?"

"That's what I was told."

"Maybe he killed MacDonald."

Jeffreys pulled a face. "Why do that? Sounds like he was some pissed because he had to go home with the goods again after all that sailing around. He'd rather have had the money."

Gordie closed his notebook. "That should do it for now. Ryan, you're now going to be formally charged with the second-degree murder in the shooting death of Diederik Haan."

"I told you that was an accident."

"That's for you and your lawyer to sort out."

Roxanne stood as well, but she had another question. "Why did you put the threatening note into Vanessa Hunt's mailbox?"

The lawyer looked puzzled. "What note?"

Ryan Jeffreys looked away from where Gordie now stood, staring at him. "I just thought she'd convince the detective to drop it."

Albright laughed. "Drop a murder investigation?"

"I mean, just stop looking for me. I thought that lady would be afraid, especially if she thought I'd already killed someone."

Joseph Burke shook his head. "You threatened a detective?"

Ryan shrugged.

Roxanne addressed herself to the lawyer. "There may be further charges coming."

Gordie opened the door and left while Roxanne arranged for the formal charges.

CHAPTER 34

MACLEAN AND ALBRIGHT FINISHED the day in the briefing room, updating the whiteboard. It felt good solving the Dab Haan murder, but they were no further ahead on the original Adam MacDonald case.

Gordie perched on the table in front of the board. "We need to go back to the beginning for Adam MacDonald."

Albright put the red marker down on the ledge of the whiteboard. "You believe Ryan then?"

MacLean nodded. "He's right that the American didn't have a motive. It was in his best interest to offload the goods, so he's out as far as I'm concerned."

"What about Gerry Jeffreys? You were so sure he was involved."

Gordie sighed. "I think he's a manipulative bastard, but as much as I hate to admit it, I can't see why he'd get on that boat in the middle of the night and get into a fight with Adam MacDonald. He was getting money for relatively low risk."

"What if he wanted to scoop the load but miscalculated and took it out on Adam?"

Gordie shrugged. "I can't see it. He doesn't seem like such a hands-on guy. But he isn't off the list. I was thinking back to your interview with the woman in Pleasant Bay. She heard a boat motoring away that night. We have a paint chip from a boat that recently rubbed up against the *Sea Child*. Now that we know the American boat is a sailing yacht, it seems unlikely that the paint came from that. They don't flake and chip so easily. Tomorrow we're in the office and we're going to figure out where that boat came from."

Roxanne nodded. "Gerry may have an unregistered boat. I'll check the records for boat sales over the last couple of years."

"And let's get some uniforms out doing a house-to-house in his neighbourhood. If he ever had a boat, someone's bound to know about it."

He stood. "Let's call it a day for now."

***

Gordie was home. He washed the cups from which he and Roxanne had had tea and then looked down at where Taz sat, hopefully waiting.

"Yes, all right. A walk on the beach will be good for both of us."

He bumped along the logging road and then they got out and walked through a rough trail amongst pine and spruce trees until they came out at the shore. He breathed deeply through his nose to fill his lungs with the fragrance of conifers blended with salt and fish. The water also seemed to inhale and exhale with a repeating swish-and-sigh sound. The small pebbles shifted inshore and out again with the force of the waves. Taz bounded off in a joyful burst of energy, and Gordie followed at a leisurely pace. He wore a tweed cap he'd once bought in Newfoundland, and it kept his hair from blowing around.

Gordie picked his way along the rocky shore, navigating around wet mounds of kelp and eelgrass as he followed Taz. He felt the stress of the past few days ease away. His shoulders dropped and neck muscles relaxed as he felt the last of the sun's warmth on the top of his head. Slowly his mind wandered away from work and he found himself thinking of Vanessa.

No point thinking about her, old boy. I'm controlling, remember? He frowned as he recalled their argument. *I don't get it. I'm not controlling. At least, I don't think.* Unbidden, an image of another woman, another argument dating back years. came to him. Margaret had said something similar.

Gordie looked at his watch. *After supper, maybe I'll give Jeannie a call.*

"Come on, Taz. Let's go home."

The dog came loping. She had a smear of something dark and smelly across the scruff of her neck and shoulder.

"Oh, Taz. What did you roll in?"

Gordie gripped her by the collar and pulled her to the water's edge. He pulled out his handkerchief and soaked it, wiping down the stinking tar-like substance from Taz. When he had soaked and wiped her several times, she was soaking wet but cleaner. "Isn't it good I have the handkerchief? People think I'm old-fashioned, but you never know when you need a hankie."

He released her, and she shook, spraying Gordie with sea water.

"I guess that serves me right for not paying attention to you earlier. Let's go. Supper's waiting, and as much as I might enjoy talking to you, you just don't give me the good advice my sister gives."

***

After a supper of bacon, eggs and tinned beans, Gordie called his sister Jean. "Hi, Jeannie. Are you OK to talk for a few minutes?"

He heard the delight in her voice. "Gordie. What a great surprise. Yes, it's a perfect time. I saw Mum this afternoon, and we were just talking about you."

"Why doesn't that surprise me?"

She laughed. "We do talk about other things, you know. We wondered when we'd see you and Vanessa down here for a visit. It's been ages."

"I've been busy with this case."

"Yes, Mum has the articles clipped out of the paper because it mentioned your name as the lead investigator. The fisherman and one of his crew, right?"

"That's the one."

"Is it going OK? You sound down."

"The case is going all right. That's not why I'm calling."

"What is it, Gordie? What's wrong?"

"Vanessa and I had a falling out."

"Oh, no. Oh, Gordie. I like her so much. What happened?"

"Jeannie, I have to ask you something, and I want you to be honest."

"OK. I always try to be honest."

"I know. So, here's the thing. She broke up with me because apparently, I'm controlling. That's not how I see myself. I respect her and I don't make a fuss if she wants one thing and I want something else. Jeannie, I care about her and want to keep her safe. So how is that controlling?"

He heard his sister sigh. "Without knowing the details of what happened, I can only speculate what she means. I'm no counsellor, Gordie, but I've taken therapy myself. I had to after what Dad put our family through, so I probably have some insight."

"OK, so share these insights."

"As a kid, you were helpless. You saw Dad thrash Mom and you couldn't do anything about it. Sometimes it was even me or you, yourself, that took the brunt of his anger. The lasting effect on me is that I have trouble trusting a man and because of that, I've never had a healthy relationship with one. For you, I think it's left you very protective of the people you love. You want to make sure nothing bad happens. Some women like that, but some will chafe against it. I think for Vanessa, it comes across as controlling. Is that possible?"

He frowned. "You're saying it's a bad thing to want to protect people I love? That doesn't make sense to me."

"It's not a bad thing, but it depends on how you do it. If you suggest getting a better lock on the door or a security camera and you make a logical argument about why it makes sense, that's one thing, but if she makes a counter-argument, about why she doesn't want those things, you have to accept that. She's a grown-up and a smart, capable woman. You say you respect her, so that means believing that she can make informed decisions for herself. Does that make sense?"

"Maybe. I don't know."

"Talk to her, Gordie. I know she cares about you. I would hate to see you just walk away without trying."

"On a more positive note, I've quit smoking."

His sister yelped. "Oh, Gordie. That's fantastic."

"Don't tell Mum. I'm not out of the woods yet. I'll tell her when I'm ready."

"Fair enough. You can do it. When you put your mind to something, you can do it."

They chatted for a few more moments, and then he hung up with a promise to come to Halifax for a visit as soon as it was possible.

***

MacLean arrived at the station early the next morning, but Albright had gotten there earlier and left a coffee on his desk. He picked it up and took a sip. "Ahh. Just the perfect temperature for drinking. Thanks."

She rolled her chair over to his desk, holding her own paper cup. "You're welcome. You look better than you have in days. Does this mean you're back on the smokes?"

"No. Maybe I'm past the worst of it. I had the best night's sleep I've had in a while. In fact, my mind is clearer than it's been in a very long time."

"That sounds positive. Have you had any brain waves?"

Gordie gestured towards the briefing room. "Follow me."

They stood in front of the whiteboard.

Gordie pointed to the photo of Ryan handing over the roll of money to Adam MacDonald. "Adam got involved in this whole gun smuggling thing because of money. He started as early as last year because even then he had hopes that his daughter would be accepted to the music school. Money. That was his motive for this illegal activity. We need to figure out what the motive was for killing him. The motive is everything."

Roxanne frowned. "Maybe someone found out, and they wanted in? Someone else wanted the money that Adam was getting?"

Gordie nodded. "Another fisherman maybe?"

Roxanne tapped the photo of Dab Haan. "Is it possible that Haan was with Adam? Haan seemed to know more about this entire enterprise than anyone else we've talked to."

Gordie continued the thought. "Adam didn't like running the boat on his own. He takes Haan with him with a promise of a cut, but then when they are out there waiting for the meeting with the American, Haan finds out his cut is going to be smaller than he expected. Adam's trying to save money after all, and now he knows for definite that his daughter has been accepted, so he decides to cut back on what he's going to give Haan."

She stands up. "Haan's pissed and goes after Adam with the gaff hook, but Adam gets it away from him, slicing open his hand. Haan is elderly, but he's still in good shape. He jumps forward and pushes Adam, who goes down, smacking his head."

Gordie shakes his head. "Wait a minute. No, this can't be right. How did Haan get off the boat and back home?"

"He waves someone down? He sees a fisherman out in a run-about and waves him over, telling him he's got engine troubles. Adam's down, maybe unconscious. It's still dark out so no one can see in and down where MacDonald's lying."

Gordie nods. "And then he hitch-hikes back to Port Hood? To be there at the wharf for his usual start time?"

"Didn't we hear Haan was a bit late that morning? And then he wanted to go home pretty soon after when it was obvious that *Sea Child* wasn't there for the morning fishing."

Other detectives began filing into the briefing room. Rob Norris came in carrying a mug but looked around. "No breakfast pastries? I figured we'd be celebrating this morning. You two are falling down on the job."

Gordie smiled. "You're right. I should have. I'll get lunch instead. How's that sound?"

Norris gave a thumbs-up. "You're forgiven."

When everyone had assembled, Gordie began with a summary of where both cases stood. When he finished taking everyone through the weapons trafficking operation, he handed it over to Albright to talk about the Adam MacDonald case. There were a few questions and theories when she explained they were now focussed on motive.

One detective called out. "Money. It's always about the money."

Norris added his thoughts. "Yeah, but maybe along with the money, it's about sex. Has the wife got a lover? She hired someone to get rid of the husband so she could have the money along with her new boyfriend?"

Albright shook her head. "We looked into that one, and no, we can't find any evidence of that."

Hennessey raised his hand. "Are we ruling out an accident, then?"

Roxanne pointed to an autopsy close-up photo. "These bruises indicate that someone grabbed Adam by the upper arms. We speculate that this assailant essentially flung Adam back against the steel locker where he hit his head, so yes, we are ruling out an accident."

Sergeant Arsenault had been seated at the back of the room. He now stood up. "Thanks to Detectives Doucette and Hennessey for their work on the Haan case. Great job closing that investigation, gentlemen. Detective Norris, you're still supporting MacLean. MacLean, if you need more resources, you can talk to me. Otherwise, Gabe and Joe, once you've finished all your reports, I've got a break-in for you."

That was the signal for everyone to leave the room.

As Roxanne went back to her desk, she waved her notebook at Gordie. "OK, I'm working on finding that boat. The witness in Pleasant Bay said it was an outboard engine she heard, which syncs up with the aluminium paint chip."

"Good. I'm going through those phone records of Adam Mac-Donald's again. I'm going back through the autopsy and forensics reports as well, just to refresh my memory. Norris is coordinating a couple of uniforms to get out around the area of Gerry Jeffreys' house to ask about a boat. Have Norris let you know what that nets."

They went off to dive into their tasks. Gordie printed off the phone records and then took them with a highlighter to the small interview room to study them.

At noon, Gordie ordered pizza for delivery and when it was delivered, invited Doucette, Hennessey, Norris and Albright to the briefing room to dig in. "As promised, lunch is served."

Gabe Doucette took a bite from a slice of pepperoni, bacon, and mushroom pizza. "I'll take our local pizza over that stuff they served up in Inverness any day."

Roxanne laughed as she tackled a slice of vegetarian pizza. "You're just used to it, that's all."

Joe Hennessey wiped his mouth with a paper napkin. "No, Gabe's right."

Gordie finished his first slice. "I'd have to agree. And guys, thanks for your work on the Dab Haan case." He stood up to read through the details on the whiteboard. "And if you have any thoughts to share on the MacDonald case, don't be shy."

Gabe took a second slice. "Not me. I'm knee-deep in reports as it is, and I've been given the quiet word from Sarge to make sure every 't' is crossed and every 'i' dotted because our Mountie friends will get a copy of everything."

Joe nodded. "We're heading over to the Correctional Centre later to have another interview with our friend, just to get some of the timing and whatnot, tightened up."

When Doucette and Hennessey finished, they left with a wave and thanks for the lunch. Gordie, Roxanne and Rob Norris stayed behind. Gordie took a sip from a can of cola. "The phone records didn't give me a lot. A short call the afternoon before Adam died, from a burner phone which we now know belonged to Ryan Jeffreys. No doubt confirming that all was a go for the pickup. Other than that, just calls we'd expect. One from Sharon at eleven-fifteen that day before, which syncs up with what Sharon told us. She had called Adam when she got the letter to acknowledge that Izzie was accepted into the school. One from Dannymac, and one from Kyle. The one from Kyle is the longest. That was in the evening after supper. I'm going to take another trip out to both Kyle and Dannymac to confirm what the calls were about.

Norris used his thumbnail to dig out a piece of meat from between his teeth and then shrugged. "Nothing from the uniforms yet, and it isn't a big area to cover. The house is out behind the hospital in Inverness, but it's not like doing a house-to-house in Sydney. Twenty houses and they're done."

"No boat, in other words."

"No boat."

Roxanne flipped open her notebook. "I've been going through all the boat rental places from Inverness to Pleasant Bay. There are ten, including private places like cottage rental parks." She looked at her list. "I've spoken to six so far and no rentals for that day. It's too early in the season for many tourists."

Gordie sighed. "And if a person was up to no good, would they go through an official boat rental place, anyway?"

Roxanne nodded. "I agree, but we have to start somewhere."

"Sure. I think tomorrow we'll be back in the area, though. I want to talk to the MacDonalds, and you might be on the ground looking for an unofficial place where a boat could be rented or borrowed."

They finished lunch, and they left the few slices that remained on the table. Roxanne would spread the word that there were a few slices for first come first served. Everyone knew they would empty the place of food in minutes.

CHAPTER 35

MACLEAN AND ALBRIGHT EACH took their own cars the next morning. They arranged to meet in Pleasant Bay at noon for lunch.

As usual, when Gordie drove past the turnoff for Parish Lane in Port Mulroy, on his way to Port Hood, he wondered if he should call Vanessa. He'd mulled it over the night before but distracted himself by spending the evening working on reports instead. *Let's see what the day brings. Maybe I'll see if she feels like meeting me for a cup of tea later.*

It was too soon to meet with Kyle. He was out fishing, but Gordie had called last night to let MacDonald Senior know he'd be dropping by and to ask if ten o'clock was too early. The time was fine and as Gordie pulled into the driveway, the elderly man was sitting out on the veranda reading the morning paper.

Gordie smiled as he approached the veranda. "Morning, Danny. Nice day, isn't it?"

Dannymac folded the newspaper and tucked it under his arm, and rose shakily out of his chair. "Yeah. It's good to get the sun on my old bones."

"We can stay out here if you prefer. This won't take long."

"I'm ready for a fresh tea. You want a cup? Or maybe an instant coffee?"

"Tea would be great, thanks."

Gordie held the storm door open as Dannymac gingerly made his way through the house and into the kitchen.

Danny put the paper on the table and shuffled over to fill the kettle and click it on.

Gordie saw the page open to the crossword puzzle. Danny had filled a few of the answers in, the writing spidery and almost illegible. "Good for you, trying out the crossword. I'm no good at those things, or any of the others, like, what is it called? Sudoku."

Danny shook his head. "I only do the crosswords in the paper. It's good to keep the mind alert. And I watch Jeopardy."

Gordie laughed. "Yeah, when I get a chance, I like that show too. It's not the same since Alex Trebek died, though."

Danny shrugged. "We all die sometime, and life goes on. I watch it for the questions, not who's asking them."

"Fair enough." The kettle boiled and clicked off and Gordie rose before Danny did and waved the older man to stay seated. "I'll get it."

Gordie emptied the pot of cold tea, rinsed it with boiling water, took two tea bags from the tin canister beside the kettle, tossed them into it and filled the pot. He set the teapot on the table and Dannymac took the cozy that lay there and set it over the pot. Gordie rinsed out the cup Dannymac had been using and took one from the draining board beside the sink for himself. He got the plastic bottle of Scotsburn 2% milk from the fridge and set it on the table. A bowl with sugar was already there, the spoon lumpy with sugar, obviously used for both spooning out sugar and stirring the tea.

Before Gordie sat down, Dannymac pointed to a cabinet above the toaster. "I've got some Fat Archies if you want one. Bring them down anyway. I'll have one."

He got out the small bakery box with half a dozen thick molasses cookies from the cabinet and put it on the table. "Do you want butter with it?"

"Ah, no. Go on ahead if you want."

Gordie shook his head. "It's been a while since I had one of these."

Danny poured out the tea for both of them and then helped himself to a Fat Archie. "So, what brings you here, then? I read in the paper that you made an arrest for the killing of Dab."

"We did. The man confessed, so that's done and dusted pretty much."

They drank their tea in silence for a moment as Gordie studied Danny. "You aren't asking why he did it. Most of the time, that's one of the first things people want to know."

Danny shrugged a bony shoulder. "OK. Why did the fella do it? I know Dab could be annoying sometimes, but it seems like an extreme way to deal with someone irritating."

"Dab may have annoyed the man, but that had nothing to do with why he was killed."

"What was it then?"

"The person we've arrested, a man named Ryan Jeffreys, was involved in weapons trafficking. Jeffreys believed Dab knew something about his operation and went over to scare Dab into staying quiet about anything he knew. The man shot Dab by accident. He only meant to threaten him, but he ended up killing him."

Danny set his half-eaten cookie down on the table beside his cup, as if he suddenly felt ill. "Jesus. Poor old Dab. He didn't deserve that."

"No, he didn't. You were friends with Dab. Did he talk to you about what he knew or thought he knew?"

Danny took a moment to top up his tea from the pot. He glanced over to Gordie's cup in a silent question about whether Gordie wanted a refill. Gordie shook his head.

"He was always telling me nonsense. It might be some conspiracy from the government one day to seeing a bobcat out behind his cabin, another day to someone having it off with someone else's wife. You never knew what foolishness he'd come up with next."

"That doesn't answer my question, Danny. Did Dab say anything specifically about weapons trafficking?"

A heartbeat of hesitation, and then he picked up his cookie again. "Not that I recall."

"Not that you recall. Are you sure?"

Danny chewed slowly. "Yep. Nothing comes back to me."

Gordie considered pursuing it but decided against it. Not here, not now. He would need to get Kyle and Danny into the station for a proper interview when the time was right.

"OK." Gordie pulled out the folded report on Adam's phone history. "I have a printout here of Adam's phone records from the days prior to his death."

He saw Dannymac blink rapidly, and he continued. "I see you called him the afternoon prior to his death. Can you tell me what you talked about?"

"I can't really remember. We talked a lot. It was probably about the business. How the day's catch was, things like that."

"You didn't call him every day, though to ask those questions."

"A lot of times he'd drop in on his way back, or Kyle would tell me, so there was no need to talk on the phone every day."

"Right. I can see that. So, if Kyle lives right here and sees you every day, why would you want to ask Adam questions about the catch?"

Danny frowned. "Just for an excuse to have a chat. He was my son, and I enjoyed talking to him."

"Fair enough."

"Wait, I remember. That was the day we found out Izzie got accepted at the school. Kyle told me, so I called Adam to congratulate him." Danny smiled, perhaps at the happy memory.

"OK. That makes sense. I'm sorry for the difficult questions,

Danny. We just need to continue to check into every avenue in case there's something people remember now that will help us find the person who assaulted Adam."

"And it wasn't this Jeffreys guy? If he killed Dab, maybe he killed Adam too?"

"It seems unlikely, but the investigation is ongoing."

Gordie finished his tea and stood. "Thank you for the tea and for answering my questions, Danny. I'll let you get back to your crossword. Don't get up."

After he left MacDonald Senior, he drove the few minutes to the wharf. Most of the boats were back by now. The Co-op team was weighing and writing slips out for the captains as they handed their catch over and sorted. Gordie saw the bright red hull of *Sea Child*. It looked as though they had already finished handing over their haul and the two young men dressed in yellow waterproof overalls were washing down the boat.

Gordie walked along the wharf to 'Sea Child's berth and called out. "Hello, is Kyle here?"

Kyle MacDonald stuck his head out from the cabin. He nodded to MacLean. "Give us a few minutes to finish up here and then come in. Maybe ten minutes. OK?"

"That's fine." Gordie waved to the shack where hot drinks and snacks were being sold. "Can I get you anything?"

Kyle shook his head. "No, thanks."

Gordie walked back down the wharf to let them finish their work. He wanted no more tea but would have loved a cigarette. To distract himself, he went and looked at the menu written in marker on a piece of Bristol board hung on the wall.

A woman in a white apron called out to him. "What can I get you, dear?"

He didn't want anything, but it seemed rude not to order now he was asked. "A double-double coffee, please."

She poured it out, tipping a generous amount of cream and sugar into the paper cup. "A dollar twenty-five, please."

Gordie fished a toonie out of his pocket and told her to keep the change from the two-dollar coin. He took the coffee and was surprised at how good it was. It was strong, hot, and successfully eased his craving for a cigarette.

When he saw the two crew members leave the *Sea Child*, Gordie drained his cup, tossed it in the garbage can beside the snack shack, and made his way back to the boat.

Kyle waved him on board. "Watch your step. The deck's slick."

Stepping carefully, he climbed on board. Kyle perched on the edge of the washboard, the wide edge around the boat and Gordie stood and faced him, but after a moment, it seemed that Kyle felt at a disadvantage to be lower than Gordie, and he rose as well.

"Well, Detective? What can I do for you?"

"A lot has happened since we last spoke, and I thought it made sense to reconnect."

"You mean because you arrested that guy who killed Dab?"

"Yes. That and how it may connect to your brother's death."

Kyle took off his yellow waterproof jacket. "Is this going to take a while?"

"It might. Are you in a hurry?"

"I'm ready to go home. I'm tired and I'm hungry."

"I'm happy to follow you home if you'd rather talk there."

Kyle sighed. "All right, then. Let's do that. I'll meet you there."

Gordie nodded and climbed back out. He went back to his car and called Roxanne as he waited for Kyle to pull out. "Hey. How's it going up there?"

"Not bad. I heard about a guy that sometimes rents out his boats and I'm on my way there now. The official outfitters were a bust."

"OK. I met with Dannymac and I'm just waiting to follow Kyle home now to have a talk with him. Looks like I'll be late by the time I get up there. I'll call you when I'm done with Kyle and unless you need me, it makes more sense to wait for you down here since you have to come back this way, anyway."

"No problem. You stay there and we'll plan to meet in Port Hood instead."

"Right. I'll call you."

He disengaged and followed Kyle. He knew he could have just gone ahead and met him there, but he didn't feel like sitting there like a mug if Kyle decided he suddenly had somewhere else he'd rather be.

Kyle went straight home and within minutes, Gordie drove past the house again, where he had so recently had tea with MacDonald Senior.

Gordie gave Kyle a few minutes in the house on his own, assuming he might want to change or freshen up. He used the time to look through Adam's phone records again and then he went up and knocked on the door.

Kyle opened the door and waved to the kitchen table. "I'm making myself a fried egg sandwich. Want one?"

"No, you're all right, thanks though. I had a Fat Archie with your father recently. Those things are like a meal in themselves."

Kyle smiled. "Dad has a sweet tooth. I'm surprised he shared with you."

"He wanted one himself, so he was forced into it, maybe. I'll pick some up for him, now that I know he likes them."

Kyle pulled a Moosehead beer from the fridge and waved it as an invitation, but Gordie shook his head. "I'm water-logged as it is."

When Kyle sat down with his meal, Gordie chatted casually with him. "How's the fishing going?"

"It's a good year so far. Prices opened at eight dollars a pound, but it's been going up every week. Last year we were getting something like five dollars, so yeah. So far, so good." He wolfed down his sandwich and then he pushed his plate away. "It's hard though. I miss Adam. I miss him every day." Kyle removed his glasses and used a tissue to polish them. When he put them back on, his eyes swam. "He always made everything look easy. He managed everything so well. Even when we were kids in school. He was good academically and good at sports. Everyone liked him." He shrugged. "Me, on the other hand. I was the kid with the pimples and glasses. Everything was a struggle and sometimes it pissed me off that everything was easy for him."

"Was it easy, though?"

"That's the thing, isn't it? I don't suppose it was. He just managed things. He was organized and worked at it, whatever *it* was. I see that now. When he had a problem, he quietly figured out a way to solve it. When I had a problem, everyone knew about it. My mom was my ally, though. He smiled, "She made things better."

"And then she died."

"Yes. I went through a bad time then. I was mad at the world."

"Is that when you went away?"

"Yeah. First Halifax and then Toronto. I had to go away to get perspective. When I lived in Toronto, I saw how some people lived." He shook his head. "That's where I saw what real problems were, and I realized what I was missing here at home. I don't take it for granted anymore and I might not be Adam, but I'll figure it all out, with help." Kyle folded his arms across his chest. "So, what did you want to talk to me about?"

"You obviously read about the arrest of Ryan Jeffreys in the killing of Dab Haan. Do you know Ryan?"

Kyle shook his head. "No. Never even heard the name before. Why'd he do it? What did Dab do to him?"

"Did you read the story in the Post?"

"Skimmed it."

"Ryan Jeffreys is being investigated by the RCMP for weapons trafficking."

Kyle nodded. "Right. I saw something about that. But Dab wasn't involved with that." Kyle snorted. "Dab wouldn't know the first thing about something like that. If it was to do with making backwoods booze, I'd say right, Dab might be involved. Guns though? No way."

"You know already that we found a box of rounds on *Sea Child*, so why are you so dismissive of the idea that Dab might have known something about that?"

Kyle frowned. "I forgot about that. Are you saying that Dab was involved? And this Jeffreys guy got in a dispute with Dab over it?"

"I'm not saying that, no. The investigation is still ongoing. I just want to know if you ever heard either Dab or Adam talk about Ryan Jeffreys?"

Kyle tightened his lips. "No. Never."

Gordie pulled out the phone records. "Although Ryan Jeffreys has confessed to shooting Dab Haan, we are still piecing together what happened to Adam. I've been looking over his phone records for the days before he died. I see that on the evening before his death, you had a fairly long conversation with him. Just over nine minutes, to be exact. This might not seem like a long chat, but considering you had spent the morning together, it seems pretty long to me. What did you talk about?"

"I can't remember. It's a few weeks ago now."

"It's the last conversation you had with your brother, and yet you can't remember what you talked about?"

He shook his head. "No. I can't remember."

Gordie folded the pages and put them back inside his jacket pocket. "As you say, a few weeks have passed now. Has anything come back to you about the time before Adam died? Any arguments you knew about? You spent a lot of time together. Surely you spoke with each other during all those hours?"

"Listen, Detective. When you're out there with the engine going, the hauler working, the wind noise and seagulls screeching, conversation is minimal. It's hard work, and we talked about what was necessary for the work. That's it."

Gordie nodded. "I see. And when you stopped for your break?"

"Again. We kept it light and easy. Half the time we just let Dab blather on about something. He could be very entertaining when he wasn't drinking. Then he was generally over the top. Dab knew all the gossip, and that's what the conversation was. Oh yeah, and about Izzie. If Adam talked about anything, it was about his daughter." Kyle sighed. "He sure loved that girl."

MacLean stood. "All right. Thank you for your time. As I said, this investigation is very much still ongoing, and we will probably need you and your father to come to the station for a formal interview at some point. Sharon has already come in, so we have her statement on file, but we will need to talk further with you and your father. For now, though, thank you for your time and I'll let you get on with your day."

Kyle sat and watched Gordie leave; his arms folded tight across his chest.

CHAPTER 36

MACLEAN CALLED ROXANNE. "I'M done with the MacDonalds. Where are you?"

He heard the excitement in her voice. "I'm on my way back down. I'll be there in about half an hour. The bakery place?"

"Sounds good. You don't want to tell me now?"

"No. You'll have to be patient. See you soon." She disengaged.

Gordie stopped at the Co-Op and picked up a newspaper. He parked in the lot for their new favourite coffee shop and waited for Roxanne to arrive. Although the paper was open and his eyes followed the lines of print, his mind was elsewhere.

Roxanne pulled in and parked next to him. He tossed the paper on the passenger seat and got out to stretch as he waited for her to park and gather her things.

He nodded and led the way. "I'm buying. What'll you have?"

"Are you having lunch?"

He nodded. "The toasted western sounds good to me." He ordered along with a coffee while Roxanne studied the menu. "Well?"

"A bowl of seafood chowder and a sparkling water, please."

He smiled. "All this focus on fishing gave you a craving?"

"I think so. And if a person's going to have seafood, this is the town to have it."

They were told the food would be delivered, so they took their drinks to a table against the wall, away from some tourists sitting by the window admiring the harbour view in loud voices. They each put their notebooks on the table but spoke about the weather and drive while they waited for the food. Once it was placed in front of them, the fragrant steam rising from Roxanne's soup, Gordie flipped open his book.

"I'll start. First, I met with Senior, who claims to have never heard our friend's name before." Roxanne nodded. This was a small village, and they were loath to mention names that might be overheard.

"Did you believe him?"

He chewed the bite of his sandwich as he thought about it. "I'm not sure I did. Well, maybe he told the truth that he had never heard the name, but he was not entirely truthful. He was cagey. I asked if…" Gordie slit his eyes over to the server, but she was talking to the tourists. "Dab had spoken to him about his theories or anything he may have heard or known. I was told no, but his body language said yes."

Roxanne dipped into her soup. "This is lovely. You should have had it. So, you figure Senior is hiding something. What about Junior?"

"Same thing. It was a useful chat. I feel I know him better. He's very authentic when he says he misses his brother, but, like Senior, I sense he isn't telling me everything. I told Junior that both of them will be asked to come to the station for a formal talk."

"Did you get anything concrete that we can explore more?"

"No, nothing specific, but it's got me thinking. OK, go on. Spill. What did you find?"

Roxanne took the last spoon of soup and wiped her mouth with the napkin. "I found the boat."

Gordie put down the cup he was about to sip from. "What?"

She grinned. "Yup. OK, here it is. It belongs to a man in Pleasant Bay. He doesn't normally rent out his boat, like he doesn't advertise or anything, but if someone calls him, he'll let it go sometimes." She flipped open her book and thumbed through to the right page. "It's a fourteen-foot Sea Nymph aluminum boat with a fifteen horsepower Evinrude outboard motor."

"Damn it, I don't care what make and model it is. You've kept me in suspense long enough. Who rented it?"

She made a face. "Carl."

"Carl? Who is that?"

"That's the million-dollar question, isn't it?"

He closed his eyes for a second. "OK, from the beginning, please."

"This man, Al MacInnis, and no, before you ask, he's not the hockey player. Well, he has this boat and if someone specifically asks him, and they don't seem dodgy, he'll rent it out. It seems that this man Carl phones him that afternoon on May 17th. He remembers because it was the same day as his mother-in-law's 90th birthday. Carl told him he was up from Halifax with a buddy, and they want to go out and do a bit of fishing. He'd gotten Al's name from someone in a local coffee shop but didn't know that person's name. MacInnis was in a hurry getting ready to go out, so he told Carl where the boat was and just to leave 50 bucks in the boathouse for him."

"That's very trusting."

"That's what I said. He told me he has never been let down by trusting people, so there you go, Gordie. You should learn from him."

Gordie snorted. "He rented his boat to a murderer."

Roxanne nodded. "I didn't quite say that to him, but I said that we strongly believed that his boat may have been used in the commission of a crime, so he must allow no one to go near it until it's been processed."

"Has it been used a lot since then?"

"Not once. It's under a tarp pulled up on his private bit of shore."

"That's a break, anyway."

"I didn't call it in yet for forensics. I wondered if your great pals in Inverness would process it for prints. Might be faster than having John Allen and the team come all the way up here?"

"Definitely. I'll give Ada Benoit a call and see what she says."

"I'm getting a tea. Do you want another coffee?"

He nodded as he made the call. "Thanks." He got through to Sergeant Benoit and explained the situation. By the time Roxanne came back with the drinks, he was off the phone.

"She's arranging a team to come here. I need the exact location to text to her."

Roxanne gave him the address and directions and once he had sent it off, they sat and enjoyed their drinks in silence for a moment.

Roxanne tilted her head. "Who do you think Carl is?"

"The prints will tell us soon enough, but I don't believe it's some random stranger that we haven't heard about yet."

"No."

"I was thinking about Adam's injuries. The more I think about it, the more personal it seems. It just doesn't feel like some deliberate, planned attack. If it was, he would have been shot or stabbed. There's too much emotion and spur-of-the moment in this killing."

"You're thinking family?"

"Or Dab Haan."

"You're giving up on Gerry Jeffreys?"

Gordie sighed. "I can't see him having the emotion for this."

"I agree."

He finished his coffee. "I have to call Sarge. Better do that before I head off. Can you come back up here tomorrow to watch over the forensics? I'm hoping they can give us the prints pretty quickly."

"Will do. You go on. I'll just finish my tea and head home to write up the reports."

***

Gordie sat in the parking lot and went through the updates with

Sergeant Arsenault, who had mixed reactions to the idea that the RCMP forensics team was called upon instead of their own resources.

"MacLean, why do we have a forensics team if we don't use them? Isn't it their job to go out to crime scenes and process them?"

"Of course, but since we're talking about the other end of the island, I made the call that it made more sense to go with the team closer by. Faster and cheaper. Our guys would waste hours just getting to the scene and back."

"That never stopped you before."

"It's only because the Mounties are already a part of the investigation. I didn't see the harm."

Gordie heard Arsenault sigh. "All right, it's done now. Saves our budget, I guess."

After he hung up, Gordie took a breath and called Vanessa. "Hi Vanessa, it's Gordie."

She laughed, the sound sending a thrill through him. "I have your number on the phone, Gordie. I know it's you. How are you?"

"Not bad. Feeling pretty good, actually. I'm just on my way home from Port Hood and believe that we're making progress."

"You'll be coming past here? Feel like a cup of tea?"

"I'd like that."

"That's settled then. I'll see you soon."

Gordie felt his heart quicken. *Just friends. We're just friends now. A cup of tea doesn't mean you're back in her good books.*

She was outside when he drove up. She had pulled her blond hair back in a loose braid, and she wore a floppy tan coloured hat. Vanessa walked towards him, her blue eyes crinkled at the corners and the dimple in her right cheek deepened.

He stood beside the car for a moment and sucked in a deep breath. "Hiya."

"Hi." She paused as though waiting.

He walked towards her and dared to kiss her on the cheek. "It's nice to see you."

"And you. Are you having a cigarette before we go in?"

He grinned. "No. I quit."

Impulsively, she grasped his hand. "Oh, Gordie. What fantastic news! How long's it been?"

"Nearly three weeks now."

"How is it going?"

"I think I'm over the worst, but I still get lots of cravings. Mostly after I've eaten, or when I'm having a coffee. Distracting myself by making phone calls, or whatever helps. I have been eating too many baked goods, but I figure I can only quit one thing at a time, so right now it's the cigarettes. Later the sweets."

She continued to hold his hand. "Then come in and have a freshly baked peanut butter, chocolate chunk cookie to go with your tea."

"Sounds good. I can't stay long, but that does sound good."

Gordie followed her into the house and through to the kitchen, where the aroma of baking filled the air. He sat at the table and enjoyed the bustle of activity as she placed cookies on a plate, filled the kettle, and set out cups and the pot for tea.

When she sat down across from him, there was a sudden awkward silence. "How's the case going? Are you allowed to say?"

"I think we're getting close to resolving things."

"Oh, that's good. All of Port Hood is on edge right now. I spoke with Lynn the other day and all she could talk about was poor Dab Haan's death and wondering what was going on with Adam's investigation. I'll be glad when it's all behind us and we can go back to thinking about the quilting fair and such things."

She rose to make the tea when the kettle boiled.

"Vanessa." Gordie was tongue-tied. "I had a talk with my sister Jean the other day."

"Oh? How is she? And how's your mum?"

He was impatient. "Fine. They're fine."

"Good."

"It's just...well, she gave me some things to think about."

"Things?"

"When I'm not so tied up with this case, I'd like to sit down and have a proper talk with you."

Vanessa poured out the tea and pushed the plate of cookies towards him. "I'd like that, Gordie. I've been doing some thinking as well."

He took a cookie but studied it and with his eyes lowered, he continued. "So, you think we might be able to talk our way through things, then?" He looked up. "I'm not great at talking about feelings, but maybe we could give it a go if you think we should."

"Yes. I think we should. I believe it will be worth the effort for both of us."

Gordie took a big sip of tea and ate the cookie like a starving man. "This is delicious."

She smiled. "I'm glad you stopped in."

"I'd love to sit here all afternoon, but I have to go." He drained his cup and stood.

Vanessa walked him back to the car. "I'll see you when I see you then. I'm so glad about the smoking, Gordie. Do you feel better for it?"

Inhaling deeply, he exhaled slowly. "I couldn't do that without coughing a few weeks ago, so yes. I do feel better."

"That's a great motivation to stick with it then."

"Oh, I'm done with them now. Once I decided, that was it."

She nodded. "I believe you. You're very strong-willed."

As Gordie drove away, he wondered if being strong-willed was a good thing or bad.

CHAPTER 37

MACLEAN BRIEFED THE TEAM in the morning while Roxanne attended the forensics collection of evidence. The boat had been under a tarp for weeks, so they were not hopeful about collecting any trace evidence, but the fingerprint team collected several good prints from the boat and outboard motor. Gordie made sure that Roxanne instructed the forensics team to collect a sample of the paint to compare to the chip recovered from *Sea Child*.

At the station, MacLean reviewed the interviews and concluded happily that the discovery of the boat was the breakthrough they needed.

While Gordie worked on reports, he had Rob Norris put in a warrant to request further phone records. If they could identify conclusively who had called Al MacInnis about renting the boat, it would add evidence to the case.

The net was closing in, and it was just a matter of time now.

***

Roxanne arrived at the station late in the afternoon. "It'll probably take 48 hours or more to get the prints back."

Gordie frowned. "Damn. I thought the Mounties were so fast at these things."

"I suspect that is fast, Gordie."

"Yeah, OK. I've sent off a note to Dr. Ingram to ask him to compare the prints from the boat to the ones collected from the gaff hook as well."

"Right. That makes sense. Dr. Ingram was out there this morning. After I left, the print guy was going over to Al MacInnis' place to collect his for exclusion."

"OK, I guess we just need patience."

Roxanne grinned. "Something you are so good at."

"I can be. And besides, that's the pot calling the kettle black, I'd say."

"You're right. I was tempted to ask if I could help with the prints, but figured I'd be more of a hinderance than a help."

"When's the last time you did any print analysis?"

"Police college."

"Yeah. Let's leave it to the experts."

Gordie stood up and stretched. "I'll do a Tim Hortons run and then maybe you, Rob and I can sit down together and map out our case to figure out where we are and what we still need."

Roxanne and Rob were in the briefing room when Gordie got back. Roxanne was busy updating the whiteboard, crossing out names and adding new ones.

"Dig in." Gordie handed around the tea for Roxanne and coffee for Rob. He flipped open the box of doughnuts and crullers and they each helped themselves.

Rob Norris nodded at the board. "So, you think you've got it figured out, do you?"

Gordie nodded. "We have to wait for the prints, but yes, I do." He took them through his thinking and the evidence they had so far.

Roxanne drew a timeline on the board which showed their theory of the killer's movements. "It would have been a rush, but we know it was do-able."

Rob sat back with a second doughnut. "Motive?"

Gordie explained what he believed.

Roxanne made more notes. "Here's what we need to pull it all together. Prints, phone records, paint chip comparison."

Gordie smiled. "And a confession."

Rob laughed. "That's always nice, but is it likely?"

MacLean shrugged. "I think so. Yes, I think so."

Norris eyed the box of doughnuts and then stood. "I better not. You two done with these?"

When they both confirmed they were, Rob took the box. "I'll put it out by the coffee machine then."

Roxanne and Rob went back to their desks to finish entering information into the system, while Gordie made his way to Sergeant Arsenault's office to give him the latest information.

***

It took three days to get the report from the Mounties on fingerprints and confirmation that the paint chip collected from Al MacInnis' boat was a match for the questioned sample taken from *Sea Child*. By then, the requested phone records were also available.

They were ready to move forward, and Gordie planned for backup from uniforms. Roxanne and Gordie met in Saint Peter's to travel together in Gordie's car.

***

It was ten in the morning and traffic was light. They were almost at their destination when Gordie cursed. "Damn. I meant to put the back seats up. When we get there, I'll go knock on the door while you do that, OK?"

"You called already to say you were coming by, didn't you? How did he react?"

"I did. I didn't give a lot of information. Just said I was coming to see him. When he asked me why, I just said that new information had come to light, and I needed to talk to him."

"What did he say?"

"He hung up without answering."

"Weird. He must know. Let's hope he doesn't do a runner."

Gordie raised his eyebrows. "Seriously?"

She shrugged. "Anything's possible."

MacLean pulled into the now familiar driveway and got out of the car, leaving Roxanne to fiddle with the back seats of his Santa Fe.

As he walked towards the house, the side door opened and Dannymac stood there pointing a shotgun. "Don't come any closer, Detective."

Gordie stopped, still a good hundred yards away. "Danny. What are you doing?"

"I've had enough of talking to you."

"Danny. It's over. We have the boat you two used. Don't be foolish now. Put the gun down." Gordie walked forward, confident that the man with whom he had shared a pot of tea a few days earlier was only bluffing.

Dannymac waved the gun. His frail arms could hardly hold the gun steady. "I'm warning you."

MacLean held up his hands but took another step. "Put it down now, Danny."

Dannymac pulled the trigger and Gordie collapsed in an explosion of pain and blood, the sound of the shot mingling with Albright's shout.

CHAPTER 38

ROXANNE CALLED ARSENAULT AS she crept towards where MacLean lay. "Officer down. MacLean's been shot. I need backup and an ambulance. Call the Mounties. We're at Danny MacDonald's place. Dannymac shot MacLean."

She kept a wary eye on the door, behind which MacDonald had disappeared, as she ran, hunched over to MacLean. "Gordie. Can you hear me?"

He opened his eyes. His voice was low. "What the hell?"

"You've been shot. I need to get you back to the car. Do you think you can stand?"

Gordie's left arm dangled, blood flowing through the shirt from his chest just below the shoulder. "I think so."

Continuing to glance at the house for any sign of MacDonald, Roxanne squatted beside Gordie and put her arm around him. "Put your arm across my shoulder and on three we're going to stand. One-two-three."

She dragged him upright and then hustled him back to the car. In the distance, Roxanne heard the wail of a siren. Albright lowered

MacLean to the ground beside the car and he sat, leaning back against the rear wheel. Opening the rear passenger door, Roxanne yanked a towel from where she had shoved it when she had been raising the back seat. She hoped he wouldn't get some terrible infection from using a dog towel to stem the flow of blood, but decided it was the lesser of the risks. She folded it into a padded square and pressed it against Gordie's pectoral muscle. "I hope Taz won't mind me using one of her towels."

He smiled weakly. "Taz will be happy to be of service."

"Can you hold this in place?"

He lifted his right hand and pressed against the towel.

Albright let go and went back to her phone where she knew Arsenault waited and she kept hearing his voice calling out faintly to find out what was happening.

"Sarge, I've got him to safety. His shoulder's a mess, but it looks like that's it."

She heard him say that the RCMP were on their way with an armed unit. "The uniforms are just arriving now. I'm putting the phone back in my pocket. I'll be back to you in a minute."

Roxanne was surprised to see Kyle MacDonald locked in the back of the cruiser. He shouted to be let out, but the two uniformed constables ignored him and ran over to where she and Gordie were down behind Gordie's SUV.

They both wore bulletproof vests. "What happened here?"

"I'm Detective Albright and this is Detective MacLean. We were here to pick up Danny MacDonald, but before we knew what was happening, he came out with a shotgun and, well, you can see what happened. Neither of us believed he would use it."

Gordie's face wasn't quite as pale as it had been. "To be fair, I think he tried to fire over my head, but he's so bloody weak that the gun dropped."

The constable, who seemed to be the senior of the two, raised his eyebrows. "That's a pretty charitable point of view."

The other one gestured back to the car. "Is that the shooter's son?"

Albright nodded. "How did you get him picked up already? I thought he'd be out fishing still."

The senior man shrugged. "We were told to get him when he came back, and he came in about half an hour ago. He wasn't too happy about being taken away, but he didn't seem too surprised."

Gordie grunted as he shifted. "Dad probably called him to say I was coming this morning."

"So, where do we go from here?"

Albright pulled out her phone. "Sarge? The uniforms have Kyle MacDonald in the back of their car. He's screaming bloody murder to be let out and go check on his father."

She nodded as he spoke. "Do not let him out. Then we have two people holed up. No one goes into that house. Just sit tight until the Mounties get there. They'll take over. How's MacLean managing?"

"Sarge wants to know how you're doing?"

Gordie nodded. "I'm OK."

"He says he's OK, but he's losing a lot of blood, Sarge. Any idea how long before the ambulance gets here?"

"It's coming from Inverness. Another 15 minutes."

"OK. I'm hanging up. I don't want the phone to run out of juice. I'll call you back when anything happens."

Roxanne looked at Gordie's pale, sweaty face. "I'm going to lay you down, Gordie. It'll help control the bleeding." She supported him as he lay down and she slipped off her jacket to roll up under his head and upper body and then pulled the duvet that Taz usually lay on, out of the back and covered him. Gordie's arm fell away from where he had been pressing the towel to his injury. "You." She pointed to the junior constable. "Move over here and keep the pressure on the towel."

He moved closer to follow Roxanne's instruction.

A passing car had pulled over, and a woman called out. "Anything I can do to help?"

The senior constable waved her on. "Please keep going. Keep this area clear."

"OK. I just live a couple of doors down. If you need anything, let me know."

Roxanne cursed. "Where are those bloody Mounties? And where is the ambulance?"

Almost as though she had conjured them, a siren wailed and an emergency vehicle from the Port Hood Volunteer Fire Department pulled alongside. There was a flurry of activity as the senior constable jogged over to speak to the new arrivals. Obviously, the first thing they were told was about the danger of a shooter, and they moved to take cover behind the vehicle, but in moments a man came running over, bent low and carrying an oxygen tank and a bag over his shoulder.

He took over from the relieved constable, peeling back the towel to look at the wound. Another volunteer crept over, carrying a foil emergency blanket. Roxanne moved out of the way to let the two do their work, feeling relieved that Gordie's welfare was now in someone else's hands.

Roxanne took a moment to look around and saw Kyle on the phone in the back of the police car. She frowned. *Who are you talking to?*

Kyle saw Roxanne watching him and gestured for her to come over. Roxanne took another look at the house and, seeing nothing, she scurried over to the police car. The window on the driver's side was open, and she crouched down to speak to him face to face through the window. "What is it?"

"My father wants to come out and give himself up."

Roxanne stepped away, hunched down beside the car and called her Sergeant. "Gordie's being looked after by the volunteer fire department guys. Listen, according to Kyle, Dannymac wants to give himself up. What do you want me to do? I've got the two uniforms here but no sign of the Mounties yet. Should I go ahead?"

"No. Wait for the Mounties. They're more experienced with this kind of situation. You got that Albright? No heroics. Wait."

"Got it."

Another ten long minutes passed, but Roxanne saw Gordie regaining some colour as he got oxygen and received a pain killer. Taz's duvet had been tossed aside, covered in blood, and Roxanne turned her eyes away from it, feeling queasy.

At last, everyone seemed to show up within minutes of each other. Two more patrol cars immediately went to block off the road and take control of the emergency vehicles coming on the scene. The ambulance arrived. They apprised the medics of Gordie's situation, and they whisked him into the ambulance and away, on the way to the hospital in Port Mulroy. At last, the Mounties arrived, and Roxanne jogged over to the Senior Officer in Charge. She explained what had happened. She pointed to Kyle in the police car. "That's his son, Kyle, and he's talked to his father over the phone. The father is ready to turn himself in."

The officer nodded. "He's a suspect as well, is that right?"

"Yes. We figured the father was pretty much innocent. A witness maybe. Kyle's the actual suspect."

He walked over and opened the back door of the car. "Kyle, right?"

"Yes. Let me go talk to him. He didn't mean it. He's a sick old man."

"Call him up and give me the phone, son."

Kyle dialed the phone. "Dad? I told them you're going to give yourself up. I'm handing the phone over to this Mountie. He'll tell you what to do."

The officer in charge spoke with Dannymac, and Roxanne stepped away, feeling lost. The whole thing had gone so wrong. She wondered where Gordie's keys were. *How do I even get home?*

The Mountie officer shouted orders. "He's coming out. Daniels and Jackson. Move up to that side door. He's going to throw out the shotgun. It should be unloaded, but don't take any chances."

Two officers crept forward and stood on either side of the door. Roxanne watched as the door opened and the shotgun, broken open to show it was unloaded, came out, held by the thin, shaking hand of Dannymac.

One officer grabbed the gun while the other shouted at the elderly man. "On your knees. Get down, get down. Hands behind your back." Danny MacDonald knelt on the landing of his steps, looking grey-faced and ready to collapse.

The second officer handcuffed and hauled MacDonald to his feet and then between them, they supported him down the steps. The officer in charge moved forward to stand in front of the old man. Then he turned and called Roxanne. "Detective, this is your arrest to make."

Roxanne widened her eyes, swallowed, and marched forward. The adrenalin that had been draining from her spiked again. She informed Danny that he was being arrested in the matter of the death of Adam MacDonald, and that additional charges would be forthcoming in the shooting of a police officer. "Do you understand the reason for your arrest?"

"Yes."

"You have the right to retain and instruct counsel without delay. You have the right to telephone any lawyer you wish." Albright went through the rest of the arrest information, finishing with a final "Do you understand?"

Dannymac looked at the ground and mumbled "yes". Then he looked up at Roxanne. "Will he be all right?"

"Detective MacLean?"

"Yes."

"I'm not sure yet. Danny, what possessed you? Why did you shoot him?"

"I was shooting at the tree. Above his head."

She shook her head and sighed. "Another one. Another guy who shot someone by accident." She frowned. "Even still. Why get out your gun at all? MacLean's only ever been respectful to you. He wanted to take you to Sydney for questioning in the comfort of his own car instead of making you go in a police car. I just don't get it."

Dannymac looked at the ground. "Can we just get this over with?"

Roxanne waved to the senior constable. "Take him in a separate vehicle from Kyle, but they both need to be taken to the station." She turned away and then back. "And can I get a lift to Saint Peter's?"

The volunteer first responders were about to pull out, and Roxanne hastened over. "Thanks, guys. You made all the difference getting here as quick as you did. Thank you."

The driver grinned. "Our pleasure. Give us a call and let us know how it all pans out." He pulled a card from his pocket and handed it to her. *Eddy Tomah.*

"Thanks, Eddy. I'm Roxanne Albright. I will."

CHAPTER 39

THE HOSPITAL RELEASED MACLEAN two days later. He was on medical leave but insisted that Roxanne pick him up and take him into the station.

When he walked into the briefing room, a series of whoops and cheers rose. Sergeant Arsenault stood at the front of the room. The whiteboard had been cleared, with only the names of Kyle and Danny MacDonald still showing.

Arsenault folded his arms and frowned at Gordie. "Detective MacLean, you are on medical leave. You shouldn't be here."

"I know, I know. I just needed to pick a few things up, and Detective Albright agreed to transcribe my reports."

His boss smiled then. "You continually surprise me, MacLean. I guess I should just be grateful you haven't dragged your service dog in with you."

"Hey. Great idea. Next time, Sarge."

"Don't call me Sarge. OK, you're here now. Sit yourself down here at the front and give us the blow by blow of what happened and why."

Gordie knew Roxanne had already gone through all the details, but he went forward anyway and perched on one of the front desks. "Well, you knew already that we had the prints back from the rental boat, so we knew that both Kyle and his father had been in that runabout. The matching paint flake verified that this boat rubbed up against *Sea Child*."

Doucette called out, "but why? I haven't heard that, yet. I thought that the older son and his father were so close?"

"They were. Even Kyle was completely engaged in the family business once he came back from his travels. That was the problem. Dab Haan found out about the weapons trafficking. Whatever he didn't know, he guessed. He wanted a piece of the business, but Adam wasn't having any of it. He was getting out anyway. Dab went to Kyle to complain. Kyle went to Dad, but Dannymac had trouble believing it. Adam was the golden boy, so it seemed impossible that he'd put the entire family business at risk like that." Gordie stopped talking, feeling his energy flag.

Roxanne took over and Gordie nodded his thanks

"Kyle and Dannymac heard from Dab about this planned meeting. He knew about it because he'd overheard Ryan and Adam making the arrangements behind the Canadian Tire. First Kyle tries to talk to Adam, which explains the nine-minute phone call. Adam tries to make out he isn't doing anything wrong, but Kyle doesn't believe him and that's when Kyle went to his father. Dannymac needs to be convinced, so Kyles says 'we'll go out and catch him at it. Maybe you'll believe it then.' So away they went in the middle of the night. Kyle gets the little runabout up and running and they go out to *Sea Child*. An argument ensues. Dannymac is heartbroken and keeps asking Adam why, and Adam explains about needing the money for the daughter's school."

Gordie nods. "And from here, things get fuzzy."

Roxanne continued. "Supposedly, Dannymac is very upset. He's yelling at Adam that all he needed to do was ask him for help. Kyle gets into it as well and accuses Adam of always needing to be right and do everything himself. He's always got to be the hero instead of just being a normal person. There's all kinds of shouting and Adam tries to get them to get away because he's afraid his contact won't come with the final shipment. Apparently, Dannymac loses it. He takes the gaff hook and swings it at Adam, who easily grabs it away and tosses it to the side."

Hennessey nods. "Makes sense. An old sick guy."

Albright nodded. "So far, it makes sense. But then Dannymac, who is still furious with Adam, grabs him, as we know from the autopsy, and shoves him. Adam falls back, hitting his head."

MacLean took over again. "Both Kyle and Danny claim that Adam had gotten up again, and they believed he was fine. By then, Dannymac had worked through his rage and just wanted to leave, so that's what they do. Kyle and Dannymac get back on the runabout and go back home. Kyle figured Adam would be back in time for the fishing and planned to continue the discussion with his brother the next day, but of course, that never happened."

Rob Norris shook his head. "Why didn't they just come forward when they found out Adam had died?"

Gordie sighed. "Afraid to lose the boat and the business because of the weapons thing. They couldn't tell a part of the story without telling all of it."

Sergeant Arsenault put a line through the two names on the whiteboard. "And now it's done. MacDonald Senior has confessed to the murder, and I'm sure there'll be a plea bargain that will reduce that down to manslaughter or less. Kyle is out on bail, for his part, which looks like it'll just be obstructing justice."

Gordie stood. "Thanks for all the support, team. I'll be taking some time to recover, but I've already called into the Old Triangle and put some money behind the bar for a celebration. I'll have to pass for the time being."

Norris laughed. "Gives us an excuse for two celebrations. Thanks, buddy."

When Roxanne and Gordie were alone at Gordie's desk, she looked at him. "You don't think it went the way Dannymac tells it, do you?"

"How could it? That sick old man grabs a strong young man and shoves him that hard?"

"Maybe if the boat lurched, just at the right moment?"

"Yeah. Maybe. I wasn't there, so we have to accept what the confession tells us."

He looked at her. "I talked to Dannymac yesterday on the phone. I had to know why he shot me. You know what he said?"

She shook her head. "I asked him that too, but he didn't answer."

"He said 'I needed people to know that I'm capable of violence.' What do you think of that?"

"He was setting up for the confession because he knew we'd be skeptical."

"But nobody wants to know that, do they? There's a confession and that's good enough for the system."

Roxanne shook her head. "Let's get this done."

***

Gordie was well enough to drive himself to court on the date when the sentencing hearing for Dannymac and Kyle was held.

After it was over, MacLean followed Kyle to his car. The young man turned to face him before getting in.

Gordie shook his head. "How can you do this to your father?"

Kyle looked over his shoulder to make sure no one else was listening. "To? Try for." He sighed. "Detective, you see my dad and think he's a sick, frail man. Maybe he is. At the same time, some people that we see as weak turn out to be the strongest people we know, and maybe it's best to have faith in their strength, set aside our own inclinations and do as they ask."

Kyle got in his car and then lowered his window. "Detective MacLean, don't imagine that I'm getting away scot-free for my role in all of this." He choked on his words. "I'll be punished every single day for the rest of my life." He raised the window, started the car and drove away, leaving Gordie to watch until Kyle was out of sight.

***

Gordie called Vanessa when he pulled out of the lot. "Hi. I'm on the way back."

Her voice was sympathetic and soothing. "Did things turn out the way you expected?"

"Pretty much. Kyle was found guilty of perverting the course of justice and was given a suspended sentence of 12 months. We originally charged Dannymac with manslaughter but did a plea deal, which took it down to assault with bodily harm. He was sentenced to 12 months, but his lawyer is already filing a petition for a conditional sentence, meaning that he'll serve his time at home. Everyone knows he won't serve out the 12 months, no matter what. His cancer is aggressive, and he doesn't have long to live. I imagine the conditional will be approved."

"What about the fact that Danny shot you?"

"I spoke with the Crown Attorney on Danny's behalf. As part of the plea package, they dropped the charges because they couldn't prove intent. He didn't intend to shoot me. It's an offence to even point a firearm at another person, but given my request and the circumstances, they dropped it."

Gordie took a breath and continued. "I heard Dannymac signed over the business."

"To Kyle, I guess?"

"Fifty percent to Kyle and fifty percent in trust to Adam's daughter Izzie. That means that half the revenues every year will go to Izzie, which Sharon will manage. It's the right thing, and Kyle seemed very content with it."

"It's all such a shame. Well, drive carefully. Taz is supervising me in the garden, but we'll be cleaned up and waiting for you by the time you get here, and then we'll all go for a good long walk along the shore."

"Sounds good, love. See you soon."

His next call was to his mother. "Hi Mum."

"Gordie. How nice to hear from you. Are you driving? You shouldn't be driving and talking to me at the same time."

Gordie laughed. "It's hands-free Mum. It's perfectly OK."

"All right, then. I just worry about you."

"No need. Mum, I've been thinking back to when I was a kid."

"Oh, you should put that all behind you. It was such a long time ago."

"I'm trying to. I just wanted to say that sometimes I remember being angry with you back then, when I was thirteen or fourteen."

He heard the disappointment in her voice. "Angry with me?"

"There were times that I thought that if you were braver, you would take us away somewhere. If we were only away from Dad, everything would be better. I wanted to look after you."

She sighed. "I did what I thought was best, Gordie. I didn't have money of my own and the idea of living on welfare, living in a tiny apartment in a rough area, didn't seem like a good option. You grew up in one house, on a street where you and Jeannie had your friends and went to the same school with everyone you knew. The bad times stand out in your mind the most, but it wasn't all bad. Your father was a binge drinker, and yes, those times were bad. He wasn't nice then, but in between, it was all right. I won't say happy, but not terrible."

"Mum, I can see that now. I'm not saying that I would counsel others to make the same choice, but I understand it now. Most importantly, I now understand that when I thought you weren't being brave enough, I was wrong. In fact, it was you being very brave. You were courageous and strong. Thanks for that, Mum. That's all I wanted to say about it."

He heard the tears in her voice. "When will I see you again? You're going back to work soon, aren't you?"

"Well, that's the other reason I'm calling. Vanessa has been helping me do some redecorating in my house, or maybe I should say, decorating."

"Are you thinking of selling? Are you two moving in together?"

"No, Mum. We've done a lot of talking and both of us agree we are content to stay as we are, each with our own home, but we spend a lot of time together. Her house is all done and renovated, so she turned her sights on my place, and I'll admit it looks better. What used to be my junk room is now an actual spare room with two beds in it. I've talked to Jeannie and if you feel like it, I'd like both of you to come up for a few days to visit before I go back to work."

"Oh yes, I'd love to."

"Then give Jean a call and let her know. The plan is that you'll come up on Tuesday and stay for three nights. If the weather cooperates, we might even go down to Big Pond to visit with Roxanne Albright and her Nana, Helen. We've all got our vaccines so we can safely go and sit outside and have a visit. You'll like Helen. They've got a new dog as well. A golden retriever named Sheba."

"I'll bring lots of cookies. Some for the dogs, and some for you."

The last call was to Roxanne Albright. "Hiya."

"Did you go to court?"

"Yeah." He reviewed the results for her. "Where are you? I'll be going past Big Pond in a few minutes."

She hesitated. "I'm sure Nana would love to see you, but I'm not at home."

"Oh, OK. I thought you were on a day off."

"I am. I'm in Port Hood."

"Good lord. Haven't you had enough of that place?"

"I'm visiting a friend."

"A friend?"

"Eddy Tomah. He's the guy who helped you when you were shot. From the Port Hood volunteer fire department."

Gordie had a vague memory of concerned brown eyes above an n-95 mask. "Well, that's great. Enjoy your day. I just wanted to let you know that my mother and sister are definitely coming next week, so I'll take you up on the invitation to visit if the weather is fine."

"That's great. I'll let Nana know. I'll give you a call on Monday once we see the forecast and we'll make a plan."

Gordie smiled. "Sounds good. Hey, Roxanne?"

"What?"

"Maybe invite Eddy."

He hung up before getting an answer.

The End

ACKNOWLEDGEMENTS

Thanks to Professor Stephen Schneider, Ph.D., Department of Criminology at Saint Mary's University in Halifax, Nova Scotia for his guidance on weapons trafficking in Canada and for pointing me to some further informative reading on the subject.

Thank you also to Shirley Brown of Antigonish, Nova Scotia for spending a good chunk of time going through the details of a day on a lobster fishing boat. You are an inspiring and amazing person and one tough lady! (Although Shirley tells me that 'there's no better place to be on a good day' than out on the water fishing!).

Thanks to Andrew Hickerson who brought his years of policing expertise to answer my questions promptly and thoroughly. I'm afraid you're on the team now Andrew, with little chance of escape!

To these experts who provided me with their experienced opinions, I apologize if I modified things for the good of the story. All inconsistencies and misrepresentation of facts are completely my own doing.

Last but not least, thanks to my 'usual suspects' of Dave Wickenden who battled through challenges to edit my book, and to Sharron

Elkouby who provided further edits and proofreading to add another project to the decades of work you've already done for me. Thanks to Jimmy Carton who serves as my first reader and always gives me solid feedback. Thank you to Robert Scozzari for another beautiful cover design.

And thank you to all the readers who have responded with such enthusiasm to Gordie MacLean.